莎士比亚 *Shakespeare*

经典名著译注丛书
JINGDIANMINGZHUYIZHUCONGSHU

威尼斯商人

The Merchant of Venice

主编◎阮珅

William Shakespeare 著

朱生豪 译

刘军平 注

湖北长江出版集团
湖北教育出版社

（鄂）新登字 02 号

图书在版编目（CIP）数据

威尼斯商人：英汉对照/（英）莎士比亚（Shakespeare, W. ）著；朱
生豪译；刘军平注. —武汉：湖北教育出版社，2013. 10
（莎士比亚经典名著译注丛书/阮坤主编）
书名原文：The Merchant of Venice
ISBN 978 - 7 - 5351 - 7002 - 6

Ⅰ. 威…　Ⅱ. ①莎… ②朱… ③刘…　Ⅲ. ①英语 - 汉语 - 对照
读物 ②喜剧 - 剧本 - 英国 - 中世纪　Ⅳ. H319. 4：I

中国版本图书馆 CIP 数据核字（2011）第 148627 号

现在读书
book.cnxianzai.com

出版　发行：湖北教育出版社　　　　　　武汉市青年路 277 号
网　　址：http://www.hbedup.com　　邮编：430015　电话：027 - 83619605

经　销：新 华 书 店
印　刷：武汉中远印务有限公司　　　（430034·武汉市硚口区长丰大道特 6 号）
开　本：880mm×1230mm　1/32　　　　　　　　　　6. 25 印张
版　次：2011 年 11 月第 1 版　　　　　　　2013 年 10 月第 4 次印刷
字　数：170 千字

ISBN 978 - 7 - 5351 - 7002 - 6　　　　　　　　　　定价：12. 50 元

如印刷、装订影响阅读，承印厂为你调换

目次
Contents

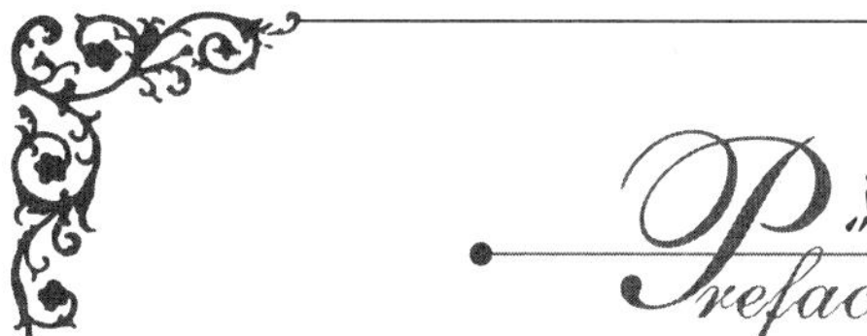

  天下书汗牛充栋。一个人穷毕生的精力发愤为学，最多不过学富五车。因此要善于择书而读。要读好书，攻名著。英国文艺复兴时期的大戏剧家、诗人威廉·莎士比亚（William Shakespeare，1564—1616）的作品就是经典名著，值得精读。马克思在青少年时代就喜欢阅读莎剧，能背诵许多台词，学以致用。

  莎士比亚出生于英国中部沃里克郡艾汶河畔斯特拉特福镇一个富裕市民家庭。大约七岁起在当地的文法学校念书。十几岁时因家庭破产而辍学，帮助父亲做生意。工作余暇，读了不少文学精品。他经常观看巡回剧团的演出，养成了对戏剧的爱好。据说他曾在乡间任教，当过家庭教师、屠宰店学徒、海员，也当过兵，还在律师事务所供过职，接触了各阶层的人，熟悉社会生活。大约在二十三岁时（1587 年），他离开家乡去伦敦谋生。到伦敦后，据考证，他先在剧院门口为看戏的绅士看管马匹，接着在剧院里打杂，为演员提词，还演过配角。后来编写剧本，成了名剧作家。

  莎士比亚在创作期间用素体诗（blank verse）写了三十七部诗剧（他和弗莱彻合作编写的《两个高贵的亲戚》除外），还写了两首长诗和一百五十四首十四行诗，在剧坛和诗坛统领风骚。他塑造了从帝王将相到下层人民群众各式各样的人物形象，描绘了文艺复兴时期新兴资产阶级逐步取代封建贵族的统治地位的历史进程和五光十色的社会背景，反映了人类经受的前所未有的伟大变革的实质，表现了他的人道主义精神与和谐理想。他的同事、好友、诗人、剧作家班·琼森称他为"时代的灵魂"。恩格斯特别赞赏他的"剧作的情节的生动性与丰富性"，并要人们更多地注意他"在戏剧发展史上的意义"。

莎士比亚既属于英国，也属于全世界；既属于文艺复兴时期，也属于千秋万代。他的创作及其思想与时间共存，无远弗届。从他逝世后近四百年来，世界各国的学者和研究人员争当弘扬莎学的"使人"，翻译、诠释其作品，探究、阐明其作品中所蕴含的义理，分析、评述其作品对世道人心所产生的作用和影响。由于有了使人，异代异域的莎士比亚和现代人越来越亲近了。

江山代有使人出。从二十世纪初到今天一百一十多年间，中国境内出了五代莎学使人，他们在莎士比亚和广大的中国读者之间起着沟通作用。

第一代使人是莎剧故事的编译者。1903 年上海达文社开风气之先，用文言文翻译出版了英国散文家查尔斯·兰姆和他的姊姊玛丽·兰姆合写的《莎士比亚故事集》中的十则故事，书名标作《澥外奇谭》。第二年，商务印书馆出版了林纾和魏易用文言文合译的上述著作的全译本（共二十则故事），书名为《英国诗人吟边燕语》。这部译作以其"雅驯隽畅"的文风豁人心目，流传浪广，对当时的文人学子包括童年时代的郭沫若产生了浪大的影响。

二十年后，在北大任教的朗巴特（Frank Alanson Lombard）教授注释了《莎士乐府原本威城商人》（1923），由商务印书馆出版。该书用英语解析词义和场景特色，评说时代背景和人物形象，便于英文水平较高的大学生通过原文注释读懂原著。可以认为，朗巴特教授是我国境内第二代莎学使人。

从二十世纪二三十年代至八九十年代，我国有众多的学者翻译了莎士比亚作品（包括剧本、十四行诗）和莎剧故事，还发表了不少精辟的莎学评著。第三代使人可谓"极半世纪之盛"。田汉在 1921 年从日文转译了悲剧《哈孟雷特》，这是首次用白话文移译的完整的莎剧（不同于文明戏时期据《吟边燕语》改编的幕表剧）。此后相继出版了其他莎剧中译本（散文译本）。最有影响的是朱生豪译的 31 部莎剧和梁实秋译的莎剧全集。前者的文笔优美流畅，素为国内莎学界和翻译界所推崇；后者的译文忠实严谨，并附有详尽的注释。还有孙大雨、卞之琳和方平等人的诗体译本，有美皆备。

第四代使人当推《莎士比亚注释丛书》的编者。商务印书馆从 1984 年起出版了裴克安主编的注释丛书，已出 18 种。书中主要用英文释义，辅以中文解说，扼要钩玄，尽发莎剧义蕴。

二十世纪九十年代初，莎氏辞典的编纂蔚然成风。第五代使人以崭新的面貌"异军突起"。从 1990 年起出版了五部各具特色的《莎士比亚辞典》。

以上作了大致的回顾，回顾是为了前瞻。湖北教育出版社于世纪之交审时度势，多方论证，认定编辑一套集莎剧原文、译文、注释于一体的新丛书的重任，落在第六代使人的肩上。为满足广大读者的需求，决定出版《莎士比亚经典名著译注丛书》，推出莎氏最著名的悲喜剧《哈姆雷特》、《罗密欧与朱丽叶》、《奥瑟罗》、《李尔王》、《麦克白》、《威尼斯商人》、《仲夏夜之梦》、《皆大欢喜》、《第十二夜》和十四行诗集共十种。本丛书借重莎士比亚原著和朱生豪译文，博采中外各注家之长，将不辱使命，在中华莎学的发展中，发挥积极的促进作用，既有助于莎氏作品的普及，又有助于读者鉴赏水平的提高，并借鉴莎剧，繁荣我国的戏剧创作，做到古为今用，外为中用，使这套丛书真正成为雅俗共赏、开卷有益的读物。大学生、研究生、莎剧爱好者、文艺工作者、文学翻译工作者、大中学英语教师和研究人员可从不同的角度出发，基于不同的要求，从丛书中得到他们期望得到的"食粮"；中学生和同等程度的英语自学者，将原文和译文对照阅读，并依靠注释，析疑辨义，含英咀华，定能升堂入室，深入理解和赏析莎士比亚原著辞旨的精髓，并怡情于原著所体现的真善美的理想境界，豁然开朗。

在编书过程中，我们参阅了 1946 西风版、1957 牛津版、1973 新哈丁·克雷格版、1974 河畔版和 1984 新企鹅版等莎剧原文本，对各种异文和某些文句的不同的排列顺序作了校正和界定。以《罗密欧与朱丽叶》为例：牛津版第一幕第四场原 68—70 行谈春梦婆的车子（chariot），现依河畔版改排在 60、61 行谈车辐（waggon-spokes）和车篷（cover）之前，这样从整体谈到局部，顺理成章；又如，牛津版第二幕前面有一段 Prologue，与第一幕前的开场诗（即总引）平起平坐，似不合章法，因此亦照河畔版把这一段话移到第二幕后面，删去 Prologue 的字样，只以"副末上念"（Enter Chorus）标目。在校勘异文中，我们看到，牛津版远远胜过河畔版。如 I.i. 26 行 "I will be cruel with the maids."（我要对他们的女人不留情面），同一场 217 行 "...in strong proof of chastity well arm'd, /From love's weak childish bow she lives unharm'd."（不让爱情稚弱的弓矢损害她的坚不可破的贞操。）以及 I. ii. 29 行 "Among fresh female buds"（在蓓蕾一样娇艳的女郎丛里）中的 cruel，unharm'd 和 female，不能用河畔版的 civil，uncharm'd 和 fennel 来分别加以替代。上下文是最好的评判者。

对待新老版本的异文，我们的取舍一概以上下文的意义为依据，不轻信"凡是新的都是好的"，不当"凡是派"或空头"维新派"。例如在《哈姆雷特》第一幕第一场中，霍拉旭谈到老哈姆雷特生前和敌人谈判的情景，一些新版本上都是这样写的："He smote the sledded Polacks on the ice."（他把那些乘雪橇的波兰人击倒在冰上。）这里的"the sledded Polacks"在第一、第二版四开本和对开本里都作 "sleaded pollax"（=his leaded poleaxe），整句意思是 "他用沉重的长柄斧敲击冰块"。据上文，上文说的是在谈判当中；据常情，在谈判当中不会也不应发动突然袭击。"两国相争，不斩来使"，何况是两国的国王进行面对面的谈判！而且莎士比亚是把老哈姆雷特作为一位理想的国王来描绘的，不会让他搞小动作。但在冰上谈判时，盛怒之下用斧头敲击冰块则是完全可能的，以这种动作表现激动情绪是合乎情理的。

本丛书使用朱生豪译文（据《莎士比亚戏剧全集》，1954 年作家出版社版），对个别错字作了必要的校勘；对原译者遗漏未译或有意删节的文句，作了补译。如 Hamlet 和 Macbeth，选用已为大多数人所接受的 "哈姆雷特" 和 "麦克白"；地名则以世界地图册上的译名为准，如 Verona—维罗纳，Tripolis—的黎波里，Crete—克里特，Genoa—热那亚等；神话中个别人物名则沿用《希腊罗马神话和〈圣经〉小辞典》中的译名，如 Jason—伊阿宋。

注释主要用中文。举凡社会习俗、历史文化、宗教传统、神话典故、版本异文、双关隐语、词的深层含义等，都作了简明扼要的阐释。为了兼顾普及和提高，在以中文释义为主的原则下，有时用英中双解，有时用英文反复解释。"一唱三叹"，以加深理解，帮助读者提高英文水平。

有些词语，英美注家注注在释义后打一个问号（?）表示存疑。本丛书编者不揣愚陋，提出了自己的浅见。如对《罗密欧与朱丽叶》I. V. 98. 行中的 the gentle sin 加了这样一个注：温存的罪过。罗密欧觉得他的粗手握着朱丽叶的纤纤玉手是 "粗野的触摸"（rough touch），是一种罪过，但这种罪过是由温存的爱促成的，所以说是 "温存的罪过"。他将以 "轻柔的吻"（a tender kiss）来抚慰 "粗野的触摸"。河畔版加注，把 the gentle sin 解作 "gentlemen 向女人求爱时必犯的错过"，恐怕是出于附会吧。

《麦克白》门房一场（Ⅱ.iii. 4—5）有一句话："Here's a farmer that hanged himself on the expectation of plenty." 也颇值得推敲。朱生豪的译文是："一定是什么乡下人，因为久盼丰收而自缢身死。"人民文学出版社校订本改为："一定是个囤积粮食的富农，眼看碰上了丰收的年头，就此上了吊。"英美一些版本都加了这样的注解：有农夫囤积粮食，等待高价出售，而 1606 年粮食丰收，谷价暴跌，故农夫自杀身亡。显然，校订本是根据上述注解改译的。这里硬把门房的一句不牵涉任何典故的话同 1606 年丰收的史实联在一起，可能失于牵强。"笺家穿凿苦求奇"，莎学中的某些考证和我国红学中的"索隐"不无类似之处。因此，本丛书编者在"盼丰收"的注释中先引用英美版本的释文，接着作了如下补充："但也有人持不同的看法，执著于从字面上诠释：'农夫在企盼丰收中上了吊'，即未能捱过荒年，做了吊死鬼兼饿死鬼。"

本丛书编者在校注中参考了西风版、新哈丁·克雷格版、河畔版、新企鹅版和梁实秋译《莎士比亚全集》等书的注释，裴克安主编《莎士比亚注释丛书》及吕荧译《仲夏夜之梦》所附的注解；还参考了梁实秋译文、人民文学出版社校订本、曹未风、曹禺、卞之琳、方平的莎剧译本及其他学者在各种报刊上发表的关于莎剧翻译的论文，在此一并致谢！

由于时间紧迫，资料有限，本丛书在考证、校勘、注疏各方面都存在不足或不妥之处，希望读者多提宝贵意见，以便再版时改进。

阮　珅

于武昌珞珈山萤斋

《威尼斯商人》导读

　　《威尼斯商人》是莎士比亚第一创作时期（1590—1600）的一部优秀喜剧，约写于1594—1598年。1598年7月22日，印刷商詹姆斯·罗伯茨托人在书业公所登记这部喜剧的书稿，书名暂定为"威尼斯商人"或"威尼斯的犹太人"。罗伯茨同莎士比亚所在的"宫内大臣剧团"有密切的联系，取得了登记出版该剧团演出本的权利。这次在登记簿上特意声明："未经宫内大臣剧团许可不得出版。"显然是为了保护版权，阻止他人出版而采取的一种做法。1600年10月28日，罗伯茨将版权转让给出版商托马斯·海伊斯，再次在书业公所登记，旋即出书，为第一版四开本，有莎士比亚署名，文本可靠，为1619年重印本和1623年第一版对开本所依据。

　　本剧的主要题材来源是意大利作家乔万尼·菲奥伦蒂诺的短篇小说集《蠢货》（写于1378年，出版于1558年）中第四天的第一个故事，一磅肉的故事本此。第二个来源是用拉丁文写的《传奇故事集》中的第66个故事。三匣择婿的故事本此。此书大约成于十三世纪末，十四世纪初。作者不可考。理查德·鲁宾逊于1577年将此书译为英语。此外还有一个老剧本《犹太人》，已失传。

　　《威尼斯商人》有三条情节线。第一条情节线是重友谊、轻资财的威尼斯商人安东尼奥和重利盘剥、吝啬而残暴的犹太富翁夏洛克之间的冲突；第二条线是安东尼奥的好友巴散尼奥向贝尔蒙脱的富家嗣女鲍细霞求婚的经过；第三条线是罗伦佐同夏洛克的女儿吉雪加恋爱的插曲。这是一条辅线。前两条主线通过法庭审判交织在一起。一磅肉的故事和三匣择婿的故事联为一体。

　　剧本一开始就展示了安东尼奥和巴散尼奥的真诚的友谊。他们两人一向过往很密，肝胆相照。巴散尼奥家道中落，经济困难，安东尼奥在钱财方面给了他很多援助。这次他因爱上了鲍细霞，需要一笔钱应酬，置备礼物，便又来向安东尼奥借钱。这时安东尼奥的全部财产都在海船上，手头很拮据，也没有可以变换现款的货物，便答应以自己的名义和信用担保，为他在威尼斯城里想办法借一笔款子。两人于是分头去打听债主。巴散尼奥打听到了夏洛克是富翁，便向他借三千块钱，由安东尼奥签立借据。以前安东尼奥曾在交易所里多次辱骂过夏洛克，骂他盘剥取利，因此他怀恨在心。现在安东尼奥求上门来，他决定利用这个机会报复他的深仇宿怨，便要安东尼奥在借约上写明，如三个月后到期不还，由债权人在债务人身上割一磅肉作为处罚。安东尼奥估计两个月之内他的商船就会带回四十倍于这笔借款的数目，坦然地签了约。可是借约过期，商船仍不见回来。夏洛克向威尼斯公爵提出控诉，一定要照约执行，割安东尼奥一磅肉。借了钱的巴散尼奥带着他的朋友葛莱西安诺乘船去贝尔蒙脱，倒是一路顺风。他向鲍细霞求婚，选中铅匣，又一举成功，享受着爱情的幸福。就在他们柔情似蜜的时刻，突然接到安东尼奥的信，说他生命操在夏洛克手里，危在旦夕。聪明敏慧的鲍细霞当即决定割舍儿女私情，要巴散尼奥先赶到威尼斯法庭搭救安东尼奥，她自己和女仆聂莉莎随后乔装为律师和书记也去法庭参加审讯。审讯中她郑重提出：夏洛克应照约行事，在安东尼奥胸口割下一磅肉，但不准流一滴血，也不得超过或少于一磅的重量，否则就要夏洛克抵命，他的财产全部充公。夏洛克终于败诉。法庭没收了他一半财产，还命令他改信基督教，并当庭写下文契，声明死后他的全部产业传给最近和他的女儿私奔的罗伦佐。审判结束后，鲍细霞和巴散尼奥、聂莉莎和葛莱西安诺一同去贝尔蒙脱过着恩爱美满的婚姻生活。安东尼奥的商船也平安到港。戏的结尾，还穿插了赠送指环的闹剧，风趣横生。

莎士比亚本着人道主义精神，乐于看到人们友好相处，和衷共济，慷慨好义，乐善互助，而不愿意看到人们怀着卑劣的贪心，使用残暴的手段，见利忘义，谋财害命。《威尼斯商人》正是在这方面表达了作者对生活的看法。剧本的主题就是歌颂慷慨互助的友谊，反对贪婪和残暴。剧中两条主线——一磅肉和三个匣子的故事相互穿插，交织出作者的主旨，人物的道白包含着作者的深刻寓意。这两条主线反映了旧法统同人道主义原则的矛盾和冲突。作者在反映矛盾和冲突中毫不含糊地对旧法统进行了强烈的谴责。

在三个匣子的故事中，旧法统同人道主义原则的矛盾表现为世俗礼法同人性的对立。对立双方是"父与女"，确切地说，是"一个活着的女儿的意志，却要被一个死了的父亲的遗嘱所钳制"（Ⅰ.2.）。

作者通过鲍细霞以形象化的语言宣告了反钳制的斗争："理性可以制定法律来约束感情，可是热情激动起来，就会把冷酷的法令蔑弃不顾；年轻人是一头不受拘束的野兔，它会跳过老年人所设立的理智的藩篱"（同上）。尽管反钳制的斗争是在遗嘱所规定的"三匣择婿"的钳制下进行，但结果毕竟是鄙弃虚荣（金匣、银匣象征虚荣）的质朴真挚的爱情（以铅匣为象征）取得了胜利，这是"无聊的世俗的礼法"（Ⅲ. 2.）所钳制不了的。

在一磅肉的故事中，旧法统同人道主义原则的矛盾表现为法律契约同人情的对立。安东尼奥是"跟一个心如铁石的对手当庭对质，一个不懂怜悯，没有一丝慈悲心的不近人情的恶汉"（Ⅳ. 1.）。而这个恶汉是以契约为后盾的。摆在莎士比亚面前的问题是：要尊重法律契约，就违反了人情；要尊重人情，就得蔑视法律契约。莎士比亚看出了这个矛盾，但找不到也不可能找到正确的解决办法。他提出法治加人道，即以慈悲作为法律的补充。这就是他开出的"药方"。人道主义者总是以仁爱、友谊相号召，以此来消除贪得无厌、唯利是图的恶行，并力图以人道慈悲的原则来改造"人对人是豺狼"的礼会。这是不可能实现的幻想，但他们的积极的思想倾向在当时所起的作用不应低估。

莎士比亚在《威尼斯商人》中对一磅肉事件的矛盾双方的褒贬态度，是非常鲜明的。他在剧本开头，就强调指出安东尼奥和巴散尼奥两人的深情厚谊。当后者把心里的打算告诉前者时，前者慨然允诺说："只要您的计划跟您向来的立身行事一样光明正大，那么我的钱囊可以让您任意取用，我自己也可以供您驱使；我愿意用我所有的力量，帮助您达到目的"（Ⅰ. 1.）。后来巴散尼奥对鲍细霞极力称赞安东尼奥的为人，说他是"一个心肠最仁慈的人，热心为善，多情尚义，在他身上存留着比任何意大利人更多的古代罗马的仁侠精神"（Ⅲ. 2.）。高利贷者夏洛克则截然相反，他毫无恻隐之心，硬要割对方的肉。因此，萨莱里奥愤怒地说道："我从来没有见过这样一个样子像人的家伙，一心一意只想残害他的同类"（同上）。葛莱西安诺在法庭上指着夏洛克的鼻子骂道："万恶不赦的狗……你的前生一定是一头豺狼……，因为你的性情正像豺狼一样残暴贪婪"（Ⅳ. 1.）。1600 年的《威尼斯商人》第一版四开本书名页的标题中，就用了"极端残暴的犹太人夏洛克"这样一些字眼，正式表明了莎士比亚对他笔下这个人物的评价。总之，莎士比亚对矛盾双方一褒一贬。褒的是一个最仁慈的人安东尼奥，这是正面人物，是人道主义思想的体现者；贬的是一个样子像人、豺狼成性的夏洛克，这是反面形象，是人道主义思想的对立面。

莎士比亚的创作意图不止于一褒一贬，从剧情发展中我们可以看出他的深刻用心在于通过夏洛克同安东尼奥的冲突反映法律契约同人情的对立，进一步揭露批判旧法制及其代表人物。随着戏剧冲突进入高潮，莎士比亚的批判也进入高潮。他因势利导，把批判的锋芒直指威尼斯的统治者。夏洛克手里有契约，心里有数：契约是神圣的，谁也不能违背或改变契约的规定。因此他气势汹汹，一定要照约割一磅肉。他在法庭上踌躇满志地说："我现在只等着执行原约"（IV. 1.）。夏洛克有恃无恐，就因为统治者、统治阶级有国家机器必然要维护为统治阶级利益服务的法律契约。这一点，安东尼奥也知道得很清楚，他说："公爵不能变更法律的规定，因为威尼斯的繁荣，完全倚赖着各国人民的来往通商，要是剥夺了异邦人应享的权利，一定会使人对威尼斯的法治精神发生重大的怀疑"（III. 3.）。鲍细霞也在法庭上宣称："在威尼斯谁也没有权力变更既成的法律；要是开了这一个恶例，以后谁都可以借口有例可援，什么坏事都可以干了"（IV. 1.）。变更或取消既成的法律，就是变更或取消统治阶级的既得利益。法律契约之所以"神圣"，之所以必须维护，原因就在于此。正因为这样，夏洛克才敢于同公爵争辩，敢于反驳公爵关于慈悲的说教，并单刀直入地揭穿他购买奴隶、虐待奴隶的底细（IV. 1.）。夏洛克辩驳的意思是：公爵可以蓄奴，他就可以要求割一磅肉，两者应同样受到法律的保护。反唇相讥，充分暴露了统治阶级法治的实质。莎士比亚让公爵大讲人道慈悲，以反对夏洛克的残暴不仁，又通过夏洛克的辩驳，来撕破这位统治者的人道主义伪装，作者的社会批判是何等透彻有力，艺术手法又足何等圆浑自然！

有人会问，既然莎士比亚对夏洛克痛加针砭，为什么又把揭露统治者的任务交给这样一个反面人物？这是一个值得讨论的问题。我们认为，这个问题既牵涉到作者的时代条件，也牵涉到他的性格描绘的艺术。

先谈谈时代条件。莎士比亚在他的第六十六首十四行诗中，曾经痛心地指出：“官府钳制着艺术的喉舌”。统治者只许人们歌功颂德，不许直言时弊。老百姓不能随便议论朝政，作家也不能在作品中任意揭统治者的疮疤。由于形格势禁，莎士比亚的创作都是利用旧题材，利用古代或外国的故事反映英国社会的现实生活。《威尼斯商人》也是如此。作者借夏洛克之口揭公爵的老底，是有其苦衷的。一方面是“借他人酒杯，浇胸中块垒”，另一方面，以恶人出恶言的形式出现，不致于罪于官府。曹雪芹写《红楼梦》不就是托假语村言，将真事隐去吗？他还无限感慨地赋了一首诗：“满纸荒唐言，一把辛酸泪。都云作者痴，谁解其中味？”寥寥二十个字，充满了愤激哀怨之情。对于莎士比亚，我们未尝不可以这样理解。

再谈谈莎士比亚的性格描绘的艺术。这位戏剧艺术大师总是多层面地在发展中描绘人物的复杂性格。在这方面，马克思和恩格斯曾给他以高度的评价。他的作品中的人物是活生生的，不是僵死的，干瘪的，就在于他在不同的时间、地点和条件下显露出不同的性格特征。夏洛克不只是贪婪残暴，刁顽狡诈，爱财如命，认钱不认人，而且有“机智”，反应快，尖刻毒辣，能言善辩，善于玩弄唇枪舌剑，攻击对方。这些性格特点适时地发挥作用，使他能够咄咄逼人，得逞于一时。他在揭露公爵时声色俱厉地说：“您要是拒绝了我，那么让你们的法律见鬼去吧”（Ⅳ.1.）！夏洛克口之所说，表明他心之所想：如果法律不是骗人的东西，它就应该成为奴役人、剥削人的保证，应该成为杀人的东西，即应该容许他割安东尼奥一磅肉。夏洛克的“慷慨陈词”，恰到好处地烘托了他的阴险狠毒的性格。

他的另一段为犹太人“请命”的道白（Ⅲ.1.），也应该这样看。莎士比亚让夏洛克讲这段话，同样是出于描绘人物性格、塑造人物形象的需要。大凡奸诈之徒，都会装腔作势，假借名义。在第三幕第一场以前，夏洛克多次谈到，他同安东尼奥发生冲突的起因是在放债的问题上。主要是由于安东尼奥“借钱给人不取利钱”，把他们“在威尼斯城里干放债这一行的利息都压低了”（Ⅰ.3.）。夏洛克知道，对此进行报复是名不正，言不顺的。为了争取舆论的同情，他便来一个急转弯，把矛盾转嫁到民族仇恨上去，并把自己装扮成种族歧视的受害者。他以犹太民族的代言人自居，采取恶人先告状的手法，给安东尼奥罗织罪名：“他曾经羞辱过我，夺去我几十万块钱的生意，讥笑着我的亏蚀，挖苦着我的盈余，侮蔑我的民族，破坏我的买卖，离间我的朋友，煽动我的仇敌。他的理由是什么？只因为我是一个犹太人……"（Ⅲ．Ⅰ．）鼓舌如簧，企图以民族恨掩盖私仇，以娓娓动听的言词掩盖他重利盘剥的罪行和割肉复仇的动机。

国内外有些评论者根据他这一段道白认为：夏洛克作为一个残暴贪婪的高利贷者，受到莎士比亚的谴责；作为一个倍受欺凌的犹太人，又得到了莎士比亚的同情。夏洛克是一般的犹太人吗？不，他不是一般的犹太人，他是一个上等犹太人，是一个犹太富翁。夏洛克是种族歧视中的受害者吗？不是。作为一个上等人，他逍遥于种族歧视之外。二十个商人、公爵以及最有名望的一些士绅，都为安东尼奥向夏洛克求情。试问，受歧视的犹太人能得到这种礼遇吗？而且，他眉头一皱，就想行贿买通官府，枉法徇私。请看第三幕第一场结尾，莎士比亚只用一两句台词就为我们提供了一个重要的线索。夏洛克指点杜拔尔："到衙门里走动走动，花费几个钱"。这就最好不过地说明，夏洛克和官府衙门是沆瀣一气的。如果不是素有勾结，平日一毛不拔的吝啬鬼，怎肯那么轻易"花费几个钱"呢？

莎士比亚始终是把夏洛克刻画为一个狠毒的高利贷者，犹太人中的恶棍，人道主义原则的对立面，不是把他刻画为受歧视的犹太人。描绘他的复杂性格，不是说明他值得同情。莎士比亚同情遭受种族歧视的普通人，但决不至于同情有钱有势、神通广大的犹太富翁，决不至于同情他心目中的"极端残暴"的反面人物。确实，这个反面人物为犹太人鸣不平的独白，包含了作者的种族平等观念。产生这方面的联想是很自然的，因为这段道白毕竟是作者写的。不过，既然作者在创作过程中将某一想法或见解"移植"到人物语言中去，我们就必须联系该人物的社会地位、说话动机、性格特征等等进行分析。夏洛克要使自己"义正词严"，立于不败之地，便假借人道名义，虚张声势，打起种族平等的旗号，披上犹太民族代言人的外衣。腔调十足，自以为得计。莎士比亚独创性地给旧题材增添这一段道白，正是为了表现夏洛克的狡黠诡诈，以便更全面地揭示这个人物的本质。

夏洛克和安东尼奥都是现实世界里的人，他们两人所体现的高利贷资本和商业资本的矛盾是现实世界里的矛盾。莎士比亚如实地反映了这个矛盾，使这出喜剧具有现实主义的生命力，这是一方面。另一方面，莎士比亚在剧中特意加进了许多笑闹取乐的场景和迷人的抒情的画面，安排了幸福的大团圆的结局，又使这出戏具有浓郁的浪漫主义气息。在威尼斯法庭审判之后，在一场紧张的冲突之后，剧作者把观众带到景色宜人的贝尔蒙脱。这里没有喧闹，没有纷争，没有憎恨，没有冲突；只有宁静、和谐，只有爱。人们置身于一片皎洁的月色之中，耳边响起了动听的音乐：

> 月光多么恬静地睡在山坡上！我们就在这儿坐下来，让音乐的声音悄悄送进我们的耳中；柔和的静寂和夜色，是最足以衬托出音乐的甜美的。……瞧，天宇中嵌满了多少灿烂的金钹；你所看见的每一颗微小的天体，在转动的时候都会发出天使般的歌声，永远应和着嫩眼的天婴的妙唱。
>
> （V．1．）

莎士比亚拿贝尔蒙脱同威尼斯相对照。威尼斯的街道、交易所和法庭是严酷的现实，贝尔蒙脱是月色和歌声交融的"世外桃源"。一个是世俗社会，一个是理想世界。剧本结尾充满了光明和欢乐的气氛。莎士比亚激情满怀，凝望着鲍细霞家里的灯光，把幻想和希望寄托在这位新女性的身上：

> 一枝小小的蜡烛，它的光照耀得多么远！一件善事也正像这支蜡烛一样，在这罪恶的世界上发出广大的光辉。
>
> （V．1．）

THE MERCHANT OF VENICE

Dramatis Personae

The Duke of Venice.
The Prince of Morocco,
The Prince of Arragon, } *suitors to Portia.*
Antonio, *a merchant of Venice.*
Bassanio, *his friend, suitor to Portia.*
Gratiano,
Solanio, } *friends to Antonio and Bassanio.*
Salerio,
Lorenzo, *in love with Jessica.*
Shylock, *a rich Jew.*
Tubal, *a Jew, his friend.*
Launcelot Gobbo, *a clown, servant to Shylock.*
Old Gobbo, *father to Launcelot.*
Leonardo, *servant to Bassanio.*
Balthazar,
Stephano, } *servants to Portia.*

Portia, *a rich heiress of Belmont.*
Nerissa, *her waiting-gentlewoman.*
Jessica, *daughter to Shylock.*

Magnificoes *of Venice, Officers of the Court of Justice, Jailer, Servants to Portia, and other Attendants.*

Scene: *Partly at Venice and partly at Belmont, the seat of Portia, on the Continent.*

剧中人物名字读音：
Antonio [æn'təuniəu]
Bassanio [bə'sɑ:niəu]
Salerio [sæ'leriəu]
Solanio [səu'lɑ:niəu]

Gratiano [ˌgrɑ:ʃi'ɑ:nəu]
Lorenzo [lɔ'renzəu]
Shylock ['ʃailɔk]
Tubal ['tju:bəl]

 莎士比亚经典名著译注丛书

剧 中 人 物

威尼斯公爵

摩洛哥亲王 ⎫
阿拉贡亲王 ⎭ 鲍细霞的求婚者

安东尼奥　威尼斯商人

巴散尼奥　他的朋友，鲍细霞的求婚者

葛莱西安诺 ⎫
索拉尼奥　 ⎬ 安、巴二人的朋友
萨莱里奥　 ⎭

罗伦佐　吉雪加的恋人

夏洛克　犹太富翁

杜拔尔　犹太人，夏洛克的朋友

朗西洛脱·高波　小丑，夏洛克的仆人

老高波　朗西洛脱的父亲

里奥那陀　巴散尼奥的仆人

包尔萨泽 ⎫
史梯番诺 ⎭ 鲍细霞的仆人

鲍细霞　贝尔蒙脱富家嗣女

聂莉莎　她的侍女

吉雪加　夏洛克的女儿

威尼斯众士绅，法庭官吏，狱吏，鲍细霞家中的仆人，及其他侍从

地点　一部分在威尼斯；一部分在大陆上的贝尔蒙脱，鲍细霞邸宅所在地

Launcelot Gobbo [ˈlɑːnslətˈgɔbəu]
Leonardo [ˌli(ː)əˈnɑːdəu]
Balthazar [ˌbælθəˈzɑː]
Stephano [ˈstefənəu]

Portia [ˈpɔːʃiə]
Nerissa [niˈrisə]
Jessica [ˈdʒesikə]

ACT I

Scene I — Venice. A Street.

Enter Antonio, Salerio, and Solanio.

Ant.   In sooth [1], I know not why I am so sad;
It wearies me, you say it wearies you;
But how I caught it, found it, or came by [2] it,
What stuff' tis [3] made of, whereof it is born,
I am to learn [4];
And such a want-wit [5] sadness makes of me,
That I have much ado [6] to know myself.

Sal.   Your mind is tossing on the ocean,
There where your argosies [7] with portly sail
Like signiors [8] and rich burghers [9] on the flood,
Or as it were the pageants [10] of the sea,
Do overpeer the petty traffickers [11]
That cur'sy [12] to them, do them reverence,
As they fly by them with their woven wings [13].

Sol.   Believe me, sir, had I such venture [14] forth,
The better part of my affections would
Be with my hopes abroad. I should be still [15]
Plucking the grass to know where sits the wind,
Piring [16] in maps for ports and piers and roads;
And every object that might make me fear
Misfortune to my ventures, out of doubt
Would make me sad.

Sal.   My wind [17] cooling my broth [18]
Would blow me to an ague [19] when I thought
What harm a wind too great might do at sea.
I should not see the sandy hour-glass run [20]

---

1. **In sooth**〔古〕：其实，真实的。

2. **came by**：acquire，得到。

3. **'tis**=it is.

4. **I ... learn**：I have still to find out, i. e. I don't know.

5. **want-wit**：（复合形容词）愚钝的，want 表示"欠缺"，"匮乏"之意。

6. **ado**：费力，艰难。much ado 即"费尽心血"。

7. **argosies**〔诗〕：大商船，船队。

8. **signiors**："先生"。（源自意大利语 signor）

9. **burghers**：市民，公民。 由 burgh（苏格兰的自治市）衍生而来。

10. **pageants**：庆典，华丽的展览。

 莎士比亚经典名著译注丛书

第一幕

第一场　威尼斯；街道

安东尼奥、萨莱里奥及索拉尼奥上。

安　真的，我不知道我为什么这样闷闷不乐，它真叫我厌烦；你们说你们见我这样子，也觉得很厌烦；可是我怎样会让忧愁沾上了身，这种忧愁究竟是怎么一种东西，它是从什么地方产生的，我却全不知道，忧愁已经使我变成了一个傻子，我简直有点自己也不懂得自己起来了。

萨　您的心是跟着您那扯着满帆的大船，在海洋上簸荡着呢；它们就像水上的达官贵绅，炫示着它们的豪华，那些小商船向它们点头敬礼，它们却睬也不睬地凌风直驶。

索　相信我，老兄，要是我也有这么一笔买卖在海外，我一定要用大部分的心思牵挂它；我一定常常拔草观测风吹的方向，在地图上查看港口码头的名字；凡是足以使我担心我的货物的命运的一切事情，不用说都会引起我的忧愁。

萨　吹凉我的粥的一口气，也会吹痛了我的心，当我想到海面上的一阵暴风，将会造成怎样的一场灾祸。一看见沙漏的时计，

---

11. **petty traffickers**: 小商贩，这里指小船。
12. **cur'sy**: curtsey 或 curtsy（西方女性）屈膝礼。
13. **woven wings**: 指船帆。
14. **venture**:（冒险的）海运货物。
15. **still**: constantly.
16. **Piring**: peering，凝视，盯着看。
17. **wind**: breath，呼吸。
18. **broth**: 肉汤，清汤。
19. **ague**: 冷颤，发冷。
20. **sandy hour-glass run**: 莎士比亚时代还未发明钟表，故计时用沙漏计时器。罗伯特·彭斯（1759—1796）在 A Red Red Rose 这首诗里曾用 the sands of life 形容人的生命有限。

But I should think of shallows and of flats [21],
And see my wealthy Andrew [22] dock'd in sand,
Vailing her high top [23] lower than her ribs
To kiss her burial. Should go to church
And see the holy edifice of stone,
And not bethink [24] me straight of dangerous rocks,
Which touching but my gentle [25] vessel's side [26]
Would scatter all her spices on the stream,
Enrobe [27] the roaring waters with my silks,
And in a word, but even now [28] worth this,
And now worth nothing? Shall I have the thought
To think on this, and shall I lack the thought
That such a thing bechanc'd [29] would make me sad?
But tell not me; I know Antonio
Is sad to think upon his merchandise.

  Ant. Believe me, no. I thank my fortune for it,
My ventures are not in one bottom [30] trusted,
Nor to one place; nor is my whole estate
Upon the fortune of this present year:
Therefore my merchandise makes me not sad.

  Sol. Why then you are in love.

  Ant.   Fie [31], fie!

  Sol. Not in love neither? Then let us say you are sad
Because you are not merry; and'twere [32] as easy
For you to laugh and leap, and say you are merry
Because you are not sad. Now by two-headed Janus [33],
Nature hath fram'd strange fellows in her time:
Some that will evermore [34] peep through their eyes,
And laugh like parrots at a bagpiper [35];
And other [36] of such vinegar aspect [37]
That they'll not show their teeth [38] in way of smile

---

21. **shallows and flats**: 浅滩和平滩。使人联想到船只的搁浅。

22. **Andrew**: 船名。1596 年英国在 Cadiz 缴获了西班牙大帆船 St. Andrew，以后许多英国人用 St. Andrew 指代船只。直到现在许多英国水手称 Royal Navy 为"The Andrew"。

23. **Vailing her high top**: 低下桅顶。**Vailing**: to lower or bow as in surrender, 低头或俯首称臣; **high top**: 桅顶。

24. **bethink**: 想起，想到。

25. **gentle**: noble.

26. **side**: 船舷。

27. **enrobe**: 使穿长袍。这里指船只触礁翻船后丝绸漂流在大海之中。

28. **but even now**: just a moment ago.

29. **bechanc'd**: 发生，遭遇。bechanc'd 即 be-chanced。这里以 ' 号代替 e, 为的是压缩音节。以 -ed 结尾的

 莎士比亚经典名著译注丛书

我就会想起海边的沙滩，仿佛看见我那艘富丽的商船倒插在沙里，船底朝天，它的高高的桅樯吻着它的葬身之地。要是我到教堂里去，看见那用石块筑成的神圣的殿堂，我怎么会不立刻想起那些危险的礁石，它们只要略微碰一碰我那艘好船的船舷，就会把满船的香料倾泻在水里，让汹涌的波涛披戴着我的绸缎绫罗，方才还是价值连城的，一转瞬间尽归乌有？要是我想到了这种情形，我怎么会不担心这种情形也许果然会发生而忧愁起来呢？不用对我说，我知道安东尼奥是因为想到他的货物而忧愁。

安　不，相信我；感谢我的命运，我的买卖的成败，并不完全寄托在一艘船上，更不是倚赖着一处地方；我的全部财产，也不会因为这一年的盈亏而受到影响，所以我的货物并不能使我忧愁。

索　啊，那么您是在恋爱了。

安　呸！哪儿的话！

索　也不是在恋爱吗？那么让我们说，您因为不快乐，所以忧愁；这就像瞧您笑笑跳跳，就说你因为不忧愁，所以快乐一样，再便当没有了。凭双头的伊阿诺斯发誓，老天造下人来，真是无奇不有：有的人老是眯着眼睛笑，好像鹦鹉见了一个吹风笛的人一样；有的人终日皱着眉头，

形容词或过去分词在诗中常以这种形式出现。

30. **one bottom**：one ship or hold of a ship，一只船，或一只船的船舱。

31. **fie**：表示嫌恶、震惊，呸！咄！如 Fie upon you，去你的。

32. **'twere**：it were，等于 it would be，莎士比亚时代的虚拟语气常不用 would 或 should。

33. **Janus**：伊阿诺斯，是罗马神话中守护门户的两面神。他的头前后各有一副面孔，同时看着两个不同的方向。一副看着过去，另一副看着未来。在古罗马的建筑物以及一般住宅的大门上，都有他的雕像。Janus 司百物之初（如人生之始，年月之始等）。January（一月）即从 Janus 脱胎而来。

34. **evermore**：总是。

35. **And laugh...bagpiper**：laugh at something that is not funny；对并不好笑的事无端发笑。苏格兰人认为风笛所演奏的庄重悲哀的音乐是欢快的。

36. **other**：其他人。

37. **vinegar aspect**：阴郁的场面。

38. **show their teeth**：发怒，作威胁姿态。

Though Nestor [39] swear the jest be laughable.

Enter Bassanio, Lorenzo, and Gratiano.

Here comes Bassanio, your most noble kinsman,
Gratiano, and Lorenzo. Fare ye well [40],
We leave you now with better company.
　　Sal. I would have stay'd till I had made you merry,
If worthier friends had not prevented [41] me.
　　Ant. Your worth [42] is very dear in my regard.
I take it your own business calls on you,
And you embrace th'occasion [43] to depart.
　　Sal. Good morrow [44], my good lords.
　　Bass. Good signiors both, when shall we laugh [45]? say, when?
You grow exceeding strange. Must it be so?
　　Sal. We'll make our leisures to attend on yours [46].

　　　　　　　　　　[Exeunt Salerio and Solanio.]

　　Lor. My Lord Bassanio, since you have found Antonio,
We two will leave you, but at dinner-time
I pray you have in mind [47] where we must meet.
　　Bass. I will not fail you [48].
　　Gra. You look not well, Signior Antonio,
You have too much respect upon the world [49].
They lose it that do buy it with much care.
Believe me you are marvellously chang'd.
　　Ant. I hold the world but as the world, Gratiano,
A stage, where every man must play a part,
And mine a sad one.
　　Gra. 　　　　　　　Let me play the fool,
With mirth and laughter let old wrinkles come,
And let my liver rather heat with wine [50].
Than my heart cool with mortifying groans.
Why should a man, whose blood is warm within,

---

39. **Nestor**：奈斯脱。据希腊神话，他是海神波赛冬的孙子，涅琉斯的儿子，多年来当希腊西海岸皮罗斯的国王。年轻时，即以英勇著称，曾参加特洛伊战争。是年长和智慧的象征。
40. **Fare ye well**：再见。ye[古]：你们，汝等。
41. **prevented**：forestalled. 占先，抢在前头。
42. **worth**：高贵的人品。
43. **embrace th'occasion**：take the chance，借此机会。
44. **morrow**：morning。
45. **laugh**：相聚，笑着谈论。
46. **We'll make...yours**：We'll make ourselves available when you are free，有时间就来奉陪。

即使奈斯脱发誓说那笑话很可笑，他也不肯露一露他的牙齿，装出一个笑容来。

巴散尼奥，罗伦佐及葛莱西安诺上。

索　您的一位最尊贵的朋友，巴散尼奥，还有葛莱西安诺，罗伦佐都来了。再见；您现在有了更好的同伴，我们可以少陪啦。

萨　倘不是因为您的好朋友来了，我一定叫您快乐了才走。

安　你们的友谊我是十分看重的。照我看来，恐怕还是你们自己有事，所以借着这个机会想抽身出去吧？

萨　早安，各位大爷。

巴　两位先生，咱们什么时候再聚在一起谈谈笑笑？你们近来跟我十分疏远，这是为了什么呢？

萨　您什么时候有空，我们一定奉陪。（萨、索下。）

罗　巴散尼奥大爷，您现在已经找到安东尼奥，我们也要少陪啦；可是请您千万别忘记吃饭的时候咱们在什么地方会面。

巴　我一定不失约。

葛　安东尼奥先生，您的脸色不大好，您把世间的事情看得太认真了。一个人在重重忧虑中过日子，就失去了人生乐趣。相信我，您近来真的大大地变了一个人啦。

安　葛莱西安诺，我把这世界不过看作一个世界，每一个人必须在这舞台上扮演一个角色，我扮演的是一个悲哀的角色。

葛　让我扮演一个小丑吧。让我在嘻嘻哈哈的欢笑声中不知不觉地老去；宁可用酒温暖我的肠胃，不要用折磨自己的呻吟冰冷我的心。为什么一个身体里面流着热血的人，

---

47. **have in mind**：别忘记，切记。

48. **I will not fail you**：I will keep my promise，我一定不失约。

49. **respect upon the world**：concern for worldly affairs，关切世俗的一些事情。

50. **And let...wine**：用酒温热了我的肝。"肝"代表情感。

Sit like his grandsire cut in alablaster [51]?
Sleep when he wakes?   and creep into the jaundies [52]
By being peevish?   I tell thee [53] what, Antonio—
I love thee, and 'tis my love that speaks—
There are a sort of men whose visages
Do cream and mantle [54] like a standing pond [55],
And do a willful stillness entertain [56],
With purpose to be dress'd in an opinion [57]
Of wisdom, gravity, profound conceit [58],
As who should say, "I am Sir Oracle [59],
And when I ope [60] my lips let no dog bark! "
O my Antonio, I do know of these [61]
That therefore only are reputed wise
For saying nothing; when I am very sure,
If they should speak, would almost damn those ears
Which hearing them would call their brothers fools [62].
I'll tell thee more of this another time;
But fish not with this melancholy bait
For this fool gudgeon [63], this opinion.
Come, good Lorenzo. Fare ye well a while,
I'll end my exhortation after dinner.

  Lor.　Well, we will leave you then till dinner-time.
I must be one of these same dumb wise men,
For Gratiano never lets me speak.

  Gra.　Well, keep [64] me company but two years moe [65],
Thou shalt not know the sound of thine own tongue [66].

  Ant.　Fare you well! I'll grow a talker for this gear [67].

  Gra.　Thanks, i 'faith [68], for silence is only commendable
In a neat's tongue [69] dried and a maid not vendible [70].

       [*Exeunt Gratiano and Lorenzo.*]

  Ant.　It is that—any thing now!

  Bass.　Gratiano speaks an infinite deal of nothing,

---

51. **Sit.. .alablaster**: 像是石膏塑的老头子似的坐着。
 grandsire〔古〕: 老人, 祖先。　**alablaster**: alabaster.
 指石膏墓碑。
52. **jaundies**: 黄疸病。
53. **thee**: 第二人称单数代词"thou"(你)的宾格。
54. **cream and mantle**: 装出一种表情(字面意义为"长
 出了浮垢"。)。
55. **like a standing pond**: 像一潭死水。　**standing**: stag-

nant. 停滞的。
56. **entertain**: 保持, 相当于 maintain。
57. **opinion**: 名声。
58. **conceit**: thought.
59. **Sir Oracle**: 神谕先生, 意指无所不晓的人。
60. **ope**〔诗〕: open.
61. **of these**: some men.
62. **call their brothers fools**: 《新约·圣经·马太福音》

要那么正襟危坐，就像他祖宗爷爷的石膏像一样呢？明明醒着的时候，为什么偏要像睡去了一般？为什么动不动翻脸生气，把自己气出了一场黄疸病来？我告诉你吧，安东尼奥——因为我爱你，所以我才对你说这样的话：世界上有一种人，他们的脸上装出一副心如止水的神气，故意表示他们的冷静，好让人家称赞他们一声智慧深沉，思想渊博；他们的神气之间，好像说，"我说的话都是纶音天语，我要是一张开嘴唇来，不许有一头狗乱叫！"啊，我的安东尼奥，我看透这一种人，他们只是因为不说话，博得了智慧的名声；可是我可以确定说一句：要是他们说起话来，听见的人，谁都会骂他们是傻瓜的。等有机会的时候，我再告诉你关于这种人的笑话吧；可是请你千万别再用悲哀作钓饵，去钓这种无聊的名誉了。来，好罗伦佐。回头见；等我吃完了饭，再来向你结束我的劝告。

罗　好，咱们在吃饭的时候再见吧。我大概也就是他所说的那种以不说话为聪明的人，因为葛莱西安诺不让我有说话的机会。

葛　嘿，你只要再跟我两年，就会连你自己说话的声音也听不出来。

安　再见，我会把自己慢慢儿训练得多说话一点的。

葛　那就再好没有了；只有干牛舌和没人要的老处女，才是应该沉默的。（葛、罗下。）

安　他说的这一番话有些什么意思？

巴　葛莱西安诺比全威尼斯城里无论哪一个人都更会拉上一大堆废话。

第 5 章第 22 节中说"凡骂弟兄是笨蛋的，难免地狱之火"。这里指因骂人而下地狱。

63. **gudgeon**：a small fish, easily caught and often used for bail, 做钓饵的小鱼。

64. **keep**：if you keep.

65. **moe**：more, 更多, 再。

66. **Thou…tongue**：you shall not know the sound of your own accent.　**shalt**：shall 的第二人称单数现在时，与 thou 连用。

67. **gear**：stuff, nonsense, 胡说。

68. **i' faith**：in faith 实在, 真。

69. **neat's tongue**：牛舌头。　**neat**：牛类（总称。单复数同形）。

70. **vendible**：能卖的, 有销路的。这里的意思是"嫁得出去的"。

More than any man in all Venice. His reasons are as
Two grains of wheat hid in two bushels of chaff；
You shall seek all day ere [71] you find them，and when
You have them，they are not worth the search.

  Ant. Well，tell me now what lady is the same
To whom you swore a secret pilgrimage [72]，
That you to-day promis'd to tell me of?

  Bass. 'Tis not unknown to you，Antonio，
How much I have disabled mine estate [73]，
By something showing a more swelling port [74]
Than my faint means would grant continuance.
Nor do I now make moan to be abridg'd [75]
From such a noble rate [76]，but my chief care
Is to come fairly [77] off from the great debts
Wherein my time [78] something too prodigal
Hath [79] left me gag'd [80]. To you，Antonio，
I owe the most in money and in love，
And from your love I have a warranty
To unburthen [81] all my plots and purposes
How to get clear of all the debts I owe.

  Ant. I pray you，good Bassanio，let me know it，
And if it stand，as you yourself still do，
Within the eye [82] of honour，be assur'd
My purse，my person，my extremest means，
Lie all unlock'd to your occasions [83].

  Bass. In my school-days，when I had lost one shaft [84]，
I shot his fellow [85] of the self-same flight [86]
The self-same way with more advised watch [87]
To find the other forth，and by adventuring both
I oft [88] found both. I urge this childhood proof [89]，
Because what follows is pure innocence.
I owe you much，and like a willful youth，

---

71. **ere**〔古、诗〕：before.

72. **pilgrimage**：朝圣。莎士比亚时代把对情人的追求比作朝圣。

73. **disabled mine estate**：荒荡了产业。disable 作 reduce 解。

74. **swelling port**：high style of living，挥霍。

75. **to be abridg'd**：to be cut down.

76. **rate**：manner of living.

77. **fairly**：体面地。

78. **time**：youth.

79. **Hath**：has，第三人称单数动词有时用 th 结尾。

80. **gag'd**：pledged，mortgaged；抵押借债。

他的道理就像藏在两桶砻糠里的两粒麦子，你必须费去整天功夫才能够把它们找到，可是找到了它们以后，你会觉得费这许多气力找它们出来，是一点不值得的。

安　好，您今天答应告诉我您立誓要去秘密拜访的那位姑娘的名字，现在请您告诉我吧。

巴　安东尼奥，我怎样为了维持我的外强中干的体面，把一份微薄的资产消耗殆尽的情形，您是知道得很明白的；对于因为家道中落而感到的生活上的紧缩，现在我倒也不以为意；我的最大的烦恼，是怎样可以解脱我背上这一重重由于浪费而积欠下来的债务。无论在钱财方面或是友谊方面，安东尼奥，我欠您的债都是顶多的；因为你我交情深厚，我才不敢大胆把我心里所打算的怎样了清这一切债务的计划全部告诉您知道。

安　好巴散尼奥，请您告诉我吧。只要您的计划跟您向来的立身行事一样光明正大，那么我的钱囊可以让您任意取用，我自己也可以供您驱使；我愿意用我所有的力量，帮助您达到目的。

巴　我在学校里练习射箭的时候，每次把一枝箭射得不知去向，便用另一支箭向着同一方向射了过去，眼睛看准了它掉在什么地方，这样往往可以把那失去的箭也找了回来。我提起这一件儿童时代的往事作为譬喻，因为我将要对您说的话，完全是一种很天真的思想，我欠了您很多的债，而且像一个不听话的孩子一样，

---

81. **Unburthen**：Unburden 的变体。

82. **eye**：sight，view，视野。

83. **occasions**：needs 需要。

84. **shaft**：箭。

85. **his fellow**：another arrow，另一支箭。　**his**：its.

86. **flight**：range.

87. **advised watch**：小心注意。

88. **forth**：out.　**oft**〔古、诗〕：often，经常。

89. **urge...proof**：urge：mention 提及。　**proof**：experience 经历。

That which I owe is lost，but if you please
To shoot another arrow that self way
Which you did shoot the first，I do not doubt,
As I will watch the aim，or [90] to find both
Or bring your latter hazard back again,
And thankfully rest [91] debtor for the first.

    Ant.　You know me well，and herein spend but [92] time
To wind about my love with circumstance [93]，
And out of doubt you do me now more wrong
In making question of [94] my uttermost
Than if you had made waste of all I have.
Then do but say to me what I should do
That in your knowledge may by me be done,
And I am prest unto [95] it；therefore speak.

    Bass.　In Belmont is a lady richly left [96],
And she is fair and，fairer than that word,
Of wondrous virtues. Sometimes [97] from her eyes
I did receive fair speechless messages.
Her name is Portia，nothing undervalu'd [98]
To Cato's daughter，Brutus' portia [99].
Nor is the wide world ignorant of her worth,
For the four winds [100] blow in from every coast
Renowned suitors，and her sunny locks [101]
Hang on her temples like a golden fleece,
Which makes her seat of Belmont Colchis' [102] strond [103]，
And many Jasons [104] come in quest of her.
O my Antonio，had I but the means
To hold a rival place with one of them,
I have a mind presages me such thrift [105]
That I should questionless be fortunate！

    Ant.　Thou know'st [106] that all my fortunes are at sea，
Neither have I money nor commodity
To raise a present sum；therefore go forth,

---

90. **or**：either.

91. **rest**：仍然是。

92. **spend but**：only waste.

93. **circumstance**：formality，circumlocution，迂回表达。

94. **making question of**：questioning the extent of my willingness，怀疑是否愿意。

95. **prest unto**：准备、打算。

96. **richly left**：of inherited wealth，继承了巨额遗产。

97. **Sometimes**：从前。

98. **nothing undervalu'd**：in no way inferior，不比谁差，毫不逊色。

99. **To... Portia**：Cato，恺多，古罗马哲学家（95—46B. C.），**Brutus**：勃鲁脱斯，古罗马政治家，其妻Portia即是Cato之女，与本剧中Portia同名。

把借来的钱一起挥霍完了；可是您要是愿意向着您放射第一枝箭的方向，再把您的第二枝箭射了过去，那么这一回我一定会把目标看准，即使不把两枝箭一起找回来，至少也可以把第二支箭交还给您，让我仍旧对于您先前给我的援助做一个知恩图报的负债者。

安　您是知道我的为人的，现在您用这种譬喻的话来试探我的友谊，不过是浪费时间罢了；要是您怀疑我不肯尽力相助，那就要比把我所有的钱一起花掉还要对我不起。所以您只要对我说我应该怎么做，如果您知道那件事是我的力量所能办到的，我一定会给您办到。您说吧。

巴　在贝尔蒙脱有一位富家的嗣女，她生得非常美貌，尤其值得称道的，她有非常卓越的德性；从她的眼睛里，我有时接到她的脉脉含情的流盼。她的名字叫做鲍细霞，比起古代恺多的女儿，勃鲁脱斯的贤妻鲍细霞来，毫无逊色。这广大的世界也没有漠视了她的好处，四方的风从每一处海岸上带来了声名藉藉的求婚者；她的披在鬓角上的光亮的长发就像是传说中的金羊毛，使得她的贝尔蒙脱住宅变成了科尔喀斯的海滨，引诱着无数的伊阿宋前来向她追求。啊，我的安东尼奥！只要我有相当的财力，可以和他们中间无论哪一个人匹敌，那么我觉得我有充分的把握，一定会达到愿望的。

安　你知道我的全部财产都在海上；我现在既没有钱，也没有可以变换做一笔现款的货物。所以我们还是去试一试我的信用，

---

100. **four winds**: 四海之内，普天之下。

101. **sunny locks**: 金黄色的头发。

102. **Colchis**: 科尔喀斯。古国名，在黑海东端。

103. **strond**: strand, shore.

104. **Jasons**: 伊阿宋，出自希腊神话，伊阿宋是伊俄尔科斯国王伊孙的儿子。伊孙的同母异父的弟兄珀利阿斯篡夺了王位，后来答应把王位让给伊阿宋，

只要他肯去科尔喀斯把金羊毛取回来。于是伊阿宋就坐了大船阿耳戈号前去，他得到了科尔喀斯国王的女儿迷迭霞的帮助，取得了金羊毛。

105. **thrift**: thriving, success, 成功。

106. **Know'st**: knowest, 词尾-est, -st在古英语中用以构成动词的第二人称单数形式，又如 goest, dost 等。

Try what my credit can in Venice do.
That shall be rack'd [107], even to the uttermost,
To furnish thee to Belmont, to fair Portia.
Go presently inquire, and so will I,
Where money is, and I no question make [108]
To have it of my trust [109], or for my sake.   [_Exeunt._]

Scene **II** — Belmont. A Room in Portia's House.

Enter Portia and Nerissa.

Por.   By my troth [110], Nerissa, my little body is a-weary of this great world.

Ner.   You would be, sweet madam, if your miseries were in the same abundance as your good fortunes are; and yet for aught I see [111], they are as sick that surfeit with too much as they that starve with nothing. It is no mean happiness therefore to be seated in the mean [112] : superfluity comes sooner by white hairs, but competency [113] lives longer.

Por.   Good sentences [114], and well pronounc'd.

Ner.   They would be better if well follow'd.

Por.   If to do were as easy as to know what were good to do, chapels had been churches, and poor men's cottages princes' palaces. It is a good divine [115] that follows his own instructions; I can easier teach twenty what were good to be done, than to be one of the twenty to follow mine own teaching. The brain may devise laws for the blood [116], but a hot temper leaps o'er [117] a cold decree—such a hare is madness the youth, to skip o'er the meshes of good counsel the cripple [118]. But this reasoning is not in the fashion to choose me a husband. O me, the word choose! I may neither choose who I would, nor refuse who I dislike; so is the will [119] of a living daughter curb'd by the will of a dead father. Is it not hard, Nerissa, that I cannot choose one, nor refuse none?

---

107. **rack'd**: extended 尽最后努力。
108. **I no question make**: 我同意。
109. **of my trust**: through confidence in my ability,凭别人对我的信任。
110. **by my troth**: by my faith. 发誓，一定；真的。
111. **for aught I see**: 就我所知。
112. **in the mean**: 不多不少，中庸之道。
113. **Competency**: adequate wealth,有一定的财富。
114. **sentences**: maxims.

看它在威尼斯城里有些什么效力吧；我一定尽最大的努力，供给你到贝尔蒙脱去见那位美貌的鲍细霞。去，我们两人就去分头打听什么地方可以借得到钱，我就用我的信用做担保，或者用我自己的名义给你借下来。（同下。）

第二场 贝尔蒙脱；鲍细霞家中一室

鲍细霞及聂莉莎上。

鲍 真的，聂莉莎，我这小小的身体已经厌倦了这个广大的世界了。

聂 好小姐，您的不幸要是跟您的好运气一样大，那么无怪您会厌倦这个世界的；可是照我的愚见看来，吃得太饱的人，跟挨着饿不吃东西的人，一样是会害病的，所以中庸之道才是最大的幸福："富贵催人生白发，布衣蔬菜易长年。"

鲍 说得好，真是金玉良言。

聂 要是能够照着它做去，那就更好了。

鲍 倘使做一件事情，就跟知道什么事情是应该做的一样容易，那么小教堂都要变成大礼拜堂，穷人的草屋都要变成王侯的宫殿了。一个好的说教师才会遵从他自己的训诲；我可以教训二十个人，吩咐他们应该做些什么事，可是要我做这二十个人中间的一个，履行我自己的教训，我就要敬谢不敏了。理智可以制定法律来约束感情，可是热情激动起来，就会把冷酷的法令蔑弃不顾；年轻人是一头不受拘束的野兔，它会跳过老年人所设立的理智的藩篱。可是我这样大发议论，是不会帮助我选择一个丈夫的。唉，说什么选择！我既不能选择我所中意的人，又不能拒绝我所憎厌的人；一个活着的女儿的意志，却要被一个死了的父亲的遗嘱所钳制。聂莉莎，像我这样不能选择，也不能拒绝，不是太叫人难堪了吗？

---

115. **divine**: clergyman, 牧师。
116. **for the blood**: to control passion 控制情感。
117. **leaps o'er**: 忽略。
118. **the meshes...cripple**: meshes, 罗网，陷阱；**good counsel**, 忠告；**the cripple** 是 good counsel 的同位语，cripple 指不能采取行动的智者。
119. **will**: 意愿，下一行中的 will 指遗嘱。

Ner.   Your father was ever virtuous, and holy men at their death have good inspirations; therefore the lott'ry [120] that he hath devis'd in these three chests of gold, silver, and lead, whereof who chooses his meaning chooses you, will no doubt never be chosen by any rightly but one who you shall rightly love. But what warmth is there in your affection towards any of these princely suitors that are already come [121]?

Por.   I pray thee over-name them, and as thou namest them, I will describe them; and according to my description level at my affection [122].

Ner.   First, there is the Neapolitan prince.

Por.   Ay, that's colt [123] indeed, for he doth nothing but talk of his horse, and he makes it a great appropriation [124] to his own good parts [125] that he can shoe [126] him himself. I am much afeard [127] my lady his mother play'd false [128] with a smith.

Ner.   Then is there the County Palentine [129].

Por.   He doth nothing but frown, as who should say, "And [130] you will not have me, choose." He hears merry tales and smiles not. I fear he will prove the weeping philosopher [131] when he grows old, being so full of unmannerly sadness in his youth. I had so rather be married to a death' shead [132] with a bone in his mouth than to either of these. God defend me from these two!

Ner.   How say you by [133] the French lord, Monsieur Le Bon?

Por.   God made him, and therefore let him pass for a man. In truth, I know it is a sin to be a mocker, but he! why, he hath a horse better than the Neapolitan's, a better bad habit of frowning than the Count Palentine; he is every man in no man [134]. If a throstle sing, he falls straight a-cap'ring [135]. He will fence with his own shadow. If I should marry him, I should marry twenty husbands. If he would despise me, I would forgive him, for if he love me to madness, I shall never requite him [136].

Ner.   What say you then to Falconbridge, the young baron of England?

---

120. **lott'ry**：抽签决定婚姻。

121. **are already come**：have already come.

122. **level at my affection**：猜猜我对他们（求婚者）的情感如何。 **level**：guess.

123. **colt**：小马驹，指毛头小伙子。在莎士比亚时代，那不勒斯人以擅长骑术著称。

124. **appropriation**：addition.

125. **good parts**：天赋，才能。

126. **shoe**：钉马掌。

127. **afeard**：afraid 的变体。

128. **play'd false**：私通。

129. **County Palentine**：County 即 count 伯爵，**Palentine** 指旧时莱茵河西岸地区。这里 County Palentine 可看作是世袭的尊称，是专有名词。

聂 老太爷生前道高德重，大凡有道君子，临终之时，必有神悟，他既然定下这抽签取决的方法，叫谁能够在这金银铅三匣之中选中了他预定的一只，便可以跟您匹配成亲，那么能够选中的人，一定是值得您倾心相爱的。可是在这些已经到来向您求婚的王孙公子中间，您对于哪一个最有好感呢？

鲍 请你列举他们的名字，当你提到什么人的时候，我就对他下几句评语，凭着我的评语，你就可以知道我对于他们各人的印象。

聂 第一个是那不勒斯的亲王。

鲍 嗯，他真是一匹小马；他不讲话则已，讲起话来，老是说他的马怎么怎么；他把能够自己替他的马装上蹄铁，当成是一件天大的本领。我很有点儿疑心他的令堂太太是跟铁匠有过勾搭的。

聂 还有那位巴拉庭伯爵呢？

鲍 他一天到晚皱着眉头，好像说，"你要是不要我，随你的便。"他听见笑话也不露一丝笑容。我看他年纪轻轻，就这么愁眉苦脸，到老来怕要变成爱哭的哲学家了。我宁愿嫁给一个骷髅，也不愿嫁给这两人中间的任何一个；上帝保佑我不要落在这两个人手里！

聂 您说那位法国贵族勒·滂先生怎样？

鲍 既然上帝造下他来，就算他是个人吧。凭良心说，我知道讥笑人家是一桩罪过，可是他！吓！他的马比那不勒斯亲王那一匹好一点，他的皱眉头的坏脾气也胜过那位巴拉庭伯爵。什么人的坏处他都有一点，可是一点没有自己的特色；听见画眉鸟唱歌，他就会手舞足蹈；见了自己的影子，也会跟它比剑。我倘然嫁给他，等于嫁给二十个丈夫，要是他瞧不起我，我会原谅他，因为即使他爱我爱到发狂，我也是永远不会报答他的。

聂 那么您说那个英国的少年男爵，福根勃立琪呢？

---

130. **And**: if.
131. **weeping philosopher**: 指古希腊哲学家 Heraclitus（540—475 B.C.）为人类的愚蠢行为而经常流泪。
132. **death's-head**: skull, 骷髅，墓碑上通常刻着骷髅和两根交叉的骨头，死亡之象征。
133. **by**: concerning.
134. **he...man**: 他做人没有自己的个性。
135. **falls straight a-cap'ring**: 开始跳起来，a 是从古英语 on 演变而来，**a-cap'ring**: to dancing.
136. **never requite him**: never love him, **requite** 是 repay 的意思。

Por.   You know I say nothing to him, for he understands not me, nor I him. He hath neither Latin, French, nor Italian, and you will come into the court and swear that I have a poor pennyworth in the English. He is a proper [137] man's picture, but alas, who can converse with a d umb show? How oddly he is suited [138]! I think he bought his doublet [139] in Italy, his round hose [140] in France, his bonnet in Germany, and his behaviour every where.

Ner.   What think you of the Scottish lord, his neighbour?

Por.   That he hath a neighbourly charity in him, for he borrow' d a box of the ear of [141] the Englishman, and swore he would pay him again when he was able. I think the Frenchman became his surety and seal' d under for another [142].

Ner.   How like you the young German, the Duke of Saxony's nephew?

Por.   Very vildly [143] in the morning, when he is sober, and most vildly in the afternoon, when he is drunk. When he is best, he is a little worse than a man, and when he is worst, he is little better than a beast. And [144] the worst fall that ever fell [145], I hope I shall make shift [146] to go without him.

Ner.   If he should offer to choose, and choose the right casket, you should refuse to perform your father's will, if you should refuse to accept him.

Por.   Therefore for fear of the worst, I pray thee set a deep glass of Rhenish wine on the contrary [147] casket, for if the devil be within, and that temptation without, I know he will choose it. I will do any thing, Nerissa, ere I will be married to a spunge [148].

Ner.   You need not fear, lady, the having any of these lords. They have acquainted me with their determinations, which is indeed to return to their home, and to trouble you with no more suit, unless you may be won by some other sort [149] than your father's imposition [150] depending on the caskets.

- -

137. **proper**: handsome.
138. **suited**: 装束。
139. **doublet**: coat, upper garment, 大衣, 上衣。
140. **round hose**: 圆腿裤、灯笼裤。
141. **borrow' d...of**: 被人打了一耳光也不还手。

142. **seal' d...another**: 签字保证他必定还人一耳光。苏格兰常联合法国对付英国, 故云。
143. **vildly**: vilely.
144. **And**: if.

 莎士比亚经典名著译注丛书

鲍 你知道我没有对他说过一句话，因为我的话他听不懂，他的话我也听不懂；他不会说拉丁话，法国话，意大利话；至于我的英国话程度的高明，你是可以替我出席法庭作证的。他的模样倒还长得不错，可是唉！谁高兴跟一个哑巴子做手势谈话呀？他的装束多么古怪！我想他的紧身衣是在意大利买的，他的短统裤是在法国买的，他的软帽是在德国买的，至于他的行为举止，那是他从四面八方学来的。

聂 您觉得他的邻居，那位苏格兰贵族怎样？

鲍 他很懂得礼尚往来的睦邻之道，因为那个英国人曾经赏给他一记耳光，他就发誓说，一有机会，立即奉还；我想那法国人是他的保人，他已经签署契约，声明将来加倍报偿哩。

聂 您看那位德国少爷，撒克逊公爵的侄子怎样？

鲍 他在早上清醒的时候，就已经很坏了，一到下午喝醉了酒，尤其坏透；当他顶好的时候，叫他是个人还有点不够资格，当他顶坏的时候，他简直比畜生好不了多少。要是最不幸的祸事降临到我身上，我也希望永远不要跟他在一起。

聂 要是他要求选择，结果居然给他选中了预定的匣子，那时候您倘然拒绝嫁给他，那不是违背了老太爷的遗命了吗？

鲍 为了预防万一起见，所以我要请你替我在错误的匣子上放好一杯满满的莱茵河葡萄酒；要是魔鬼在他的心里，诱惑在他的面前，我相信他一定会选了那一只匣子的。什么事情我都愿意做，聂莉莎，只要不让我嫁给一个酒鬼。

聂 小姐，您放心吧，您再也不会嫁给这些贵人中间的任何一个的。他们已经把他们的决心告诉了我，说除了您父亲所规定的用选择匣子决定取舍的办法以外，要是他们不能用别的方法取得您的应允，那么他们决定动身回国，不再麻烦您了。

---

145. **fall ... fell**: befall ... befell.
146. **make shift**: contrive 努力做到。
147. **contrary**: wrong.

148. **spunge**: sponge, drunkard, 醉鬼。
149. **sort**: manner, way.
150. **imposition**: condition, 条件。

Por.　If I live to be as old as Sibylla [151], I will die as chaste as Diana [152], unless I be obtain'd by the manner of my father's will.　I am glad this parcel [153] of wooers are so reasonable, for there is not one among them but I dote on [154] his very absence, and I pray God grant them a fair departure.

Ner.　Do you not remember, lady, in your father's time, a Venetian, a scholar and a soldier, that came hither in company of the Marquis of Montferrat?

Por.　Yes, yes, it was Bassanio—as I think, so was he call'd.

Ner.　True, madam; he, of all the men that ever my foolish eyes look'd upon, was the best deserving a fair lady.

Por.　I remember him well, and I remember him worthy of thy praise.

Enter [155] a servant.

How now, what news?

Serv.　The four strangers for you, madam, to take their leave; and there is a forerunner come from a fift [156], the Prince of Morocco, who brings word the Prince his master will be here tonight.

Por.　If I could bid the fift welcome with so good heart as I can bid the other four farewell, I should be glad of his approach.　If he have the condition [157] of a saint, and the complexion [158] of a devil, I had rather he should shrive me [159] than wive me.

Come, Nerissa. Sirrah [160], go before [161].

Whiles we shut the gate upon one wooer, another knocks at the door.

[*Exeunt.*]

---

151. **Sibylla**：希腊神话中年长的女预言家。阿波罗答应她的寿命同她手里的沙子数目一样长。

152. **Diana**：罗马神话中的月亮女神，贞洁爱情的象征，Diana 也是狩猎女神。这句话的意思是：即使我像西比拉一样长寿，也要死得像黛安娜一样贞洁。

153. **parcel**：一群人。

鲍　要是没有人愿意照我的父亲的遗命把我娶去，那么即使我活到一千岁，也只好终身不嫁。我很高兴这一群求婚者都是这么懂事，因为他们中间没有一个人我不是唯望其速去的；求上帝赐给他们一路顺风吧！

聂　小姐，您还记不记得，当老太爷在世的时候，有一个跟着蒙脱佛拉侯爵到这儿来的才兼文武的威尼斯人？

鲍　是的，是的，那是巴散尼奥；我想这是他的名字。

聂　正是，小姐，照我这双痴人的眼睛看起来，他是一切男子中间最值得匹配一位佳人的。

鲍　我很记得他，他果然值得你夸奖。

一仆人上。

鲍　啊！什么事？

仆　小姐，那四位客人要来向您告别；另外还有第五位客人，摩洛哥亲王，差了一个人先来报信，说他的主人亲王殿下今天晚上就要到这儿来了。

鲍　要是我能够竭诚欢迎这第五位客人，就像我竭诚欢送那四位客人一样，那就好了。假如他有圣人般的德性，偏偏生着一副魔鬼样的面貌，那么与其让他做我的丈夫，还不如让他听我的忏悔。来，聂莉莎。正是——

垂翅狂蜂方出户，寻芳浪蝶又登门。（同下。）

---

154. **dote on**: 爱上某人。
155. **enter**: 上场。注意在戏剧中表示"上场"，第三人称单数不加-s。
156. **fift**: fifth.
157. **condition**: 性情，气质。
158. **complexion**: 外貌，长相。
159. **shrive me**: 听我的忏悔并赦罪。
160. **Sirrah**〔古〕: 来，喂。通常是对下属打招呼。
161. **go before**: 走在前面。

Scene **III** — Venice. A Public Place.

Enter Bassanio and Shylock.

Shy.　　Three thousand ducats [162].well.

Bass.　　Ay，sir，for three months.

Shy.　　For three months，well.

Bass.　　For the which，as I told you，Antonio shall be bound.

Shy.　　Antonio shall become bound [163]，well.

Bass.　　May you stead [164] me?　Will you pleasure [165] me?
Shall I know your answer?

Shy.　　Three thousand ducats for three months，and Antonio bound.

Bass.　　Your answer to that.

Shy.　　Antonio is a good man.

Bass.　　Have you beard any imputation to contrary?

Shy.　　Ho，no，no，no，no!　my meaning in saying he is a good
man is to have you understand me that he is sufficient.　Yet his means
are in supposition [166]：he hath an argosy bound to Tripolis [167]，another
to the Indies；I understand moreover upon the Rialto [168]，he hath a third
at Mexico，a fourth for England，and other ventures he hath，squand'
red [169] abroad.　But ships are but boards，sailors but men；there be land-rats
and water-rats，water-thieves and land-thieves，I mean pirates，and then
there is the peril of waters，winds，and rocks. The man is notwithstanding
sufficient.　Three thousand ducats：I think I may take his bond.

Bass.　　Be assur'd you may.

Shy.　　I will be assur'd I may；and that I may be assur'd，I will
bethink me.　May I speak with Antonio?

Bass.　　If it please you to dine with us.

Shy.　　Yes, to smell pork, to eat of the habitation which your prophet
the Nazarite [170] conjur'd the devil into.　I will buy with you，sell with you，

162.**ducats**：威尼斯金币，约相当于四分之一到二分之
　　一英镑。
163.**bound**：under bond，立契约。

164.**stead**：帮助。
165.**pleasure**：满足愿望。
166.**in supposition**：not in existence，不存在。

第三场 威尼斯；广场

巴散尼奥及夏洛克上。

夏　三千块钱，嗯？

巴　是的，先生，三个月为期。

夏　三个月为期，嗯？

巴　我已经对你说过了，这一笔钱可以由安东尼奥签立借据。

夏　安东尼奥签立借据，嗯？

巴　你愿意帮助我吗？你愿意应承我吗？可不可以让我知道你的答复？

夏　三千块钱，借三个月，安东尼奥签立借据。

巴　你的答复呢？

夏　安东尼奥是个好人。

巴　你有没有听见人家说过他不是个好人？

夏　啊，不，不，不，不；我说他是个好人，我的意思是说他是个有
　　身价的人。可是他的财产却还有些问题：他有一艘商船开到的黎
　　波里，另外一艘开到印度群岛，我在交易所里还听人说起，他有
　　第三艘船在墨西哥，第四艘到英国去了，此外还有遍布在海外各
　　国的买卖；可是船不过是几块木板钉起来的东西，水手也不过是
　　血肉之躯，岸上有旱老鼠，水里也有水老鼠，有岸上的贼，也有
　　海上的贼——我是说海盗！还有风波礁石各种的危险。不过虽然
　　这么说，他这个人是靠得住的。三千块钱，我想我可以接受他的
　　契约。

巴　你放心吧，不会有错的。

夏　我一定要放了心才敢把债放出去，为了放心，还是让我再考虑考
　　虑吧。我可不可以跟安东尼奥谈谈？

巴　不知道你愿不愿意陪我们吃一顿饭？

夏　是的，叫我去闻猪肉的味道，吃你们那拿撒勒先知把魔鬼赶进去
　　的脏东西的身体！我可以跟你们做买卖，讲交易，

---

167. **Tripolis**: 利比亚首都的黎波里。
168. **Rialto**: 威尼斯商业交易所。
169. **squand'red**: 挥霍，浪费。

170. **the Nazarite**: 拿撒勒先知，指耶稣基督，因为耶稣
　　出生在 Nazareth。此句暗指耶稣把魔鬼赶进猪群，
　　故犹太人不吃猪肉。

talk with you, walk with you, and so following; but I will not eat with you, drink with you, nor pray with you. What news on the Rialto? Who is he comes here?

Enter Antonio.

Bass.   This is Signior Antonio.

Shy.   [*Aside.*]   How like a fawning publican [171] he looks!
I hate him for he is a Christian;
But more, for that in low simplicity [172]
He lends out money gratis [173], and brings down
The rate of usance [174] here with us in Venice.
If I can catch him once upon the hip [175],
I will feed fat the ancient grudge [176] I bear him.
He hates our sacred nation, and he rails
Even there where merchants most do congregate
On me, my bargains, and my well-won thrift,
Which he calls interest. Cursed be my tribe
If I forgive him!

Bass.   Shylock, do you hear?

Shy.   I am debating of my present store,
And by the near guess of my memory,
I cannot instantly raise up the gross [177]
Of full three thousand ducats. What of that?
Tubal a wealthy Hebrew of my tribe,
Will furnish me. But soft [178]. how many months
Do you desire?   [*To Antonio.*]   Rest you fair, good signior,
Your worship was the last man in our mouths.

Ant.   Shylock, albeit I neither lend nor borrow
By taking nor by giving of excess [179],
Yet to supply the ripe wants [180] of my friend,
I'll break a custom.   [*To Bassanio.*]   Is he yet possess'd [181]
How much ye would?

Shy.   Ay, ay, three thousand ducats.

---

171. **fawning publican**：巴结讨好的税吏。可能 Shylock 把 Antonio 看成一个收税官。税吏拿走了商人的合法收益。也可把 publican 看做是巴结讨好顾客的小旅馆老板。（参见《新约·圣经·路加福音》第 18 章第 10—14 节。）

172. **low simplicity**：这两个词都有褒贬含义。**low**=(1) humble, (2) base; **simplicity**=(1) honest plainness, (2)folly. 夏洛克说此话时有明显的讥讽意味。

173. **gratis**：无偿地。

 莎士比亚经典名著译注丛书

谈天散步，以及诸如此类的事情，可是我不能陪你们吃东西喝酒做祷告。交易所里有些什么消息？那边来的是谁？

安东尼奥上。

巴 这位就是安东尼奥先生。

夏 （*旁白*。）他的样子多么像一个摇尾乞怜的税吏！我恨他因为他是个基督徒，可是尤其因为他是个傻子，借钱给人不取利钱，把咱们在威尼斯城里干放债这一行的利息都压低了。要是我有一天抓住他的把柄，一定要痛痛快快地向他报复我的深仇宿怨。他憎恶我们神圣的民族，甚至在商人会集的地方当众辱骂我，辱骂我的交易，辱骂我辛辛苦苦赚下来的钱，说那些都是盘剥得来的肮脏钱。要是我饶过了他，让我们的民族永远没有翻身的日子。

巴 夏洛克，你答应吗？

夏 我正在估计我手头的现款，照我大概记得起来的数目，要一时凑足三千块钱，恐怕办不到。可是那没有关系，我们族里有一个犹太富翁杜拔尔，可以供给我必要的数目。且慢！您打算借几个月？（*向安*。）您好，好先生，刚才我们正谈到您。

安 夏洛克，虽然我跟人家互通有无，从来不讲利息，可是为了我的朋友的急需，这回我要破一次例。（*向巴*。）他有没有知道你需要多少？

夏 嗯，嗯，三千块钱。

---

174. **usance**：利息。

175. **catch...hip**：摔跤术语，抓住臀部作为有利的支撑点将对手摔倒。

176. **feed...grudge**：痛痛快快地一报旧仇。

177. **gross**：总数。

178. **soft**：stop，且慢。

179. **excess**：利息。

180. **ripe wants**：urgent needs 急需。

181. **possess'd**：informed，被告知。

Ant.   And for three months.

Shy.   I had forgot — three months — [*to Bassanio.*]   you told me so.
Well then, your bond; and let me see — but hear you,
Methoughts [182] you said you neither lend nor borrow
Upon advantage [183].

Ant.   I do never use it [184].

Shy.   When Jacob graz'd his uncle Laban's sheep [185]—
This Jacob from our holy Abram [186] was
(As his wise mother wrought in his behalf [187])
The third possessor [188]; ay, he was the third—

Ant.   And what of him?   did he take interest?

Shy.   No, not take interest, not as you would say
Directly int'rest. Mark what Jacob did:
When Laban and himself were compremis'd [189]
That all the eanlings [190] which were streak'd and pied [191]
Should fall as Jacob's hire [192], the ewes being rank [193]
In end of autumn turned to the rams,
And when the work of generation [194] was
Between these woolly breeders in the act,
The skillful shepherd pill'd me [195] certain wands,
And in the doing of the deed of kind [196],
He stuck them up before the fulsome [197] ewes,
Who then conceiving did in eaning [198] time
Fall parti-colour'd lambs [199], and those were Jacob's.
This was a way to thrive, and he was blest;
And thrift is blessing, if men steal it not.

Ant.   This was a venture, sir, that Jacob serv'd for,
A thing not in his power to bring to pass,
But sway'd and fashion'd [200] by the hand of heaven.
Was this inserted [201] to make interest good [202]?
Or is your gold and silver ewes and rams?

---

182. **Methoughts**: it seemed to me, 即 methought.
183. **advantage**: 利息。
184. **I...it**: 我从没有这种习惯。   **use it**: make it my practice.
185. **When...sheep**: 夏洛克引用《旧约·圣经·创世纪》第 30 章第 27—43 节的例子为自己辩护。以撒叫他儿子雅各到外公彼士利家里，娶他舅舅拉班的女儿之一为妻。拉班有两个女儿叫利亚和拉洁。

雅各看中拉洁貌美，为拉班工作了七年，愿娶拉洁为妻。拉班辩解说，大女未嫁岂可嫁小女，若雅各要娶拉洁就得再为拉班牧羊七年。
186. **Abram**: 亚伯兰（后上帝改其名为阿伯拉罕），犹太人圣祖，见《旧约·圣经·创世纪》第 17 章。
187. **wrought in his behalf**: 为他设计，为他而做。
188. **possessor**: 继承人。
189. **compremis'd**: compromised, 同意。

安　三个月为期。

夏　我倒忘了，正是三个月，（向巴。）您对我说过的。好，您的借据呢？让我瞧一瞧。可是听着，好像您说您从来借钱不讲利息。

安　我从来不讲利息。

夏　当雅各替他的舅父拉班牧羊的时候——这个雅各是我们圣祖亚伯兰的后裔，他的聪明的母亲设计使他做第三代的族长，是的，他是第三代——

安　为什么说起他呢？他也是取利息的吗？

夏　不，不是取利息，不是像你们所说的那样直接取利息。听好雅各用什么手段：拉班跟他约定，生下来的小羊凡是有条纹斑点的，都归雅各所有，作为他的牧羊的酬劳；到晚秋的时候，那些母羊因为淫情发动，跟公羊交合，这个狡狯的牧人就乘着这些毛畜正在进行传种工作的当儿，削好了几根木棒，插在淫浪的母羊的面前，它们这样怀下了孕，一到生产的时候，产下的小羊都是有斑纹的，所以都归雅各所有。这是致富的妙法，上帝也祝福他；只要不是偷窃，会打算盘总是好事。

安　雅各虽然幸而获中，可是这也是他按约应得的酬报；上天的意旨成全了他，却不是出于他自己的力量。你提起这一件事，是不是要证明取利息是一件好事？还是说金子银子就是你的公羊母羊？

---

190. **eanlings**：小羊羔。

191. **pied**：variegated in colour，有条纹的，斑驳的，指羊羔身上的条纹和斑点。

192. **hire**：工薪。

193. **rank**：in heat，发情。

194. **generation**：生殖、繁殖。

195. **pill'd me**：peeled 剥好；削好。　**me**：冗语。只为加强语气，无实际意义。

196. **kind**：nature，天性。指交配。

197. **fulsome**：多产的。

198. **eaning**：产小羊。

199. **Fall parti-coloured lambs**：产下条纹斑驳的羊羔　**Fall**：let fall，give birth to，生产，产下；**parti-coloured**：斑驳的。

200. **sway'd and fashion'd**：被支配，左右。

201. **this inserted**：指 the story from the Bible 提起这段故事。

202. **make interest good**：justify taking interest. 为索取利息找借口。

Shy.　I cannot tell, I make it breed as fast.
But note me, signior.

　Ant.　　　　　　Mark [203] you this, Bassanio,
The devil can cite Scripture [204] for his purpose.
An evil soul producing holy witness
Is like a villain with a smiling cheek,
A goodly apple rotten at the heart.
O, what a goodly outside [205] falsehood hath!

　Shy.　Three thousand ducats — 'tis a good round sum [206].
Three months from twelve; then let me see, the rate —

　Ant.　Well, Shylock, shall we be beholding [207] to you?

　Shy.　Signior Antonio, many a time and oft
In the Rialto you have rated [208] me
About my moneys and my usances.
Still have I borne it with a patient shrug
For suff' rance is the badge of all our tribe [209].
You call me misbeliever, cut-throat [210] dog:
And spet [211] upon my Jewish gaberdine [212],
And all for use [213] of that which is mine own.
Well then, it now appears you need my help.
Go to [214] then, you come to me, and you say,
"Shylock, we would have moneys [215]," you say so—
You, that did void [216] your rheum upon my beard,
And foot me as you spurn [217] a stranger cur
Over your threshold; moneys is your suit [218].
What should I say to you? Should I not say,
"Hath a dog money? Is it possible
A cur can lend three thousand ducats? " Or
Shall I bend low and in a bondman's key [219],
With bated breath [220] and whisp' ring humbleness.
Say this：

---

203. **Mark**: 你看，你听。
204. **Scripture**:《圣经》。
205. **goodly outside**: 堂皇的外表。
206. **round sum**: 整数目。
207. **beholding**: beholden, indebted, 指是否可指望（对方）帮忙。
208. **rated**: reviled, 辱骂。

209. **For suff' rance...tribe**: 忍耐是我们民族的标记。
　　suff' rance: patience, 耐心；**badge**: mark, 标记。
210. **cut-throat**: 凶残的。
211. **spet**: spit, 吐唾液。
212. **gaberdine**: 粗糙布料做成的宽大长袍。
213. **use**: 双关，一指使用，二指 usury, 利息。

夏　这我倒不能说；我只是叫它像母羊生小羊一样地快快生利息。可是先生，你听我说。

安　你听，巴散尼奥，魔鬼也会引证《圣经》来替自己辩护哩。一个指着神圣的名字作证的恶人，就像一个脸带笑容的奸徒，又像一只外观美好中心腐烂的苹果。唉，奸伪的表面是多么动人。

夏　三千块钱，这是一笔可观的整数。十二个月里算三个月，让我看看利钱应该有多少。

安　好，夏洛克，我们可不可以仰仗你这一次？

夏　安东尼奥先生，好多次您在交易所里骂我，说我盘剥取利，我总是忍气吞声，耸耸肩膀，没有跟您争辩，因为忍受迫害，本来是我们民族的特色。您骂我异教徒，杀人的狗，把唾沫吐在我的犹太长袍上，只因为我用我自己的钱博取几个利息。好，看来现在是您要来向我求助了；也罢；您跑来见我，您说，"夏洛克，我们要几个钱；"您这样对我说。您把唾沫吐在我的胡子上，用您的脚踢我，好像我是您门口的一条野狗一样；现在您却来问我要钱，我应该怎样对您说呢？我要不要这样说，"一条狗会有钱吗？一条恶狗能够借人三千块钱吗？"或者我应不应该弯下身子，像一个奴才似的低声下气，恭恭敬敬地说，

---

214. **Go to**: term of remonstrance，现在好了，相当于 very well then.

215. **moneys**: 当时 money 可用复数形式，但语法上仍作单数看。

216. **void**: 吐痰。

217. **spurn**: kick, 踢。

218. **suit**: 目的。

219. **in a bondman's key**: humble voice 奴才的腔调。

220. **bated breath**: 低声。

"Fair sir, you spet on me on Wednesday last,
You spurn'd me such a day, another time
You call'd me dog; and for these courtesies
I'll lend you thus much moneys? "

  Ant. I am as like to call thee so again,
To spet on thee again, to spurn thee too.
If thou wilt lend this money, lend it not
As to thy friends, for when did friendship take
A breed for barren metal [221] of his friend?
But lend it rather to thine enemy,
Who if he break [222], thou mayst with better face
Exact [223] the penalty.

  Shy.   Why, look you how you storm [224]!
I would be friends with you, and have your love,
Forget the shames that you have stain'd me with,
Supply your present wants, and take no doit [225]
Of usance for my moneys, and you'll not hear me.
This is kind I offer.

  Bass. This were [226] kindness.

  Shy.   This kindness will I show.
Go with me to a notary, seal me there
Your single bond [227]; and in a merry sport [228]
If you repay me not on such a day,
In such a place, such sum or sums as are
Express'd in the condition, let the forfeit [229]
Be nominated for [230] an equal [231] pound
Of your fair flesh, to be cut off and taken
In what part of your body pleaseth me.

  Ant. Content, in faith, I'll seal to such a bond,
And say there is much kindness in the Jew.

  Bass. You shall not seal to such a bond for me,
I'll rather dwell in my necessity [232].

---

221. **A breed for barren metal**: 希腊哲学家亚里士多德认为，金银不应该生利息，所以收利息是不合理的。breed 指利息，barren metal 指金银币。
222. **break**: 破产。
223. **Exact**: 作动词用，索要。
224. **storm**: 发怒。
225. **doit**: a fraction of a farthing. 几文钱，面值很小的钱币。
226. **were**: would be.
227. **single bond**: 只由借方签字，不需公证人签署的契约。

 莎士比亚经典名著译注丛书

"好先生，您在上星期三用唾沫吐在我身上；有一天您用脚踢我；还有一天您骂我狗；为了报答您这许多恩典，所以我应该借给您这么些钱吗？"

安　我恨不得再这样骂你唾你踢你。要是你愿意把这钱借给我，不要把它当作借给你的朋友——哪有朋友之间通融几个臭钱也要斤斤计较地计算利息的道理？——你就把它当作借给你的仇人吧；倘使我失了信用，你尽管拉下脸来照约处罚就是了。

夏　哎哟，瞧您生这么大的气！我愿意跟您交个朋友，大家挺要好的；您从前加在我身上的种种羞辱，我愿意完全忘掉，您现在需要多少钱，我愿意如数供给您，而且不要您一个子儿的利息；可是您却不愿意听我说下去。我这完全是一片好心哩。

巴　这倒果然是一片好心。

夏　我要叫你们看看我到底是不是一片好心。跟我去找一个公证人，就在那儿签好了约；我们不妨开个玩笑，在约里载明要是您不能按照约中所规定的条件，在什么日子什么地点，还给我一笔什么数目的钱，就得随我的意思，在您身上的任何部分割下一磅白肉，作为处罚。

安　很好，就这么办吧；我愿意签下这样一张约，还要对人家说这个犹太人的心肠倒不坏呢。

巴　我宁愿安守贫困，不能让你为了我的缘故签这样的约。

---

228. **in a merry sport**：闹着玩。
229. **forfeit**：惩罚。
230. **nominated for**：如所说的那样。
231. **equal**：exact 精确的。
232. **dwell in my necessity**：继续受穷。　**dwell**：remain, 保持；**necessity**：匮乏。

Ant.　Why,　fear not,　man,　I will not forfeit it.
Within these two months,　that's a month before
This bond expires,　I do expect return
Of thrice three times the value of this bond.

　　Shy.　O father Abram,　what these Christians are,
Whose own hard dealings [233] teaches them suspect
The thoughts of others!　Pray you tell me this：
If he should break his day [234],　what should I gain
By the exaction [235] of the forfeiture [236]?
A pound of man's flesh taken from a man
Is not so estimable [237],　profitable neither,
As flesh of muttons,　beefs,　or goats.　I say,
To buy his favour,　I extend this friendship.
If he will take it,　so,　if not,　adieu [238];
And for my love I pray you wrong me not [239].

　　Ant.　Yes,　Shylock,　I will seal unto this bond.

　　Shy.　Then meet me forthwith at the notary's;
Give him direction for this merry bond,
And I will go and purse the ducats straight,
See to my house,　left in the fearful [240] guard
Of an unthrifty knave [241],　and presently
I'll be with you.

　　Ant.　　　　Hie thee [242],　gentle Jew.　[*Exit Shylock.*]
The Hebrew will turn Christian,　he grows kind.

　　Bass.　I like not fair terms [243] and a villain's mind.

　　Ant.　Come on,　in this there can be no dismay [244],
My ships come home a month before the day [245].　[*Exeunt.*]

---

233. **hard dealings**：硬心肠的事。注意这里 dealings 同
　　moneys 一样是单数名词。
234. **break his day**：fail to pay on the due date，到期违约。
235. **exaction**：强制（执行）。

236. **forfeiture**：被罚的数目。
237. **estimable**：值钱。
238. **adieu**〔法语〕：再见。
239. **wrong me not**：别冤屈了我。wrong 作动词用。

女 老兄，你怕什么；我决不会受罚的。就在这两个月之内，离契约的满期还有一个月，我就可以有三个三倍这借款的数目进门。

夏 亚伯兰老祖宗啊！瞧这些基督徒因为自己待人刻薄，所以疑心人家对他们不怀好意。请您告诉我，要是他到期不还，我照着约上规定的条款向他执行处罚了，那对我又有什么好处？从人身上割下来的一磅肉，它的价值可以比得上一磅羊肉，牛肉，或是山羊肉吗？我为了要博得他的好感，所以才向他买这样一个交情；要是他愿意接受我的条件，很好，否则就算了。千万请你们不要误会了我这一番诚意。

安 好，夏洛克，我愿意签约。

夏 那么就请您先到公证人的地方等我，告诉他这一张游戏的契约怎样写法；我就去马上把钱凑起来，还要回到家里去瞧瞧，让一个靠不住的奴才看守着门户，有点放心不下；然后我立即就来瞧您。

安 那么你去吧，善良的犹太人。（夏下。）这犹太人快要变做基督徒了，他的心肠变得好多啦。

巴 我不喜欢口蜜腹剑的人。

安 好了好了，这又有什么要紧？再过两个月，我的船就要回来了。（同下。）

---

240. **fearful**: arousing anxiety 使人焦急，不放心。
241. **unthrifty knave**: 乱花钱的奴才。
242. **Hie thee**: hasten，去吧，请快一点。
243. **fair terms**: fair language 好听的话。
244. **dismay**: 担心。
245. **the day**: 指契约到期那天。

ACT II

Scene I — Belmont. A Room in Portia's House.

Flourish cornets. Enter the Prince of Morocco, and his Followers;

Portia, Nerissa, and their Train [1].

    Mor.   Mislike [2] me not for my complexion,
The shadowed livery of the burnish'd sun [3],
To whom I am a neighbour and near bred [4].
Bring me the fairest creature northward born,
Where Phoebus' [5] fire scarce thaws the icicles,
And let us make incision for your love,
To prove whose blood is reddest [6], his or mine.
I tell thee, lady, this aspect [7] of mine
Hath fear'd the valiant; by my love, I swear
The best-regarded virgins of our clime [8]
Have lov'd it too. I would not change this hue [9],
Except to steal your thoughts, my gentle queen.

    Por.   In terms [10] of choice I am not soly [11] led
By nice [12] direction of a maiden's eyes;
Besides, the lott'ry of my destiny
Bars me the right of voluntary choosing.
But if my father had not scanted [13] me,
And hedg'd [14] me by his wit to yield myself
His wife who wins me by that means I told you,
Yourself, renowned Prince, then stood as fair
As any comer I have look'd on yet
For my affection.

    Mor.   Even for that I thank you;
Therefore I pray you lead me to the caskets
To try my fortune. By this scimitar [15]

---

1. **Train:** 一行人，随从。
2. **mislike:** dislike，不喜欢。
3. **The shadow'd...sun:** 光明的太阳给我的黑色制服；黑色制服指黑皮肤。
4. **near bred:** 近亲。
5. **Phoebus:** the sun god，希腊神话中的太阳神。即 Apollo。他是宙斯的儿子。权力很大，主管光明、青春、医药、畜牧、音乐、诗歌，并代表宙斯宣告圣谕。
6. **Whose blood is reddest:** 最勇敢的男子。
7. **aspect:** visage，长相。
8. **clime:** climate，转指国土。

第二幕

 **第一场** 贝尔蒙脱；鲍细霞家中一室

喇叭奏花腔。摩洛哥亲王率侍从；鲍细霞，聂莉莎及婢仆等同上。

摩　不要因为我的肤色而憎厌我；我是骄阳的近邻，我这一身黝黑的制服，便是它的威严的赐予。给我到阳光溶化不了冰柱的极北，找一个最白皙姣好的人来，让我们刺血察验对您的爱情，看看究竟是他的血红还是我的血红。我告诉你，小姐，我这副容貌曾经吓破了勇士的肝胆；可是凭着我的爱情起誓，我们国土里最有声誉的少女也曾为它害过相思。我不愿变更我的肤色，除非为了取得您的欢心，我的温柔的女王！

鲍　讲到选择这一件事，我倒并不单单凭信一双善于挑剔的少女的眼睛；而且我的命运由抽签决定，自己也没有任意取舍的权力，可是我的父亲倘不曾用他的远见把我束缚住了，使我只能委身于按照他所规定的方法赢得我的男子，那么您，声名卓著的王子，在我的心目中，您跟我已经看到的那些求婚者有同样的赢得我的机会。

摩　单是您这一番美意，已经使我万分感激了；所以请您带我去瞧瞧那几个匣子，试一试我的命运吧。凭着这一柄曾经手刃波斯王，

---

9. **hue**: colour of the skin. 皮肤颜色。
10. **terms**: respect.
11. **soly**: solely, 唯一。
12. **nice**: 挑三拣四的。

13. **scanted**: stinted, 限制。
14. **hedg'd**: confined, 制约。
15. **scimitar**: 阿拉伯的弯刀。

That slew the Sophy [16] and a Persian prince
That won three fields of Sultan Solyman [17],
I would o'erstare [18] the sternest eyes that look,
Outbrave the heart most daring on the earth,
Pluck the young sucking cubs from the she-bear,
Yea, mock the lion when'a [19] roars for prey,
To win thee, lady. But alas the while!
If Hercules and Lichas [20] play at dice
Which is the better man, the greater throw
May turn by fortune from the weaker hand;
So is Alcides [21] beaten by his page,
And so may I, blind fortune leading me,
Miss that which one unworthier may attain,
And die with grieving.

Por.　　　　　You must take your chance,
And either not attempt to choose at all,
Or swear before you choose, if you choose wrong
Never to speak to lady afterward
In way of marriage; therefore be advis'd [22].

Mor.　Nor will not [23]. Come bring me unto my chance.

Por.　First, forward to the temple [24]; after dinner
Your hazard [25] shall be made.

Mor.　　　　　Good fortune then!
To make me blest or cursed'st [26] among men.　*[Cornets and exeunt.]*

Scene **II** — Venice. A Street.

Enter Launcelot Gobbo.

Laun.　Certainly my conscience will serve [27] me to run from this Jew my master. The fiend is at mine elbow and tempts me, saying to me, "Gobbo, Launcelot Gobbo, good Launcelot," or "good Gobbo," or

---

16. **Sophy**: Shah of Persia 波斯国王的称号。
17. **Sultan Solyman**: 被波斯王子击败的土耳其苏丹 (1496?—1566)，1520—1566 在位。
18. **o'erstare**: outstare，直视对方。
19. **'a**: he，他（或它），这里指狮子。
20. **Hercules and Lichas**: Hercules，罗马神话中的大力士赫邱里斯（即希腊神话中的赫拉克勒斯），他一生除暴安民，神勇无敌，完成了十二项伟大业绩。Lichas 是 Hercules 的仆人和朋友。
21. **Alcides**: Hercules 的别名。
22. **be advis'd**: 三思而行。

并且使一个三次战败苏里曼苏丹的波斯王子授首的宝剑起誓，我要瞪眼吓退世间最狰狞的猛汉，跟全世界最勇武的壮士比赛胆量，从母熊的胸前夺下哺乳的小熊；当一头饿狮咆哮攫食的时候，我要向它揶揄侮弄，为了要博得你的垂青，小姐。可是唉！即使像赫邱里斯那样的盖世英雄，要是跟他的奴仆赌起骰子来，也许是弱手赌赢，赫邱里斯就是这样败在奴仆手里。我现在听从着盲目的命运的指挥，也许结果终于失望，眼看着一个不如我的人把我的意中人挟走，而自己在悲哀中死去。

鲍　您必须试一试运气，或者死了心放弃选择的尝试，或者当您开始选择以前，先立下一个誓言，要是选得不对，终身不再向任何女子求婚，所以还是请您考虑考虑吧。

摩　我的主意已决，不必考虑了；来，带我去试我的运气吧。

鲍　第一先到教堂里去；吃过了饭，您就可以试试您的命运。

摩　好，成功失败，在此一举！正是不挟美人归，壮士无颜色。

（奏喇叭；众下。）

第二场　威尼斯；街道

朗西洛脱·高波上。

朗　要是我从我的主人这个犹太人的家里逃走，我的良心是一定要责备我的。可是魔鬼拉着我的臂膀，引诱着我，对我说，"高波，朗西洛脱·高波，好朗西洛脱，

---

23. **Nor will not**: will not violate the condition. 莎士比亚时代常用双重否定表示强调的否定。
24. **to the temple**: 去教堂起誓。
25. **hazard**: 冒险，机会。
26. **blest or cursed'st**: 最幸福或最遭殃。'st（即-est。' 号代替 e）表示形容词的最高级。
27. **serve**: allow，encourage，鼓励。

"good Launcelot Gobbo, use your legs, take the start, run away." My conscience says, "No; take heed, honest Launcelot, take heed, honest Gobbo," or as aforesaid, "honest Launcelot Gobbo, do not run, scorn running with thy heels [28]." Well, the most courageous fiend bids me pack [29]. "Fia [30]!" says the fiend; "away!" says the fiend; "for the heavens [31], rouse up a brave mind," says the fiend, "and run." Well, my conscience, hanging about the neck of my heart, says very wisely to me, "My honest friend Launcelot, being an honest man's son" — or rather an honest woman's son, for indeed my father did something smack [32], something grow to [33], he had a kind of taste [34] — well, my conscience says, "Launcelot, bouge [35] not." "Bouge," says the fiend. "Bouge not," says my conscience. "Conscience," say I, "you counsel well." "Fiend," say I, "you counsel well." To be rul'd by my conscience, I should stay with the Jew my master, who (God bless the mark [36]) is a kind of devil; and to run away from the Jew, I should be rul'd by the fiend, who, saving your reverence, is the devil himself. Certainly the Jew is the very devil incarnation [37], and in [38] my conscience, my conscience is but a kind of hard conscience, to offer to counsel me to stay with the Jew. The fiend gives the more friendly counsel: I will run, fiend; my heels are at your commandement, I will run.

Enter old Gobbo with a basket.

Gob.　Master young man, you, I pray you, which is the way to Master Jew's?

Laun.　[*Aside.*]　O heavens, this is my true-begotten [39] father, who being more than sand-blind [40], high gravel-blind [41], knows me not. I will try confusions [42] with him.

Gob.　Master young gentleman, I pray you, which is the way to Master Jew's?

---

28. **with thy heels:** 双关：①愤怒地；②用脚后跟跑。
29. **pack:** be off, 打点行李离开。
30. **Fia:** 走吧。（应为意大利语 via, 意思是"begone!"）
31. **for the heavens:** 为了上帝的缘故。
32. **did something smack:** 有点毛病。
33. **grow to:** 渐渐严重起来。
34. **a kind of taste:** 有放荡的习性。
35. **bouge:** budge, 用于否定句, 移动的意思。
36. **God bless the mark:** =Save the mark! 不要见怪；不客气地说（常用作插入语）。同下文 saving your reverence,（说句难听的语；上帝恕我这样说）意思相当, 都是交谈时表示歉意的客套话。

拔起你的腿来，开步，走！”我的良心说，“不，留心，老实的朗西洛脱；留心，老实的高波；”或者就是这么说，“老实的朗西洛脱·高波，别逃跑；用你的脚跟把逃跑的念头踢得远远的。”好，那个大胆的魔鬼却劝我卷起铺盖滚蛋；“去呀！”魔鬼说，“去呀！看在老天的面上，提起勇气来，跑吧！”好，我的良心挽住我心里的脖子，很聪明地对我说，“朗西洛脱我的老实朋友，你是一个老实人的儿子”——或者还不如说一个老实妇人的儿子，因为我的父亲的确有点儿不大那个，有点儿很丢脸的坏脾气；——好，我的良心说，“朗西洛脱，别动！”魔鬼说，“动！”我的良心说，“别动！”“良心，”我说，“你说得不错；”“魔鬼，”我说，“你说得有理。”要是听良心的话，我就应该留在我的主人那犹太人家里，上帝恕我这样说，他也是一个魔鬼；要是从犹太人的地方逃走，那么我就要听从魔鬼的话，对不住，他本身就是魔鬼。可是我说，那犹太人一定就是魔鬼的化身，凭良心说话，我的良心劝我留在犹太人的地方，未免良心太狠。还是魔鬼的话说得像个朋友。我要跑，魔鬼，我的脚跟听从着你的指挥；我一定要逃跑。

老高波提篮上。

高　年轻的先生，请问一声，到犹太老爷的家里怎么走？

朗　（旁白。）天啊！这是我的亲生父亲，他的眼睛因为有八九分盲，所以不认识我。待我把他戏弄一下。

高　年轻的少爷先生，请问一声，到犹太老爷的家里怎么走？

---

37. **incarnation**：为 incarnate 之误，Gobbo 父子均是粗人，但喜欢用大字眼，可笑的用词错误（malapropism）造成了一种喜剧效果。

38. **in**: by.

39. **true-begotten**：亲生的。

40. **sand-blind**: partly blind，半瞎。

41. **high gravel-blind**：高波自己杜撰的词，意思是几乎全瞎。

42. **try confusions**：高波套用 try conclusions（尝试、试验）作如是说。

Laun.　Turn up on your right hand at the next turning, but at the next turning of all, on your left; marry [43], at the very next turning, turn of no hand, but turn down indirectly to the Jew's house.

Gob.　Be God's sonties [44], 'twill be a hard way to hit. Can you tell me whether one Launcelot, that dwells with him, dwell with him or no?

Laun.　Talk you of young Master Launcelot? 　[*Aside*.]　Mark me now, Now will I raise the waters [45]. —Talk you of young Master Launcelot?

Gob.　No master, sir, but a poor man's son. His father, though I say't, is an honest exceeding poor man and, God be thank'd, well to live [46].

Laun.　Well, let his father be what' a will, we talk of young Master Launcelot.

Gob.　Your worship's friend and Launcelot, sir.

Laun.　But I pray you, *ergo* [47], old man, *ergo*, I beseech you, talk you of young Master Launcelot.

Gob.　Of Launcelot, an't [48] please your mastership.

Laun.　*Ergo*, Master Launcelot. Talk not of Master Launcelot, father [49], for the young gentleman, according to Fates and Destinies, and such odd sayings, the Sisters Three [50], and such branches of learning, is indeed deceas'd, or as you would say in plain terms, gone to heaven.

Gob.　Marry, God forbid, the boy was the very staff of my age, my very prop [51].

Laun.　[*Aside*.]　Do I look like a cudgel or a hovel-post [52], a staff [53], or a prop? —Do you know me, father?

Gob.　Alack [54] the day, I know you not, young gentleman, but I pray you tell me, is my boy, God rest his soul, alive or dead?

Laun.　Do you not know me, father?

Gob.　Alack, sir, I am sand-blind, I know you not.

Laun.　Nay, indeed if you had your eyes you might fail of the knowing me; it is a wise father that knows his own child [55]. Well, old man, I will tell you news of your son. Give me your blessing; truth will come to light; murder cannot be hid long; a man's son may, but in the end truth will out.

- -

43. **marry**（int.）〔古〕：哎呀！哟！由 by Virgin Mary（凭圣母马利亚起誓）演变而来。

44. **Be God's sonties**：当时一种流行而无确定意义的起誓用语。　**Be**：by；**sonties**：little saints（？）。

45. **raise the waters**：模仿魔术师的语言。双关：(1)使事情乱套；(2)使人流眼泪。

46. **well to live**：with a good livelihood，生活得不错。与前句话意思相反。可能高波以为这话的意思是"身体不错"（in good health）。

47. **ergo**〔拉丁〕：therefore.

48. **an't**：if it.

朗　你在转下一个弯的时候，往右手转过去；但是下一次转弯的时候，往左手转过去，再下一次转弯的时候，什么手也不用转，曲曲弯弯地转下去，就转到那犹太人的家里了。

高　哎哟，这条路可不容易走哩！您知道不知道有一个住在他家里的朗西洛脱，现在还在不在他家里？

朗　你说的是朗西洛脱少爷吗？（*旁白。*）瞧着我吧，现在我要诱他流起眼泪来了。——你说的是朗西洛脱少爷吗？

高　不是什么少爷，先生，他是一个穷人的儿子；他的父亲，不过我说一句，是个老老实实的穷光蛋，多谢上帝，他还活得好好的。

朗　好，不要管他的父亲是个什么人，咱们讲的是朗西洛脱少爷。

高　他是您少爷的朋友，他就叫朗西洛脱。

朗　但是我请求你，所以老人家我要问你，你说的是朗西洛脱少爷吗？

高　是朗西洛脱，少爷。

朗　所以就是朗西洛脱少爷。老人家，你别提起朗西洛脱少爷啦；因为这位年轻的少爷，根据天命气数鬼神这一类阴阳怪气的说法，是已经去世啦，或者说得明白点是已经归天啦。

高　哎哟，天哪！这孩子是我老年的拐杖，我的唯一的靠傍哩。

朗　（*旁白。*）我难道像一根棒儿，或是一根柱子吗？——爸爸，您不认识我吗？

高　唉，我不认识您，年轻的少爷；可是请您告诉我，我的孩子——上帝安息他的灵魂！——究竟是活着还是死了？

朗　您不认识我吗，爸爸？

高　唉，少爷，我是个瞎子；我不认识您。

朗　唔，真的，您就是眼睛明亮，也许会不认识我，只有聪明的父亲才会知道他自己的儿了。好，老人家，让我告诉您关于您儿子的消息吧。请您给我祝福；真理总会显露出来，杀人的凶手总会给人捉住；儿子虽然会暂时躲了过去，事实到临了总是瞒不过的。

---

49. **father**: 对老年人的普通称呼。小高波并没有暴露自己是老高波的儿子的身份。
50. **Sisters Three**: 希腊神话中的命运三女神，即 Clotho, Lachesis 和 Atropos。
51. **prop**: 靠山；支撑。
52. **hovel-post**: 柱子，拐棍。
53. **staff**: 拐杖。
54. **Alack**(int.)：alas.
55. **it...child**: 高波把谚语"it is a wise child that knows his own father"倒过来说。意思是"只有聪明的父亲才了解自己的儿子"。

Gob.   Pray you, sir, stand up. I am sure you are not Launcelot, my boy.

Laun.   Pray you let's have no more fooling about it, but give me your blessing. I am Launcelot, your boy that was, your son that is, your child that shall be.

Gob.   I cannot think you are my son.

Laun.   I know not what I shall think of that; but I am Launcelot, the Jew's man, and I am sure Margery your wife is my mother.

Gob.   Her name is Margery indeed. I'll be sworn, if thou be Launcelot, thou art mine own flesh and blood. Lord worshipp'd might he be, what a beard [56] hast thou got! Thou hast got more hair on thy chin than Dobbin my fill-horse [57] has on his tail.

Laun.   It should seem then that Dobbin's tail grows backward [58]. I am sure he had more hair of his tail than I have of my face when I last saw him.

Gob.   Lord, how art thou chang'd! How dost thou and thy master agree [59]? I have brought him a present. How' gree you now?

Laun.   Well, well; but for mine own part, as I have set up my rest [60] to run away, so I will not rest till I have run some ground [61]. My master's a very Jew. Give him a present! give him a halter [62]. I am famish'd in his service; you may tell [63] every finger I have with my ribs. Father, I am glad you are come; give me your present to one Master Bassanio, who indeed gives rare new [64] liveries. If I serve not him. I will run as far as God has any ground. O rare fortune, here comes the man. To him, father, for I am a Jew if I serve the Jew any longer.

Enter Bassanio, with Leonardo and other Followers.

Bass.   You may do so, but let it be so hasted that supper be ready at the farthest by five of the clock. See these letters deliver'd, put the liveries to making, and desire Gratiano to come anon [65] to my lodging.

[*Exit a servant.*]

Laut.   To him, father.

Gob.   God bless your worship !

- -

56. **what a beard**: 老高波把小高波的头发当成了胡子。此时小高波可能低着头。

57. **Dobbin my fill-horse**: Dobbin 马名，fill-horse 套车的马。

58. **grows backward**: ①越长越短; ②长在不该长的地方。

59. **agree**: get along, 相处; 合得来。

高　少爷，请您站起来。我相信您一定不会是朗西洛脱，我的孩子。

朗　废话少说，请您给我祝福：我是朗西洛脱，从前是您的孩子，现在是您的儿子，将来也还是您的小子。

高　我不能想象您是我的儿子。

朗　那我倒不知道应该怎样想法了；可是我的确是在犹太人家里当仆人的朗西洛脱，我也相信您的妻子玛葛蕾就是我的母亲。

高　她的名字果真是玛葛蕾。你倘然真的就是朗西洛脱，那么你是我的亲生血肉了。上帝果然灵圣！你长了多长的一把胡子啦！你脸上的毛，比我那拖车子的马儿道平尾巴上的毛还多呐！

朗　这样看起来，那么道平的尾巴一定是越长越短的，我还清楚记得，上一次我看见他的时候，他尾巴上的毛比我脸上的毛多得多哩。

高　上帝啊！你多么变了样子啦！你跟主人合得来吗？我给他带了点儿礼物来了。你们现在合得来吗？

朗　合得来，合得来；可是从我自己这一方面讲，我既然已经决定逃跑，那么非到跑了一程路之后，我是决不会停止下来的。我的主人是个十足的犹太人；给他礼物！还是给他一根上吊的绳子吧。我替他做事情，把身体都饿瘦了；您可以用我的肋骨摸出我的每一条手指来。爸爸，您来了我很高兴。把您的礼物送给一位巴散尼奥大爷吧，他是会赏漂亮的新衣服给佣人穿的。我要是不能服侍他，我宁愿跑到地球的尽头去。啊，运气真好！正是他来了。到他跟前去，爸爸，我要是再继续服侍这个犹太人，连我自己都要变成犹太人了。

　　巴散尼奥率里奥那陀及其他侍从上。

巴　你们就这样做吧，可是要赶快点儿，晚饭顶迟必须在五点钟预备好。这几封信替我分别送出；叫裁缝把制服做起来；回头再请葛来西安诺立刻到我的寓所里来。（一仆下。）

朗　上去，爸爸。

高　上帝保佑大爷！

---

60. **set up my rest**: 下定决心。

61. **some ground**: some distance 一些距离。

62. **halter**: hangman's noose 上吊的绳子。

63. **tell**: 数，计算。

64. **rare new**: very new 崭新的。

65. **anon**: 立即。

Bass.   Gramercy [66], wouldst thou aught [67] with me?

Gob.   Here's my son, sir, a poor boy—

Laun.   Not a poor boy, sir, but the rich Jew's man, that would, sir, as my father shall specify [68]—

Gob.   He hath a great infection [69], sir, as one would say, to serve—

Laun.   Indeed the short and the long is, I serve the Jew, and have a desire, as my father shall specify—

Gob.   His master and he saving your worship's reverence are scarce cater-cousins [70]—

Laun.   To be brief, the very truth is that the Jew, having done me wrong, doth cause me, as my father, being I hope an old man, shall frutify [71] unto you—

Gob.   I have here a dish of doves that I would bestow upon [72] your worship, and my suit is —

Laun.   In very brief, the suit is impertinent [73] to myself, as your worship shall know by this honest old man, and though I say it, though old man, yet poor man, my father.

Bass.   One speak for both.   [*To Launcelot.*]   What would you?

Laun.   Serve you, sir.

Gob.   That is the very defect [74] of the matter, sir.

Bass.   I know thee well, thou hast obtain'd thy suit [75].
Shylock thy master spoke with me this day,
And hath preferr'd thee [76], if it be preferment [77]
To leave a rich Jew's service, to become
The follower of so poor a gentleman.

Laun.   The old proverb [78] is very well parted [79] between my master Shylock and you, sir: you have the grace of God, sir, and he hath enough.

Bass.   Thou speak'st it well. Go, father, with thy son.
Take leave of thy old master, and inquire
My lodging out.   [*To his followers.*]   Give him a livery
More guarded [80] than his fellows'; see it done.

---

66. **Gramercy**（int.）：=（grand mercy）many thanks, 多谢。
67. **aught**: anything.
68. **specify**: 指出, 说明, 证明。
69. **infection**: 系 affection 之误。老高波同儿子一样, 没有受过多大教育, 但喜欢用大字眼, 结果漏洞百出, 贻笑大方。
70. **cater-cousins**: good friends 好朋友。
71. **fruitify**: 系 certify（证明）之误用, 造成喜剧效果。
    fruitify: 多结果实, 使多产。
72. **bestow upon**: 赏赐。此处用词不当, 因为老高波比 Bassanio 的身份低。

 莎士比亚经典名著译注丛书

巴　谢谢你，有什么事？

高　大爷，这一个是我的儿子，一个苦命的孩子——

朗　不是苦命的孩子，大爷，我是犹太富翁的跟班，不瞒大爷说，我想要——我的父亲可以给我证明——

高　大爷，正像人家说的，他一心一意地想要侍候——

朗　总而言之一句话，我本来是侍候那个犹太人的，可是我很想要——我的父亲可以给我证明——

高　不瞒大爷说，他的主人跟他有点儿意见不合——

朗　干脆一句话，实实在在说，这犹太人欺侮了我，他叫我——我的父亲是个老头子，我希望他可以替我向您证明——

高　我这儿有一盘烹好的鸽子赏给大爷，我要请求大爷一件事，——

朗　废话少说，这请求是关于我的事情，这位老实的老人家可以告诉您；不是我说一句，我这父亲虽然是个老头子，却是个苦人儿。

巴　让一个人说话。（向朗。）你究竟要什么？

朗　侍候您，大爷。

高　正是这一件事。大爷。

巴　我认识你；我可以答应你的要求；你的主人夏洛克今天曾经向我说起，要把你举荐给我。不去侍候一个有钱的犹太人，反要来做一个穷绅士的跟班，其实这不是提拔你。

朗　大爷，一句老古话刚好由我的主人夏洛克跟您来平分。他有的是钱，您有的是上帝的恩惠。

巴　你说得很好。老人家，你带着你的儿子，先去向他的旧主人告别，然后再来打听我的住址。（向侍从。）给他做一身比别人格外鲜艳一点的制服，不可有误。

---

73. **impertinent**: 系 pertinent 之误，be pertinent to，与某人某事有关。

74. **defect**: 系 effect 之误。effect（大意），相当于 gist。

75. **suit**: 双关：（1）制服；（2）请求。

76. **preferr'd thee**: 推荐你。

77. **preferment**: promotion 提升，提拔。

78. **old proverb**: 指"He that hath the grace of God hath enough."这句谚语：上帝的恩惠等于大量财富。

79. **parted**: divided.

80. **guarded**: ornamented with braid or the like，镶边。

Laun.　Father, in. I cannot get a service, no, I have ne' er a tongue in my head, well!　[*Looking on his palm*.]　If any man in Italy have a fairer table [81], which doth offer to swear upon a book [82], I shall have good fortune. Go to, here's a simple line of life! Here' s a small trifle of [83] wives! Alas, fifteen wives is nothing! Aleven [84] widows and nine maids is a simple coming-in [85] for one man. And then to scape [86] drowning thrice, and to be in peril of my life with the edge of a feather-bed [87], here are simple scapes. Well, if Fortune be a woman, she' s a good wench for this gear [88]. Father, come, I'll take my leave of the Jew in the twinkling.

[*Exeunt Launcelot and Old Gobbo*.]

Bass.　I pray thee, good Leonardo, think on this：
These things being bought and orderly bestowed,
Return in haste, for I do feast tonight
My best esteem'd acquaintance. Hie thee, go.

Leon.　My best endeavours shall be done herein.

Enter Gratiano.

Gra.　Where's your master?

Leon.　　　　　　　　Yonder, sir, he walks.　[*Exit*.]

Gra.　Signior Bassanio!

Bass.　Gratiano!

Gra.　I have suit to you.

Bass.　　　　　　　You have obtain'd it.

Gra.　You must not deny me; I must go with you to Belmont.

Bass.　Why then you must. But hear thee, Gratiano：
Thou art too wild, too rude, and bold of voice—
Parts [89] that become thee happily enough,
And in such eyes as ours appear not faults,

---

81. **table**：palm，手掌，用于看相算命。

82. **swear upon a book**：手放在（圣经）上起誓。此处指说真话。

83. **small trifle of**：有一些。

84. **Aleven**：eleven.

85. **simple coming-in**：微薄的收入。指十一个女人算不了什么。

86. **scape**：escape，逃走，逃出。

朗　爸爸，进去吧。我不能得到一个好差使吗？我生了嘴不会说话吗？好，（视手掌。）在意大利要是有谁生得一手比我还好的掌纹，我一定会交好运的。好，这儿是一条笔直的寿命线；这儿有不多几个老婆；唉！十五个老婆算得什么，十一个寡妇，再加上九个黄花闺女，对于一个男人也不算太多啊。还要三次溺水不死，有一次几乎在一张天鹅绒的床边送了性命，好险呀好险！好，要是命运之神是个女的，她倒是个很好的娘儿。爸爸，来，我要用一霎眼的功夫向那犹太人告别。（朗西洛脱及老高波下。）

巴　好里奥那陀，请你记好，这些东西买到以后，把它们安排停当，就赶紧回来，因为我今晚要宴请我的最有名望的相识；快去吧。

里　我一定给您尽力办去。

　　葛莱西安诺上。

葛　你家主人呢？

里　他就在那边走着，先生。（下。）

葛　巴散尼奥大爷！

巴　葛莱西安诺！

葛　我要向您提出一个要求。

巴　我答应你。

葛　您不能拒绝我；我一定要跟您到贝尔蒙脱去。

巴　啊，那么我只好让你去了。可是听着，葛莱西安诺，你这个人太随便，太不拘礼节，太爱高声说话了，这几点本来对于你是再合适不过的，在我们的眼睛里也不以为嫌，

87. **feather-bed**: 婚床。

88. **gear**: business, 生意。

89. **Parts**: 品性。

But where thou art not known，why，there they show
Something too liberal [90]．Pray thee take pain
To allay with some cold drops of modesty [91]
Thy skipping [92] spirit，lest through thy wild behaviour
I be misconst'red [93] in the place I go to，
And lose my hopes.

  Gra．   Signior Bassanio，hear me：
If I do not；put on a sober habit [94]，
Talk with respect [95]，and swear but now and then，
Wear prayer-books in my pocket，look demurely [96]，
Nay more，while grace is saying hood mine eyes [97]
Thus with my hat，and sigh and say amen，
Use all the observance [98] of civility，
Like one well studied in a sad ostent [99]
To please his grandma，never trust me more.

  Bass． Well，we shall see your bearing [100].
  Gra． Nay，but I bar tonight [101]，you shall not gauge [102] me
By what we do tonight.

  Bass．   No，that were pity.
I would entreat you rather to put on
Your boldest suit of mirth，for we have friends
That purpose merriment [103]．But fare you well，
I have some business.

  Gra． And I must to Lorenzo and the rest，
But we will visit you at supper-time. [*Exeunt.*]

Scene **III** — The Same. A Room in Shylock's House.

Enter Jessica and Launcelot.

  Jes． I am sorry thou wilt leave my father so.
Our house is hell，and thou，a merry devil，
Didst rob it of some taste of tediousness.

---

90. **liberal**：放肆。
91. **modesty**：moderation，节制。
92. **skipping**：不计后果的。
93. **misconst'rd**：misconstrued，错认为。
94. **put on a sober habit**：假装严肃的样子。
 habit：行为，外表。

95. **with respect**：庄重地。
96. **demurely**：清醒，严肃。
97. **while grace...eyes**：Hats were worn during meals but removed during grace. 吃饭时戴帽子，但祷告时取下来。此处指在祈祷时用帽子遮住眼睛，假装虔诚。

可是在陌生人的地方，那就好像有点儿放肆啦。请你千万留心在你的活泼的天性里尽力放进几分冷静进去，否则人家见了你这样狂放的行为，也许会对我发生误会，害我不能达到我的希望。

葛　巴散尼奥大爷，听我说。我一定会装出一副安详的态度，说起话来恭而敬之，难得赌一两句咒，口袋里放一本祈祷书，脸孔上堆满了庄严；不但如此，在念食前祈祷的时候，我还要把帽子拉下来遮住我的眼睛，叹一口气，说一句"阿门"；我一定遵守一切礼仪，就像人家有意装得循规蹈矩，去讨他老祖母的欢喜一样。要是我不照这样的话做去，您以后不用相信我好了。

巴　好，我们倒要瞧瞧你装得像不像。

葛　今天晚上可不算；您不能按照我今天晚上的行动来判断我。

巴　不，那未免太杀风景了。我倒要请你今天晚上痛痛快快地欢畅一下，因为我已经跟几个朋友约定，大家都要尽兴狂欢。现在我还有点事情，等会儿见。

葛　我也要去找罗伦佐，还有那些人；晚饭的时候我们一定来看您。（各下。）

第三场　同前；夏洛克家中一室

吉雪加及朗西洛脱上。

吉　你这样离开我的父亲，使我很不高兴；我们这个家是一座地狱，幸亏有你这淘气的小鬼，多少解除了几分闷气。

---

98. **observance**: 礼仪。

99. **sad ostent**: 庄重的外貌。

100. **bearing**: 行为举止。

110. **bar tonight**: 今晚除外。

102. **gauge**: 据……判断。

103. **purpose merriment**: 打算尽情欢乐。

But fare thee well, there is a ducat for thee,
And, Launcelot, soon at supper shalt thou see
Lorenzo, who is thy new master's guest.
Give him this letter, do it secretly,
And so farewell. I would not have my father
See me in talk with thee.

  Laun. Adieu, tears exhibit [104] my tongue. Most beautiful pagan, most sweet Jew! If a Christian did not play the knave and get thee [105], I am much deceiv'd. But adieu, these foolish drops [106] do something drown my manly spirit. Adieu!

  Jes. Farewell, good Launcelot. [*Exit Launcelot.*]
Alack, what heinous sin is it in me
To be ashamed to be my father's child!
But though I am a daughter to his blood,
I am not to his manners [107]. O Lorenzo,
If thou keep promise, I shall end this strife,
Become a Christian and thy loving wife. [*Exit.*]

Scene IV —The Same. A Street.

Enter Gratiano, Lorenzo, Salerio, and Solanio.

  Lor. Nay, we will slink away [108] in supper-time,
Disguise us at my lodging, and return
All in an hour.

  Gra. We have not made good preparation.

  Sal. We have not spoke us yet of torch-bearers [109].

  Sol. Tis vile [110], unless it may be quaintly ordered [111],
And better in my mind not undertook.

  Lor. 'Tis now but four of clock, we have two hours
To furnish us.

Enter Launcelot with a letter.

---

104. **exhibit**: 乃 inhibit 之误用。

105. **if a Christian...thee**: 要不是一个基督教徒和你妈偷情生下了你。**play the knave** 意思是幽会，偷情；**get** 是 beget（出生）之意。

106. **drops**: 眼泪。

107. **manners**: 道德、品行。

可是再会吧，朗西洛脱，这一块钱你且拿了去；你在晚饭的时候，可以看见一位叫做罗伦佐的，是你新主人的客人，这封信你替我交给他，留心别让旁人看见。现在你快去吧，我不敢让我的父亲瞧见我跟你谈话。

朗 再见！眼泪哽住了我的舌头，顶美丽的异教徒，顶温柔的犹太人！倘不是一个基督徒跟你母亲私通，生了你下来，就算我有眼无珠。再会吧！这些傻气的泪点，快要把我的男子气概都淹没啦。再见！

吉 再见，好朗西洛脱。（朗下。）唉，我真是罪恶深重，竟会羞于做我父亲的孩子！可是虽然我在血统上是他的女儿，在行为上却不是他的女儿。罗伦佐啊！你要是能够守信不渝，我将要结束我的内心的冲突，皈依基督教，做你的亲爱的妻子。（下。）

第四场　同前；街道

葛莱西安诺，罗伦佐，萨莱里奥，索拉尼奥同上。

罗 不，咱们就在吃晚饭的时候溜了出去，在我的寓所里化装好了，只消一点钟功夫就可以把事情办好回来。

葛 咱们还没有好好儿准备过呢。

萨 咱们还没有提到过拿火炬的人。

索 那一定要搞得很体面，否则叫人瞧着笑话；依我看来，还是不用了吧。

罗 现在还不过四点钟；咱们还有两个钟头可以准备起来。

朗西洛脱持函上。

---

108. **slink away**：溜掉。
109. **torch-bearer**：拿火把的人。
110. **'Tis vile**：It is too poor. 糟糕。
111. **quaintly ordered**：办得很像样。

Friend Launcelot, what's the news?

Laun.   And it shall please you to break up this [112], it shall seem to signify.

Lor.   I know the hand [113]; in faith, 'tis a fair hand,
And whiter than the paper it writ on
Is the fair hand that writ.

Gra.   Love-news, in faith.

Laun.   By your leave, sir.

Lor.   Whither goest thou [114]?

Laun.   Marry, sir, to bid my old master the Jew to sup tonight with
my new master the Christian.

Lor.   Hold here [115], take this. Tell gentle Jessica
I will not fail her, speak it privately.
Go, gentlemen,   [*Exit Launcelot.*]
Will you prepare you for this masque tonight?
I am provided of a torch-bearer.

Sal.   Ay, many, I'll be gone about it straight [116].

Sol.   And so will I.

Lor.   Meet me and Gratiano
At Gratiano's lodging some hour hence.

Sal.   'Tis good we do so.   [*Exeunt Salerio and Solanio.*]

Gra.   Was not that letter from fair Jessica?

Lor.   I must needs tell thee all. She hath directed
How I shall take her from her father's house,
What gold and jewels she is furnish'd with,
What page's suit she hath in readiness.
If e'er the Jew her father come to heaven,
It will be for his gentle [117] daughter's sake,
And never dare misfortune cross her foot [118],
Unless she do it under this excuse,
That she is issue [119] to a faithless [120] Jew.
Come go with me, peruse [121] this as thou goest.
Fair Jessica shall be my torch-bearer.   [*Exeunt.*]

---

112. **break up this**: 拆开（此信）。

113. **hand**: handwriting, 笔迹。

114. **Whither goest thou**？ : Where are you going? 你去
     哪儿?

115. **Hold here**: take this, 把这个拿去。

116. **straight**: at once, 立即，马上。

罗　朗西洛脱朋友，你带什么消息来了？

朗　请您把这封信拆开来，说不定它就会告诉您的。

罗　我认识这笔迹；这几个字写得真好看；写这封信的那双手，是比这信纸还要洁白的。

葛　一定是情书。

朗　大爷，小的告辞了。

罗　你还要到哪儿去？

朗　呃，大爷，我要去请我的旧主人犹太人今天晚上陪我的新主人基督徒吃饭。

罗　慢着，这几个钱赏给你；你去回复温柔的吉雪加，我不会误她的约；留心说话的时候别给旁人听见。各位，去吧。（朗下。）你们愿意去准备今天晚上的假面舞会吗？我已经有了一个拿火炬的人了。

萨　是，我立刻就去准备起来。

索　我也就去。

罗　再过一点钟左右，咱们大家在葛莱西安诺的寓所里相会。

萨　很好。（萨、索同下。）

葛　那封信不是美丽的吉雪加写给你的吗？

罗　我必须把一切都告诉你。她已经教我怎样带着她逃出她父亲的家里，告诉我她随身带了多少金银珠宝，已经准备好怎样一身小童的服装。要是她的父亲那个犹太人有一天会上天堂，那一定因为上帝看在他善良的女儿面上特别开恩；厄运再也不敢侵犯她，除非借口说她的父亲是一个奸诈的犹太人。来，跟我一块儿去；你可以一边走一边读这封信。美丽的吉雪加将要替我拿着火炬。（同下。）

---

117. **gentle**：双关：(1)tender，温柔；(2)Gentile，非犹太人的。

118. **foot**：i. e. path，way.

119. **issue**：后裔。

120. **faithless**：不虔诚的。

121. **peruse**：细读。

Scene **V** — The Same. Before Shylock's House.

Enter Shylock and Launcelot.

Shy. Well, thou shalt see, thy eyes shall be thy judge,
The difference of old Shylock and Bassanio. —
What, Jessica! —Thou shalt not gurmandize [122],
As thou hast done with me—What, Jessica! —
And sleep and snore, and rend apparel out [123] —
Why, Jessica, I say!

    Laun.   Why, Jessica!

    Shy. Who bids thee call? I do not bid thee call.

    Laun. Your worship was wont to tell me I could do nothing without bidding.

Enter Jessica.

    Jes. Call you? what is your will?

    Shy. I am bid forth [124] to supper, Jessica.
There are my keys. But wherefore should I go?
I am not bid for love, they flatter me,
But yet I'll go in hate, to feed upon
The prodigal Christian. Jessica, my girl,
Look to my house. I am right loath to go;
There is some ill a-brewing towards my rest,
For I did dream of money-bags tonight [125].

    Laun. I beseech you, sir, go. My young master doth expect your reproach [126].

    Shy. So do I his [127].

    Laun. And they have conspir'd together. I will not say you shall see a masque, but if you do, then it was not for nothing that my nose fell ableeding [128] on Black Monday [129] last at six a'clock i'th' morning, falling out that year on Ash We'n'sday [130] was four year in th' afternoon.

---

122. **gurmandize**: gormandize, 贪吃。

123. **rend apparel out**: 扯破衣服。

124. **bid forth**: bidden forth, 被邀请。

125. **to night**: last night.

126. **reproach**: 责备, 乃 approach(coming)之误用。

127. **So do I his**: So do I expect his reproach.

128. **nose fell a-bleeding**: 流鼻血, 不祥之兆。

第五场　同前；夏洛克家门前

夏洛克及朗西洛脱上。

夏　好，你就可以知道，你就可以亲眼瞧瞧夏洛克老头子跟巴散尼奥有什么不同啦。——喂，吉雪加！——我家里容得你狼吞虎咽，别人家里是不许你这样放肆的；——喂，吉雪加！——还让你睡觉打鼾，把衣服胡乱撕破；——喂，吉雪加！

朗　喂，吉雪加！

夏　谁叫你喊的！我没有叫你喊呀。

朗　您老人家不是常常怪我一定要等人家吩咐了才会做事吗？

吉雪加上。

吉　您叫我吗？有什么吩咐？

夏　吉雪加，人家请我去吃晚饭；这儿是我的钥匙，你好生收管着。可是我去干什么呢？人家又不是真心邀请我，他们不过拍拍我的马屁而已。可是我因为恨他们，倒要去这一趟，受用受用这个浪子基督徒的酒食。吉雪加，我的孩子，留心照看门户。我实在有点不愿意去；昨天晚上我做梦看见钱袋，恐怕不是个吉兆。

朗　老爷，清您一定去；我家少爷在等着您赏光呢。

夏　我也在等着他赏我一记耳光哩。

朗　他们已经商量好了；我并不说您可以看到一场假面舞会，可是您要是果然看到了，那就怪不得我在上一个黑色星期一早上六点钟会流起鼻血来啦，那一年正是在圣灰节星期三第四年的下午。

---

129. **Black Monday**: 黑色星期一。指 1360 年的复活节星期一，4 月 14 日，天气极其寒冷，英王爱德华进攻巴黎，兵士多冻死。故人们认为这一天不吉利。

130. **Ash We'n'sday**: （基督教）圣灰星期三，四旬节（复活节前四十日）的第一天。　We'n'sday=Wednesday.

Shy.　What, are there masques?　Hear you me, Jessica:

Lock up my doors, and when you hear the drum

And the vile squealing of the wry-neck'd fife [131],

Clamber not you up to the casements then,

Nor thrust your head into the public street

To gaze on Christian fools with varnish'd faces [132];

But stop my house's ears, I mean my casements;

Let not the sound of shallow fopp'ry [133] enter

My sober house.　By Jacob's staff [134] I swear

I have no mind of feasting forth [135] tonight;

But I will go.　Go you before me, sirrah,

Say I will come.

　　Laun.　I will go before, sir.　Mistress, look out at window for all

this [136]—

　　　　　　There will come a Christian by,

　　　　　　Will be worth a Jewess' eye.　[*Exit*.]

　Shy.　What says that fool of Hagar's offspring [137], ha?

　Jes.　His words were "Farewell, mistress!" —nothing else.

　Shy.　The patch is kind enough, but a huge feeder,

Snail-slow in profit [138], and he sleeps by day

More than the wild-cat.　Drones hive not with me,

Therefore I part with him, and part with him

To one that I would have him help to waste

His borrowed purse.　Well, Jessica, go in,

Perhaps I will return immediately.

Do as I bid you, shut doors after you;

Fast bind, fast find—

A proverb never stale in thrifty mind [139].　[*Exit*.]

　Jes.　Farewell, and if my fortune be not cross'd,

I have a father, you a daughter, lost.　[*Exit*.]

---

131. **wry-neck'd fife**: fife-player with head twisted to one side, 歪脖子的吹笛者, 同上文 drum 一样, fife 既可指乐器又可指演奏乐器的人。

132. **varnish'd faces**: 面罩; 假面。

133. **fopp'ry**: 愚蠢。

134. **by Jacob's staff**: 凭雅各的牧羊杖。参见《旧约·圣经·创世纪》第 32 章第 10 节。

135. **of feasting forth**: dining out, 外出吃饭。

136. **for all this**: despite all that Shylock has said. 不管夏洛克说什么。

137. **Hagar's offspring**: 夏甲为犹太人始祖亚伯兰正妻撒拉的婢女。撒拉因无子, 劝亚伯兰纳夏甲为妾。夏甲生子后, 遭撒拉妒忌, 并与其子一道遭斥逐。参见《旧约·圣经·创世纪》第 12 章第 14 节。夏甲的后裔, 即"贱种"之谓。

夏　怎么！还有假面舞会吗？听好，吉雪加，把家里的门锁了；听见
　　鼓声和弯笛子的怪叫声音，不许爬到窗格子上张望，也不要伸出
　　头去，瞧那些脸上涂得花花绿绿的傻基督徒们打街道上走过。所
　　有的窗都给我关起来，别让那些无聊的胡闹的声音钻进我的清静
　　的屋子里。凭着雅各的牧羊杖发誓，我今晚真有点不想出去参加
　　什么宴会。可是就去这一次吧。小子，你先回去，说我就来了。

朗　那么我先去了，老爷。小姐，留心看好窗外；"跑来一个基督徒，
　　不要错过好姻缘"（下。）

夏　嘿，那个夏甲的傻瓜后裔说些什么？

吉　没有说什么，他只是说，"再会，小姐。"

夏　这蠢才人倒还好，就是食量太大；做起事来，慢吞吞像条蜗牛一
　　般；白天睡觉的本领，比野猫还胜过几分；我家里可容不得懒惰
　　的黄蜂，所以才打发他走了，让他去跟着那个靠借债过日子的败
　　家精，正好帮他消费，好，吉雪加，进去吧；也许我一会儿就回
　　来，记住我的话，把门随手关了。"缚得牢，跑不了"，这是一句
　　千古不磨的至理名言。（下。）

吉　再会；要是我的命运不跟我作梗，那么我将要失去一个父亲，你
　　也要失去一个女儿了。（下。）

---

138. **profit**：improvement，proficiency，进展，效率。　　139. **A proverb…mind**：在节俭人心里永不陈腐的格言。

Scene VI — The Same.

Enter Gratiano and Salerio, masqued.

Gra.   This is the penthouse [140] under which Lorenzo
Desir'd us to make stand.

Sal.   His hour is almost past.

Gra.   And it is marvel he out-dwells his hour,
For lovers ever run before the clock.

Sal.   O, ten times faster Venus' pigeons [141] fly
To seal love's bonds new made, than they are wont
To keep obliged faith unforfeited!

Gra.   That ever holds. Who riseth from a feast
With that keen appetite that he sits down?
Where is the horse that doth untread [142] again
His tedious measures with the unbated fire [143]
That he did pace them first?   All things that are,
Are with more spirit chased than enjoy'd
How like a younger [144] or a prodigal
The scarfed bark [145] puts from her native bay,
Hugg'd and embraced by the strumpet wind [146]!
How like the prodigal doth she return,
With over-weather'd ribs and ragged sails,
Lean, rent [147], and beggar'd by the strumpet wind!

Enter Lorenzo.

Sal.   Here comes Lorenzo, more of this hereafter [148].

Lor.   Sweet friends, your patience for my long abode [149];
Not I but my affairs have made you wait.
When you shall please to play the thieves for wives.
I'll watch as long for you then. Approach,
Here dwells my father [150] Jew. Ho! who's within?

---

140. **penthouse**: 屋檐。
141. **Venus' pigeons**: 驾驶维纳丝双轮车的鸽子。维纳
丝是罗马神话中爱和美的女神,即希腊神话中的
阿芙洛狄特。
142. **untread**: retrace, 走回头路。
143. **unbated fire**: 不减弱的精神。 **fire**=spirit.
144. **younger**: i.e.younger son, 意指"浪子"。
145. **scarfed bark**: 挂满旗帜的船只。
146. **strumpet wind**: 狂浪的风, **strumpet** 指妓女。此
处将船比作浪子,大风比作娼妓。

第六场　同前

葛莱西安诺及萨莱里奥戴假面同上。

葛　这儿屋檐下便是罗伦佐叫我们守望的地方。

萨　他约定的时间快要过去了。

葛　他会迟到真是件怪事。因为恋人们总是赶在时钟的前面的。

萨　啊！维纳丝的鸽子飞去缔结新欢的盟约，比之履行旧日的诺言，总是要快上十倍。

葛　那是一定的道理。谁在席终人散以后，他的食欲还像初入座时候那么强烈？哪一匹马在冗长的归途上，会像它起程时那么长驱疾驰？世间的任何事物，追求时的兴致总要比享用时的兴致浓烈。一艘新下水的船只扬帆出港的当儿，多么像一个娇养的少年，给那轻狂的风儿爱抚搂抱！可是等到它回来的时候，船身已遭风日的侵蚀，船帆也变成了百结的破衲，它又多么像一个落魄的浪子，给那轻狂的风儿肆意欺凌！

罗伦佐上。

萨　罗伦佐来啦；这些话你留着以后再说吧。

罗　两位好朋友，累你们久等了，对不起得很；实在是因为我有点事情，急切里抽身不出。等你们将来也要偷妻子的时候，我一定也替你们守这么些时候。过来，这儿就是我的犹太岳父所住的地方。喂！里面有人吗？

---

147. **rent**: 破烂。

148. **more of this hereafter**: 以后再谈。

149. **abode**: delay，耽误。

150. **father**: 岳父。

Enter Jessica above in boy's clothes.

  Jes. Who are you? tell me for more certainty,
Albeit I'll swear that I do know your tongue.
  Lor. Lorenzo, and thy love.
  Jes. Lorenzo, certain, and my love indeed,
For who love I so much? And now who knows
But you, Lorenzo, whether I am yours?
  Lor. Heaven and thy thoughts are witness that thou art.
  Jes. Here, catch this casket, it is worth the pains.
I am glad 'tis night, you do not look on me,
For I am much asham'd of my exchange [151].
But love is blind, and lovers cannot see
The pretty follies that themselves commit,
For if they could, Cupid [152] himself would blush
To see me thus transformed to a boy.
  Lor. Descend, for you must be my torch-bearer.
  Jes. What, must I hold a candle to my shames?
They in themselves, good sooth, are too too light [153].
Why, 'tis an office of discovery [154], love,
And I should be obscur'd.
  Lor.   So are you, sweet,
Even in the lovely garnish [155] of a boy.
But come at once,
For the close [156] night doth play the runaway,
And we are stay'd for at Bassanio's feast.
  Jes. I will make fast the doors, and gild myself
With some more ducats, and be with you straight. [*Exit above.*]
  Gra. Now by my hood, a gentle, and no Jew.
  Lor. Beshrow [157] me but [158] I love her heartily,
For she is wise, if I can judge of her,

---

151. **exchange**: 指换上了男孩的衣服。
152. **Cupid**: 丘比特,罗马神话中的小爱神。
153. **light**: 双关:(1)明亮,(2)轻狂。

154. **'tis...discovery**: 举火炬的全部作用就是让别人看到自己。
155. **garnish**: dress,服装,装束。

吉雪加男装自上方上。

吉 你是哪一个？我虽然认识你的声音，可是为了免得错认了人，请你把名字告诉我。

罗 我是罗伦佐，你的爱人。

吉 你果然是罗伦佐，也的确是我的爱人，谁会使我爱得像爱你一样呢？罗伦佐，除了你之外，谁还知道我究竟是不是属于你的？

罗 上天和你的思想，都可以证明你是属于我的。

吉 来，把这匣子接住了，你拿了去大有好处的。幸亏在夜里，你瞧不见我，我改扮成这个怪样子，怪不好意思哩。可是恋爱是盲目的，恋人们瞧不见他们自己所干的傻事；要是他们瞧得见的话，那么丘比特瞧见我变成一个男孩子，也会脸红起来哩。

罗 下来吧，你必须替我拿着火炬。

吉 怎么！我必须拿着烛火，照亮自己的羞耻吗？像我这样子，已经太轻狂了，应该遮掩遮掩才是，怎么反而要在别人面前露脸？

罗 亲爱的，你穿上这一身漂亮的男孩子衣服，人家不会认出你来的。快来吧，夜色已经在不知不觉中深了起来，巴散尼奥在等着我们去赴宴呢。

吉 让我把门窗关好，再收拾些银钱带在身边，然后立刻就来。

（自上方下。）

葛 凭着我的头巾发誓，她真是个基督徒，不是个犹太人。

罗 我从心底里爱着她。要是我有判断的能力，那么她是聪明的；

---

156. **close**: secret.

157. **Beshrow**〔古〕: beshrew, evil befall（weakened curse），咒语。

158. **but**: 如果不。

And fair she is, if that mine eyes be true,
And true she is, as she hath prov'd herself;
And therefore, like herself, wise, fair, and true,
Shall she be placed in my constant soul.

Enter Jessica.

What, art thou come? On, gentlemen, away!
Our masquing mates by this time for us stay [159].

[Exit with Jessica and Salerio.]

Enter Antonio.

Ant.   Who's there?
Gra.   Signior Antonio!
Ant.   Fie [160], fie, Gratiano, where are all the rest?
'Tis nine a'clock—our friends all stay for you.
No masque tonight, the wind is come about,
Bassanio presently will go aboard.
I have sent twenty out to seek for you.
Gra.   I am glad on't. I desire no more delight
Than to be under sail [161], and gone tonight.   *[Exeunt.]*

Scene VII — Belmont. A Room in Portia's House.

Flourish cornets. Enter Portia with the Prince of Morocco and their Trains.

Por.   Go, draw aside the curtains and discover [162]
The several caskets to this noble prince.
Now make your choice.
Mor.   This first, of gold, who this inscription bears,
"Who chooseth me shall gain what many men desire";
The second, silver, which this promise carries,
"Who chooseth me shall get as much as he deserves";

----

159. **stay**: wait, 等待。   160. **Fie**(int.)：呸，呸。

要是我的眼睛没有欺骗我，那么她是美貌的；她已经替自己证明她是忠诚的；像她这样又聪明，又美丽，又忠诚，怎么不叫我把她永远放在自己的灵魂里呢？

吉雪加上。

罗　啊，你来了吗？朋友们，走吧！我们的舞伴们现在一定在那儿等着我们了。（罗、吉、萨同下）

安东尼奥上。

安　那边是谁？

葛　安东尼奥先生！

安　咦，葛莱西安诺！还有那些人呢？现在已经九点钟啦，我们的朋友们大家在那儿等着你们。今天晚上的假面舞会取消了，风势已转，巴散尼奥就要立刻上船。我已经差了二十个人来找你们了。

葛　那好极了；我巴不得今天晚上就开船出发。（同下。）

第七场　贝尔蒙脱；鲍细霞家中一室

喇叭奏花腔。鲍细霞及摩洛哥亲王各率侍从上。

鲍　去把帐幕揭开，让这位尊贵的王子瞧瞧那几个匣子。现在请殿下自己选择吧。

摩　第一只匣子是金的，上面刻着这几个字："谁选择了我，将要得到众人所希求的东西。"第二只匣子是银的，上面刻着这样的约许："谁选择了我，将要得到他所应得的东西。"

---

161. **under sail**：开船。　　162. **discover**：reveal，打开，让人看。

This third, dull lead, with warning all as [163] blunt,
"Who chooseth me must give and hazard all he hath."
How shall I know if I do choose the right?

    Por.　The one of them contains my picture, Prince：
If you choose that, then I am yours withal [164].

    Mor.　Some god direct my judgment! Let me see,
I will survey th' inscriptions back again.
What says this leaden casket?
"Who chooseth me must give and hazard all he hath."
Must give—for what? for lead, hazard for lead?
This casket threatens. Men that hazard all
Do it in hope of fair advantages；
A golden mind stoops not to shows of dross.
I'll then nor give nor hazard aught for lead.
What says the silver with her virgin hue?
"Who chooseth me shall get as much as he deserves."
As much as he deserves! pause there, Morocco,
And weigh thy value with an even [165] hand.
If thou beest rated by thy estimation [166],
Thou dost deserve enough, and yet enough
May not extend so far as to the lady；
And yet to be afeard of my deserving
Were but a weak disabling [167] of myself.
As much as I deserve! Why, that's the lady.
I do in birth deserve her, and in fortunes,
In graces, and in qualities of breeding；
But more than these, in love I do deserve.
What if I stray'd no farther, but chose here?
Let's see once more this saying grav'd in gold：
"Who chooseth me shall gain what many men desire."
Why, that's the lady, all the world desires her.

---

163. **all as**：equally, 同样地。
164. **withal**：therewith, 同样, 同时。

165. **even**：impartial, 不偏袒的。

第三只匣子是用沉重的铅打成的，上面刻着像铅一样冷酷的警告："谁选择了我，必须准备把他所有的一切作为牺牲。"我怎么可以知道我选得错不错呢？

鲍　这三只匣子中间，有一只里面藏着我的小像；您要是选中了那一只，我就是属于您的了。

摩　求神明指示我！让我看；我且把匣子上面刻着的字句再倒过来推敲一遍。这一个铅匣子上面说些什么？"谁选择了我，必须准备把他所有的一切作为牺牲。"必须准备牺牲；为什么？为了铅吗？为了铅而牺牲一切吗？这匣子说的话儿倒有些吓人。人们为了希望得到重大的利益，才会不惜牺牲一切；一颗贵重的心，决不会屈躬俯就鄙贱的外表；我不愿为了铅的缘故而作任何的牺牲。那个色泽皎洁的银匣子上面说些什么？"谁选择了我，将要得到他所应得的东西。"得到他所应得的东西！且慢，摩洛哥，把你自己的价值作一下公正的估计吧。照你自己判断起来，你应该得到很高的评价，可是也许凭着你这几分长处，还不配娶到这样一位小姐，然而我要是疑心我自己不够资格，那未免太小看自己了。得到我所应得的东西！当然那就是指这位小姐而说的；讲到家世，财产，人品，教养，我在哪一点上配不上她？可是超乎这一切之上，凭着我这一片深情，也就应该配得上她了。那么我不必迟疑，就选了这一个匣子吧。让我再瞧瞧那金匣子上说些什么话："谁选择了我，将要得到众人所希求的东西。"啊，那正是这位小姐了；整个儿的世界都希求着她，

---

166. **estimation**：价值。　　　　　167. **disabling**：贬值。

From the four corners of the earth they come
To kiss this shrine [168], this mortal breathing saint.
The Hyrcanian [169] deserts and the vasty wilds
Of wide Arabia are as throughfares [170] now
For princes to come view fair Portia.
The watery kingdom [171], whose ambitious head [172]
Spets in the face of heaven, is no bar [173]
To stop the foreign spirits, but they come
As o'er a brook to see fair Portia.
One of these three contains her heavenly picture.
Is't like that lead contains her? 'Twere damnation
To think so base a thought; it were too gross
To rib her cerecloth [174] in the obscure grave.
Or shall I think in silver she's immur'd [175],
Being ten times undervalued to tried gold [176]?
O sinful thought! Never so rich a gem [177]
Was set in worse than gold. They have in England
A coin that bears the figure of an angel [178]
Stamp'd in gold, but that's insculp'd upon;
But here an angel [179] in a golden bed
Lies all within. Deliver me the key.
Here do I choose, and thrive I as I may [180]!

    Por. There take it, Prince, and if my form [181] lie there,
Then I am yours. [*He unlocks the golden casket*.]
    Mor. O hell! what have we here?
A carrion Death [182], within whose empty eye
There is a written scroll! I'll read the writing. [*Reads*.]

      "All that glisters is not gold,
      Often have you heard that told;
      Many a man his life hath sold [183]
      But my outside [184] *to behold.*
      Gilded tombs do worms infold.

---

168. **shrine**: image, 形象。
169. **Hyrcanian**: 里海东南的蛮荒之地。
170. **throughfares**: thoroughfares, 大道。
171. **The watery kingdom**: 茫茫大海。
172. **ambitious head**: 波浪。
173. **bar**: barrier, 障碍。
174. **To rib her cerecloth**: 用蜡布包裹尸体, **rib** 有包裹的意思。
175. **immured**: 藏, 围, 禁闭。
176. **Being ten...gold**: 比炼过的真金要贱十倍。
     tried: tempered, 冶炼过的。
177. **gem**: 宝石。

从地球的四角他们迢迢而来，顶礼这位尘世的仙真：赫堪尼亚的沙漠和广大的阿拉伯的辽阔的荒野，现在已经成为各国王子们前来瞻仰美貌的鲍细霞的通衢大道；把唾沫吐在天庭面上的傲慢不逊的海洋，也不能阻止外邦的远客，他们越过汹涌的波涛，就像跨过一条小河一样，为了要看一看鲍细霞的绝世姿容。在这三只匣子中间，有一只里面藏着她的天仙似的小像。难道那铅匣子里会藏着她吗？想起这样一个卑劣的思想，就是一种亵渎。就算这里面放着她的寿衣也都嫌罪过。那么她是会藏在那价值只有纯金十分之一的银匣子里面吗？啊，罪恶的思想！这样一颗珍贵的珠宝，决不会装在比金子低贱的匣子里。英格兰有一种钱币是用黄金铸造的，上面有天使的像，不过那是浮雕在外面的，而这里的天使睡在金床上却藏在里面。把钥匙交给我；我已经选定了，但愿我的希望能够成就！

鲍　亲王，请您拿着这钥匙；要是这里边有我的小像，我就是您的了。（打开金匣。）

摩　哎哟，该死！这是什么，一个死人的骷髅，那空空的眼眶里藏着一张有字的纸卷。让我读一读上面写着什么。　（读。）

　　　　"光闪闪的不全是黄金，

　　　　古人的说话没有骗人；

　　　　多少世人出卖了一生，

　　　　不过看到了我的外形，

　　　　蛆虫占据着镀金的坟。

---

178. **angel**: 刻有天使像的金币，价值十先令。
179. **angel**: 指 Portia 的雕像。
180. **and...may**: 但愿我能成功。
181. **form**: 雕像。

182. **Death**: death's head，骷髅。
183. **life hath sold**: 丧失性命。
184. **outside**: 外表。

Had you been as wise as bold,
Young in limbs, in judgment old [185],
Your answer had not been inscroll'd [186].
Fare you well, your suit is cold [187]."
Cold indeed, and labour lost:
Then farewell heat [188], and welcome frost!
Portia, adieu. I have too griev'd a heart
To take a tedious leave; thus losers part [189].

       [*Exit with his Train. Flourish cornets.*]

  ***Por*.** A gentle riddance [190]. Draw the curtains, go.
Let all of his complexion [191] choose me so. [*Exeunt.*]

Scene VIII — Venice. A Street.

Enter Salerio and Solanio.

  ***Sal*.** Why, man, I saw Bassanio under sail,
With him is Gratiano gone along;
And in their ship I am sure Lorenzo is not.
  ***Sol*.** The villain Jew with outcries rais'd [192] the Duke,
Who went with him to search Bassanio's ship.
  ***Sal*.** He came too late, the ship was under sail,
But there the Duke was given to understand
That in a gondilo [193] were seen together
Lorenzo and his amorous Jessica.
Besides, Antonio certified the Duke
They were not with Bassanio in his ship.
  ***Sol*.** I never heard a passion so confus'd,
So strange, outrageous, and so variable
As the dog Jew did utter in the streets.
"My daughter! O my ducats! O my daughter!
Fled with a Christian! O my Christian ducats!
Justice! the law! my ducats, and my daughter!

----

185. **Young...old**: 四肢壮健，见识老成。将 old 放在句
  末是为了押韵。

186. **inscroll'd**: set down here. 记载在这里。

187. **suit is cold**: 求婚无效。 **cold**: without influence or
  power.

188. **heat**: 爱情。farewell heat, 摩洛哥亲王前面已发誓
  不再谈婚姻，与爱情永别。

189. **part**: 离开。

你要是又大胆又聪明，

　　手脚壮健，见识却老成，

　　就不会得到这样回音：

　　再见，劝你冷却这片心。"

冷却这片心；真的是枉费辛劳！

永别了，热情！欢迎，凛冽的寒飔！

再见，鲍细霞；悲伤塞满了心胸，

莫怪我这败军之将去得匆匆。（率侍从下；喇叭奏花腔。）

鲍　他去得倒还知趣。把帐幕拉下。但愿像他一样肤色的人，都像他一样选不中。（同下。）

 威尼斯；街道

萨莱里奥及索拉尼奥上。

萨　啊，朋友，我看见巴散尼奥开船，葛莱西安诺也跟他同船去；我相信罗伦佐一定不在他们船里。

索　那个恶犹太人大呼小叫地吵到公爵那儿去，公爵已经跟着他去搜巴散尼奥的船了。

萨　他去迟了一步，船已经开出。可是有人告诉公爵，说他们曾经看见罗伦佐跟他的多情的吉雪加在一艘平底船里；而且安东尼奥也向公爵证明他们并不在巴散尼奥的船上。

索　我从没有听见别人会这样大发雷霆，这样古怪，这样凶狠，这样反常，像那犹太狗在街上一路乱叫乱喊，"我的女儿！啊，我的银钱！啊，我的女儿！跟一个基督徒逃走啦！啊，我的基督徒的银钱！公道啊！法律啊！我的银钱，我的女儿！

---

190. **a gentle riddance**：轻轻地打发走了。

191. **his complexion**：语意双关：(1)指他那种人；(2)指与他同肤色的人。

192. **rais'd**：roused，惊醒。

193. **gondilo**：gondola，平底游艇。

A sealed bag, two sealed bags of ducats,
Of double ducats, stol'n from me by my daughter!
And jewels, two stones, two rich and precious stones,
Stol'n by my daughter! Justice! find the girl,
She hath the stones upon her, and the ducats."

  Sal. Why, all the boys in Venice follow him,
Crying, his stones, his daughter, and his ducats.

  Sol. Let good Antonio look he keep his day [194],
Or he shall pay for this.

  Sal.   Marry. well rememb'red.
I reason'd [195] with a Frenchman yesterday,
Who told me, in the Narrow Seas [196] that part
The French and English, there miscarried [197]
A vessel of our country richly fraught [198].
I thought upon Antonio when he told me,
And wish'd in silence that it were not his.

  Sol. You were best to tell Antonio what you hear,
Yet do not suddenly, for it may grieve him.

  Sal. A kinder gentleman treads not the earth.
I saw Bassanio and Antonio part：
Bassanio told him he would make some speed
Of his return; he answered, "Do not so,
Slubber [199] not business for my sake, Bassanio,
But stay the very riping of the time;
And for [200] the Jew's bond which he hath of me,
Let it not enter in your mind of love [201].
Be merry, and employ your chiefest thoughts
To courtship, and such fair ostents [202] of love
As shall conveniently [203] become you there."
And even there, his eye being big with tears,
Turning his face, he put his hand behind him,

---

194. **look he keep his day**：保证到期还钱。
195. **reason'd**：talked.
196. **the Narrow Seas**：指英吉利海峡。
197. **miscarried**：失事，完蛋。
198. **fraught**：装载。
199. **Slubber**：hurry over, do in slovenly manner, 潦草办事。
200. **for**：as for.

一袋封好的，两袋封好的银钱，都是两块头的银钱，给我的女儿偷去了！还有珠宝！两颗宝石，两颗珍贵的宝石，都给我的女儿偷去了！公道啊！把那女孩子找出来！她身边带着宝石，还有银钱。"

萨　威尼斯城里所有的小孩子们，都跟在他背后，喊着他的宝石，他的女儿，他的银钱。

索　安东尼奥应该留心那笔债款不要误了期，否则他要在他身上报复的。

萨　对了，你想起得不错。昨天我跟一个法国人谈天，他对我说起，在英法二国之间的狭隘的海面上，有一艘从咱们国里开出去的满载着货物的船只出了事了。我一听见这句话，就想起安东尼奥，并默默地祷告，但愿那艘船不是他的才好。

索　你最好把你听见的消息告诉安东尼奥；可是你要轻描淡写地说，免得害他着急。

萨　世上没有一个比他更仁厚的君子。我看见巴散尼奥跟安东尼奥分别，巴散尼奥对他说他一定尽早回来，他就回答说："不必，巴散尼奥，不要为了我的缘故而误了你的正事，你等到一切事情圆满完成以后再回来吧；至于我在那犹太人那里签下的约，你不必放在心上，你只管高高兴兴，一心一意去求婚，施展你的全副精神，去博得美人的欢心吧。"说到这里，他的眼睛里已经噙着一包眼泪，他就回转身去，把他的手伸到背后，

---

201. **enter...love**：（让此事）打扰你的爱心。　　　203. **conveniently**：适宜地。
202. **ostents**：shows.

And with affection wondrous sensible [204]
He wrung Bassanio's hand, and so they parted.

  Sol. I think he only loves the world for him.
I pray thee let us go and find him out
And quicken his embraced heaviness [205]
With some delight or other.

  Sal.   Do we so. [*Exeunt.*]

Scene IX — Belmont. A Room in Portia's House.

Enter Nerissa, with a Servitor.

  Ner. Quick, quick, I pray thee, draw the curtain straight [206];
The Prince of Arragon hath ta'en his oath,
And comes to his election [207] presently.

Flourish cornets. Enter the Prince of Arragon,

Portia, and their Trains.

  Por. Behold, there stand the caskets, noble Prince.
If you choose that wherein I am contain'd,
Straight shall our nuptial rites be solemniz'd;
But if you fail, without more speech, my lord,
You must be gone from hence immediately.

  Ar. I am enjoin'd by oath to observe three things:
First, never to unfold to any one
Which casket'twas I chose; next, if I fail
Of the right casket, never in my life
To woo a maid in way of marriage;
Lastly,
If I do fail in fortune [208] of my choice,
Immediately to leave you, and be gone.

  Por. To these injunctions [209] every one doth swear
That comes to hazard for my worthless self.

----

204. **sensible**: intense, 强烈的。   206. **straight**: 马上，立刻。
205. **quicken...heaviness**: 减轻他的愁绪。 **quicken**: light-
  en, enliven; **heaviness**: sorrow.

亲亲热热地握着巴散尼奥的手，他们就这样分别了。

索　我看他只是为了他的缘故才爱这世界的。咱们现在就去找他，想些开心的事儿替他解解愁闷，你看好不好？

萨　很好很好。（同下。）

第九场　贝尔蒙脱；鲍细霞家中一室

聂莉莎及一仆人上。

聂　赶快，赶快，扯开那帐幕；阿拉贡亲王已经宣过誓，就要来选匣子啦。

喇叭奏花腔。阿拉贡亲王及鲍细霞各率侍从上。

鲍　瞧，尊贵的王子，那三个匣子就在这儿；您要是选中了有我的小像藏在里头的那一只，我们就可以立刻举行婚礼；可是您要是失败了的话，那么殿下，您必须立刻离开这儿。

阿　我已经宣誓遵守三项条件：第一，不得告诉任何人我所选的是哪一只匣子；第二，要是我选错了匣子，终身不得再向任何女子求婚；第三，要是我选不中，必须立刻离开此地。

鲍　为了我这微贱的身子来此冒险的人，没有一个不曾立誓遵守这几个条件。

---

207. **election**: choice，选匣子。
208. **fortune**: 运气。

209. **injunctions**: 戒律。

    Ar.   And so have I address'd me [210]. Fortune now
To my heart's hope! Gold, silver, and base lead.
"Who chooseth me must give and hazard all he hath."
You shall look fairer ere I give or hazard.
What says the golden chest? Ha, let me see:
"Who chooseth me shall gain what many men desire."
What many men desire! That many may be meant
By [211] the fool multitude that choose by show,
Not learning more than the fond [212] eye doth teach
Which pries not to th'interior, but like the martlet [213]
Builds in the weather [214] on the outward wall,
Even in the force and road of casualty [215].
I will not choose what many men desire,
Because I will not jump [216] with common spirits
And rank me with the barbarous multitude.
Why then to thee, thou silver treasure house,
Tell me once more what title thou dost bear:
"Who chooseth me shall get as much as he deserves."
And well said too; for who shall go about
To cozen [217] fortune, and be honourable
Without the stamp [218] of merit? Let none presume
To wear an undeserved dignity.
O that estates [219], degrees, and offices
Were not deriv'd [220] corruptly, and that clear [221] honour
Were purchas'd by the merit of the wearer!
How many then should cover that stand bare [222]!
How many be commanded that command [223]?
How much low peasantry would then be gleaned [224]
From the true seed of honour [225]? and how much honour
Pick'd from the chaff and ruin [226] of the times
To be new varnish'd [227]? Well, but to my choice:

---

210. **address'd me**: 我已做好准备。
211. **By**: for.
212. **fond**: 愚蠢的。
213. **martlet**: martin, 燕子。
214. **in the weather**: 室外。
215. **Even...casualty**: exposed to every hazard; in the very

pathway of destructive forces, 不管一路上有什么危险。 **force**: power; **casualty**: mischance.
216. **jump**: agree, 同意。
217. **cozen**: cheat, 欺骗。
218. **stamp**: 标记, 品行, 官印。

阿　我也是这样宣誓过了。但愿命运满足我的心愿！一只是金的，一只是银的，还有一只是下贱的铅的。"谁选择了我，必须准备把他所有的一切作为牺牲。"你要我为你牺牲，应该再好看一点才是。那个金匣子上面说的什么？"谁选择了我，将要得到众人所希求的东西。"众人所希求的东西！那"众人"也许是指那无知的群众，他们只知道凭着外表取人，信赖着一双愚妄的眼睛，不知道窥察到内心，就像暴风雨中的燕子，把巢筑在屋外的墙壁上，自以为可保万全，不想到灾祸就会接踵而至。我不愿选择众人所希求的东西，因为我不愿随波逐流，与庸俗的群众为伍。那么还是让我瞧瞧你吧，你这白银的宝库；待我再看一遍刻在你上面的字句："谁选择了我，将要得到他所应得的东西。"说得好，一个人要是自己没有几分长处，怎么可以妄图非分？尊荣显贵，原来不是无德之人所可以忝窃的。唉！要是世间的爵禄官职，都能够因功授赏，不藉钻营，那么多少脱帽侍立的人将会高冠盛服，多少发号施令的人将会唯唯听命，多少卑劣鄙贱的渣滓可以从高贵的种子中间筛分出来，多少隐阖不彰的贤才异能，可以从世俗的糠秕中间剔选出来，大放它们的光泽！闲话少说，还是让我考虑考虑怎样选择吧。

---

219. **estates**：status，高位。
220. **deriv'd**：inherited，gained，继承，得到。
221. **clear**：illustrious，显赫的。
222. **cover...bare**：wear their hats，who must now bare their heads（in the presence of their social superiors）.（在上司面前）脱帽侍立的人该戴上帽子。
223. **be...command**：become servants instead of masters，应成为仆人而不是主人。
224. **gleaned**：separated，分开，分出来。
225. **seed of honour**：贵族。
226. **ruin**：糟粕，渣滓。
227. **new vanish'd**：重新装潢。

"Who chooseth me shall get as much as he deserves."
I will assume desert. Give me a key for this,
And instantly unlock my fortunes here.   [*He unlocks the silver casket.*]

    Por.   Too long a pause for that which you find there.

    Ar.   What's here? the portrait of a blinking idiot,
Presenting me a schedule [228]! I will read it.
How much unlike art thou to Portia!
How much unlike my hopes and my deservings!
"Who chooseth me shall have as much as he deserves" !
Did I deserve no more than a fool's head?
Is that my prize? Are my deserts [229] no better?

    Por.   To offend and judge are distinct offices [230],
And of opposed natures.

    Ar.   What is here?   [*Reads.*]

        "The fire seven times tried [231] this:
        Seven times tried that judgment is,
        That did never choose amiss.
        Some there be that shadows kiss,
        Such have but a shadow's bliss.
        There be fools alive, *iwis [232]*,
        Silver' d o' er, *and so was this.*
        Take what wife you will to bed,
        I will ever be your head [233].
        So be gone, *you are sped [234]."*
Still more fool I shall appear
By the time I linger here.
With one fool's head I came to woo,
But I go away with two.
Sweet, adieu. I'll keep my oath,
Patiently to bear my wroth [235].   [*Exit Arragon with his Train.*]

---

228. **schedule**: 纸卷。
229. **deserts**: merits, 应有的地位, 功绩, 美德。
230. **To...offices**: 犯罪和审判是完全不同的两回事, 意思是自己挑错了, 不能由自己来评奖。
231. **tried**: 冶炼。

“谁选择了我，将要得到他所应得的东西。”那么我有擅了，把这
匣子上的钥匙给我，让我立刻打开藏在这里面的我的命运。（开
银匣。）

鲍　您在这里面瞧见些什么？怎么呆住了一声也不响？

阿　这是什么？一个眯着眼睛的傻瓜的画像，上面还写着字句！让我
　　读一下看。唉！你跟鲍细霞相去得多么远！你跟我的希望、我的
　　应得之份又相去得多么远！难道我只配得到你这样一个东西吗？
　　“谁选择了我，将要得到他所应得的东西。”难道我只应该得到一
　　副傻瓜的嘴脸吗？那便是我的奖品吗？我不该得到好一点的东西
　　吗？

鲍　毁谤和评判，是两件作用不同，性质相反的事。

阿　这儿写着什么？（读。）

　　　　　“这银子在火里烧过七遍；
　　　　　那永远不会错误的判断，
　　　　　也必须经过七次的试炼。
　　　　　有的人终身向幻影追逐，
　　　　　只好在幻影里寻求满足。
　　　　　我知道世上尽有些呆鸟。
　　　　　空有着一个镀银的外表；
　　　　　随你娶一个怎样的妻房，
　　　　　摆脱不了这傻瓜的皮囊；
　　　　　去吧，先生，莫再耽搁时光！”

　　我要是再留在这儿发呆，
　　愈显得是个十足的蠢材；
　　顶一颗傻脑袋来此求婚，
　　带两个蠢头颅回转家门。
　　别了，美人，我愿遵守誓言，
　　默忍着心头愤怒的熬煎。（阿率侍从下。）

---

232. **iwis**〔古〕：certainly.

233. **I will ever be your head**：意思是 You will always be
　　a fool（你总是一个傻瓜）。这里的"I"是小丑画像
　　（fool's head）自称。

234. **sped**：快走，滚蛋。

235. **wroth**：ruth 的变体，意为不幸的命运。

Por.   Thus hath the candle sing'd the moth.
O, these deliberate [236] fools, when they do choose,
They have the wisdom by their wit [237] to lose.
    Ner.   The ancient saying is no heresy,
Hanging and wiving [238] goes by destiny.
    Por.   Come draw the curtain, Nerissa.

Enter a Servant.

    Ser.   Where is my lady?
    Por.   Here; what would my lord [239]?
    Ser.   Madam, there is alighted at your gate
A young Venetian, one that comes before
To signify th'approaching of his lord,
From whom he bringeth sensible regreets [240]:
To wit [241] (besides commends and courteous breath [242]),
Gifts of rich value. Yet [243] I have not seen
So likely [244] an embassador [245] of love.
A day in April never came so sweet.
To show how costly [246] summer was at hand,
As this fore-spurrer [247] comes before his lord.
    Por.   No more, I pray thee. I am half afeard
Thou wilt say anon [248] he is some kin to thee,
Thou spend'st such high-day wit [249] in praising him.
Come, come, Nerissa, for I long to see
Quick Cupid's post [250] that comes so mannerly.
    Ner.   Bassanio. Lord Love, if thy will it be!   [*Exeunt.*]

---

236. **deliberate**: calculating, 绞尽脑汁。
237. **wit**: wisdom, 智慧。
238. **wiving**: 娶妻, 在两个抽象名词 (Hanging and wiving) 后谓语动词仍用单数。
239. **my lord**: Portia 取笑仆人用的称呼。

240. **sensible regreets**: tangible greetings, 具体可感的敬意, 即真诚的敬意。
241. **To wit**: that is, 即是。
242. **breath**: speech, 口头客套。
243. **Yet**: up till now, 到现在。

鲍 正像飞蛾在烛火里伤身，
　　这些傻瓜们自恃着聪明，
　　免不了被聪明误了前程。

聂 古话说得好，上吊娶媳妇，
　　都是一个人注定的天数。

鲍 来，聂莉莎，把帐幕拉下了。
　　一仆人上。

仆 小姐呢？

鲍 在这儿；尊驾有什么见教。

仆 小姐，门口有一个年轻的威尼斯人，说是来通知一声，他的主人就要来啦；他说他的主人叫他先来向小姐致意，除了一大堆恭维的客套以外，还带来了几件很贵重的礼物。小的从来没有见过这么一位体面的爱神的使者，预报繁茂的夏季快要来临的四月的天气，也不及这个为主人先驱的俊仆的温雅。

鲍 请你别说下去了吧，你把他称赞得这样天花乱坠，我怕你就要说他是你的亲戚了。来，来，聂莉沙，我倒很想瞧瞧这一位爱神差来的体面的使者。

聂 巴散尼奥——爱神啊，但愿这是你的意旨！（下。）

---

244. **likely**：promising，有希望的。
245. **embassador**：即 ambassador。
246. **costly**：富有的。
247. **fore-spurrer**：打前站的骑手。

248. **anon**：马上，接着。
249. **high-day wit**：节假庆典即兴捧场的智慧。
250. **post**：messenger，信使。

ACT Ⅲ

Scene Ⅰ — Venice. A Street.

Enter Solanio and Salerio.

Sol.　Now what news on the Rialto?

Sal.　Why, yet it lives there uncheck'd[1] that Antonio hath a ship of rich lading[2] wrack'd on the Narrow Seas; the Goodwins[3], I think they call the place; a very dangerous flat[4], and fatal, where the carcasses of many a tall ship lie buried, as they say, if my gossip Report[5] be an honest woman of her word.

Sol.　I would[6] she were as lying a gossip in that as ever knapp'd[7] ginger or made her neighbours believe she wept for the death of a third husband. But it is true, without any slips of prolixity[8], or crossing the plain highway of talk[9], that the good Antonio, the honest Antonio, — O that I had a title good enough to keep his name company! —

Sal.　Come[10], the full stop.

Sol.　Ha, what sayest thou? Why, the end is, he hath lost a ship.

Sal.　I would it might prove the end of his losses.

Sol.　Let me say 'amen' betimes[11], lest the devil cross my prayer, for here he comes in the likeness of[12] a Jew.

Enter Shylock.

How now, Shylock, what news among the merchants?

Shy.　You knew, none so well, none so well as you, of my daughter's flight.

Sal.　That's certain. I for my part knew the tailor that made the wings she flew withal[13].

Sol.　And Shylock for his own part knew the bird was flidge[14], and then it is the complexion[15] of them all to leave the dam[16].

---

1. **uncheck'd**: unhindered, not denied, 未否认。
2. **rich lading**: 装运贵重物品。
3. **the Goodwins**: 泰晤士河入海处的浅滩，又叫 Goodwin Sands。
4. **flat**: 浅滩。

5. **my gossip Report**: 即 Dame Rumour, 饶舌妇, gossip 最初的字面意义是教父（母），后用来指女性的密友，逐渐演变成现在的意义。
6. **I would**: I wish, 但愿。

第 三 幕

第一场 威尼斯；街道

　　索拉尼奥及萨莱里奥上。

索　交易所里有什么消息？

萨　他们都在那里说安东尼奥有一艘满装着货物的船在海峡里倾覆了；那地方的名字好像是古特温，是一处很危险的沙滩，听说有许多大船的残骸埋葬在那里，要是那些传闻之辞是确实可靠的话。

索　我但愿那些谣言就像那些吃饱了饭没事做，嚼嚼生姜，或者一把鼻涕一把眼泪地假装为了她第三个丈夫死去而痛哭的那些婆子们所说的鬼话一样靠不住。可是那的确是事实，——不说啰哩啰嗦的废话，也不说枝枝节节的闲话——这位善良的安东尼奥，正直的安东尼奥——啊，我希望我有一个可以充分形容他的好处的字眼！——

萨　好了好了，别说下去了吧。

索　哈！你说什么！总结一句话，他损失了一艘船。

萨　但愿这是他最末一次的损失。

索　让我赶快喊"阿门"，免得给魔鬼打断了我的祷告，因为他已经扮成一个犹太人的样子来啦。

　　夏洛克上。

索　啊，夏洛克！商人中间有什么消息？

夏　有什么消息！我的女儿逃走啦，这件事情是你比谁都格外知道得详细的。

萨　那当然啦，就是我也知道她飞走的那对翅膀是哪一个裁缝替她做的。

索　夏洛克自己也何尝不知道，她羽毛已长，当然要离开娘家啦。

---

7. **knapp'd**: chewed，嚼。
8. **slips of prolixity**: wordy lies，赘言，废话。
9. **crossing...talk**: departing from plain speech，信口胡说。
10. **Come**(int.)：得了，表示厌烦的情绪。
11. **betimes**: 赶快地。
12. **in the likeness of**: 化装成。
13. **withal**: with。
14. **flidge**: 生有羽毛的；快会飞的。
15. **complexion**: 本性；自然倾向。
16. **dam**: 母亲（指母鸟）。

Shy.   She is damn'd for it.

Sal.   That's certain, if the devil may be her judge.

Shy.   My own flesh and blood to rebel!

Sol.   Out upon it, old carrion, rebels it at these years [17]?

Shy.   I say, my daughter is my flesh and my blood.

Sal.   There is more difference between thy flesh and hers than between jet [18] and ivory; more between your bloods than there is between red wine and Rhenish [19]. But tell us, do you hear whether Antonio have had any loss at sea or no?

Shy.   There I have another bad match [20]. A bankrout [21], a prodigal, who dare scarce show his head [22] on the Rialto, a beggar, that was us'd to come so smug upon the mart [23]: let him look to his bond. He was wont to call me usurer, let him look to his bond. He was wont to lend money for a Christian cur'sy [24], let him look to his bond.

Sal.   Why, I am sure if he forfeit thou wilt not take his flesh. What's that good for?

Shy.   To bait fish withal— if it will feed nothing else, it will feed my revenge. He hath disgrac'd me, and hind'red [25] me half a million, laugh'd at my losses, mock'd at my gains, scorn'd my nation, thwarted my bargains, cool'd my friends, heated [26] my enemies; and what's his reason? I am a Jew. Hath not a Jew eyes? Hath not a Jew hands, organs, dimensions [27], senses, affections, passions; fed with the same food, hurt with the same weapons, subject to the same diseases, heal'd by the same means, warm'd and cool'd by the same winter and summer, as a Christian is? If you prick us, do we not bleed? If you tickle us, dowe not laugh? If you poison us, do we not die? And if you wrong us, shall we not revenge? If we are like you in the rest, we will resemble you in that. If a Jew wrong a Christian, what is his humility [28]? Revenge. If a Christian wrong a Jew, what should his sufferance be by Christian example? why, revenge. The villainy you teach me, I will execute, and it shall go hard but I will better the instruction [29].

---

17. **rebels...years**：Solanio 故意误解 Shylock 的意思。因为上一行 Shylock 说自己的"亲生骨肉"用了 flesh and blood 这个短语，此短语既有"亲生骨肉"的意思，又有性欲冲动（sensual desires）的含义。

18. **jet**：黑玉，大理石。

19. **Rhenish**：white wine，白葡萄酒。

20. **match**：bargain，买卖，生意。

21. **bankrout**：破产的人。

22. **show his head**：露面。

23. **smug upon the mart**：衣冠楚楚地上市场，mart 即 market。

夏　她干出这种不要脸的事来，死了一定要下地狱。

萨　倘然魔鬼做她的判官，那是当然的事情。

夏　我自己的血肉跟我造反！

索　亏你说得出口，老东西！难道你这年纪还有肉欲冲动么？

夏　我说我的女儿是我的血肉。

萨　你的肉跟她的肉比起来，比黑炭和象牙还差得远；你的血跟她的血比起来，比红葡萄酒和白葡萄酒还差得远。可是告诉我们，你听没听见人家说起安东尼奥在海上遭到了损失？

夏　说起他，又是我的一桩倒霉事情。这个败家精，这个破落户，他不敢在交易所里露一露脸；他平常到市场上来，穿着得多么齐整，现在可变成一个叫化子啦。让他留心他的借约吧；他老是骂我盘剥取利；让他留心他的借约吧；他是本着基督徒的精神，放债从来不取利息的；让他留心他的借约吧。

萨　我相信要是他不能按约偿还借款，你一定不会要他的肉的；那有什么用处呢？

夏　拿来钓鱼也好；即使他的肉不中吃，至少也可以出出我这一口气。他曾经羞辱过我，夺去我几十万块钱的生意，讥笑着我的亏蚀，挖苦着我的盈余，侮蔑我的民族，破坏我的买卖，离间我的朋友，煽动我的仇敌；他的理由是什么？只因为我是一个犹太人。难道犹太人没有眼睛吗？难道犹太人没有五官四肢，没有知觉，没有感情，没有血气吗？他不是吃着同样的食物，同样的武器可以伤害他，同样的医药可以治疗他，冬天同样会冷，夏天同样会热，就像一个基督徒一样吗？你们要是用刀剑刺我们，我们不是也会出血的吗？你们要是搔我们的痒，我们不是也会笑起来的吗？你们要是用毒药谋害我们，我们不是也会死的吗？那么要是你们欺侮了我们，我们难道不会复仇吗？要是在别的地方我们都跟你们一样，那么在这一点上也是彼此相同的。要是一个犹太人欺侮了一个基督徒，那基督徒应该怎样？报仇呀。要是一个基督徒欺侮了一个犹太人，那么照着基督徒的榜样，那犹太人应该怎样？报仇呀。你们已经把残虐的手段教给我，我一定会照着你们的教训实行，而且还要加倍奉敬哩。

---

24. **cur'sy**：courtesy，礼貌，好意。

25. **hind'red**：妨碍。

26. **heated**：煽动。到这个动词为止 Shylock 一连用了八个动词，这种平行结构进一步增强了语气和说服力。

27. **dimensions**：身体各部分。

28. **humility**：忍受。和下一行的 sufferance 同义。

29. **and it...instruction**：it will be my fault if I do not improve on the lessons that the Christians have taught me, 我若不变本加厉地报复你们，那才是我的过错呢。

Enter a Servant.

Serv.　Gentlemen, my master Antonio is at his house, and desires to speak with you both.

Sal.　We have been up and down to seek him.

Enter Tubal.

Sol.　Here comes another of the tribe; a third cannot be match'd. unless the devil himself turn Jew.　[*Exeunt Solanio, Salerio, and servant.*]

Shy.　How now, Tubal, what news from Genoa?　Hast thou found my daughter?

Tub.　I often came where I did hear of her, but cannot find her.

Shy.　Why [30], there, there, there, there!　A diamond gone, cost me two thousand ducats in Frankford [31]!　The curse never fell upon our nation till now, I never felt it till now.　Two thousand ducats in that, and other precious, precious jewels.　I would my daughter were dead at my foot, and the jewels in her ear!　Would she were hears'd [32] at my foot, and the ducats in her coffin!　No news of them?　Why, so: and I know not what's spent in the search.　Why thou—loss upon loss!　the thief gone with so much, and so much to find the thief, and no satisfact ion, on revenge, nor no ill luck stirring but what lights a' [33] my shoulders, no sighs but a' my breathing, no tears but a' my shedding.

Tub.　Yes, other men have ill luck too.　Antonio, as I heard in Genoa—

Shy.　What, what, what? ill luck, ill luck?

Tub.　Hath an argosy cast away, coming from Tripolis.

Shy.　I thank God, I thank God.　Is it true, is it true?

Tub.　I spoke with some of the sailors that escap'd the wrack.

Shy.　I thank thee, good Tubal, good news, good news!　Ha, ha!　Heard in Genoa?

---

30. **Why**（int.）: 哎呀！哟！
31. **Frankford**: Frankfort, 德国的法兰克福, 当时以买卖
　　珠宝著名。

一仆人上。

仆　两位先生，我家主人安东尼奥在家里要请两位过去谈谈。

萨　我们正在到处找他呢。

杜拔尔上。

索　又是一个他的族中人来啦；世上再也找不到第三个像他们这样的人，除非魔鬼自己也变成了犹太人。（索、萨及仆下。）

夏　啊，杜拔尔！热那亚有什么消息？你有没有找到我的女儿？

杜　我所到的地方，往往听见人家说起她，可是总找不到她。

夏　哎呀，糟糕！糟糕！糟糕！我在法兰克福出两千块钱买来的那颗钻石也丢啦！诅咒到现在才降落到咱们民族头上；我到现在才觉得它的厉害。那一颗钻石就是两千块钱，还有别的贵重的贵重的珠宝。我希望我的女儿死在我的脚下，那些珠宝都挂在她的耳朵上；我希望她就在我的脚下入土安葬，那些银钱都放在她的棺材里！不知道他们的下落吗？哼，我不知道为了寻访他们，又花去了多少钱。你这你这——损失上再加损失！贼子偷了这么多走了，还要花这么多去寻访贼子，结果仍旧是一无所得，出不了这一口怨气。只有我一个人倒霉，只有我一个人叹气，只有我一个人流眼泪！

杜　倒霉的不单是你一个人。我在热那亚听人家说，安东尼奥——

夏　什么？什么？什么？他也倒了霉吗？他也倒了霉吗？

杜　——有一艘从的黎波里来的大船，在途中触礁。

夏　谢谢上帝！谢谢上帝！是真的吗？是真的吗？

杜　我曾经跟几个从那船上出险的水手谈过话。

夏　谢谢你，好杜拔尔。好消息，好消息！哈哈！什么地方？在热那亚吗？

32. **hears'd**：coffined，入殓。
33. **nor no=no. a'**：on，of.

Tub.　Your daughter spent in Genoa, as I heard, one night four-score ducats.

Shy.　Thou stick'st a dagger in me. I shall never see my gold again. Fourscore ducats at a sitting, fourscore ducats!

Tub.　There came divers [34] of Antonio's creditors in my company to Venice that swear he cannot choose but break [35].

Shy.　I am very glad of it. I'll plague him, I'll torture him. I am glad of it.

Tub.　One of them show'd me a ring that he had of your daughter for a monkey.

Shy.　Out upon her! Thou torturest me, Tubal. It was my turkis [36], I had it of Leah when I was a bachelor. I would not have given it for a wild erness of monkeys.

Tub.　But Antonio is certainly undone.

Shy.　Nay [37], that's true, that's very true. Go, Tubal, fee me an officer [38], bespeak him a fortnight before. I will have the heart of him if he forfeit, for were he out of Venice I can make what merchandise I will [39]. Go, Tubal, and meet me at our synagogue [40]; go, good Tubal, at our synagogue, Tubal.　[*Exeunt*.]

Scene **II** — Belmont. A Room in Portia's House.

Enter Bassanio, Portia, Gratiano, Nerissa, and Attendants.

Por.　I pray you tarry, pause a day or two
Before you hazard, for in choosing [41] wrong
I lose your company; therefore forbear a while.
There's something tells me (but it is not love)
I would not lose you, and you know yourself.
Hate counsels not in such a quality [42].

---

34. **divers**: various, 不同的。
35. **choose but break**: 避免破产。
36. **turkis**: turquoise, 绿宝石。
37. **Nay**: 可不是, 对, (=why, well)。

杜　听说你的女儿在热那亚一个晚上花去八十块钱。

夏　你把一把刀戳进我心里！我再也瞧不见我的银子啦！一下子就是八十块钱！八十块钱！

杜　有几个安东尼奥的债主跟我同路到威尼斯来，他们肯定地说他这次一定要破产。

夏　我很高兴。我要摆布摆布他；我要叫他知道些厉害。我很高兴。

杜　有一个人给我看一个指环，说是你女儿用它向他买一头猴子的。

夏　该死该死！杜拔尔，你提起这件事，真叫我心里难过；那是我的绿玉指环，是我的妻子莉霞在我没有结婚的时候送给我的；即使人家拿一大群猴子来向我交换，我也不愿把它给人。

杜　可是安东尼奥这一次一定完了。

夏　对了，这是真的，一点不错。去，杜拔尔，现在离开借约满期还有半个月，你先给我到衙门里走动走动，花费几个钱。要是他愆了约，我要挖出他的心来；只要威尼斯没有他这个人，我做起买卖来就可以随心所欲了。去，去，杜拔尔，咱们在会堂里见面。好杜拔尔，去吧；会堂里再见，杜拔尔。（各下。）

第二场　贝尔蒙脱；鲍细霞家中一室

巴散尼奥，鲍细霞，葛莱西安诺，聂莉莎及侍从等上。

鲍　请您不要太急，停一两天再选吧；因为要是您选得不对，咱们就不能再在一块儿，所以请您暂时缓一下吧。我心里仿佛有一种什么感觉，可是那不是爱情，它告诉我我不愿失去您；您一定也知道，嫌憎是不会向人说这种话的。

---

38. **fee me an officer**：花钱给我请一位警吏。
39. **make...will**：随意做我的买卖。
40. **synagogue**：犹太人教堂。
41. **in choosing**：if you choose.
42. **quality**：方式。

But lest you should not understand me well—
And yet a maiden hath no tongue but thought [43] —
I would detain you here some month or two
Before you venture for me. I could teach you
How to choose right, but then I am forsworn.
So will I never be, so may you miss me.
But if you do, you'll make me wish a sin.
That I had been forsworn. Beshrow your eyes,
They have o'erlook'd [44] me and divided me:
One half of me is yours, the other half yours—
Mine own, I would say: but if mine, then yours,
And so all yours. O, these naughty [45] times
Puts bars between the owners and their rights!
And so though yours, not yours. Prove it so [46],
Let fortune go to hell for it, not I.
I speak too long, but'tis to peize [47] the time,
To eche [48] it, and to draw it out in length,
To stay you from election.

  Bass.   Let me choose,
For as I am, I live upon the rack.

  Por. Upon the rack, Bassanio! then confess
What treason there is mingled with your love.

  Bass. None but that ugly treason of mistrust,
Which makes me fear th'enjoying of my love;
There may as well be amity and life
'Tween snow and fire, as treason and my love.

  Por. Ay, but I fear you speak upon the rack,
Where men enforced [49] do speak any thing.

  Bass. Promise me life, and I'll confess the truth.

  Por. Well then, confess and live.

  Bass.   Confess and love

---

43. **a maiden...thought**: 一个小姐只有心里想，难以启齿。 45. **naughty**: wicked, 残忍。
44. **o'erlook'd**: 施魔法；迷惑；摄住。 46. **Prove it so**: 如果真是如此。

一个女孩儿家本来只好心里想，不该信口说话，可是惟恐您不能懂得我的意思，我真想留您在这儿住上一两个月，然后再让您为我而冒险一试。我可以教您怎样选才不会有错；可是这样我就要违犯了誓言，那是断断不可的；然而那样您也许会选错；要是您选错了，您一定会使我起了一个有罪的愿望，懊悔我不该为了不敢背誓而忍心让您失望。顶可恼的是您这一双眼睛，它们已经对我施了魔法，把我分成两半：半个我是您的，还有那半个我也是您的——不，我的意思是说那半个我是我的，可是既然是我的，也就是您的，所以整个儿的我都是您的。唉！都是这可恶的时代，使人们不能享受他们合法的权利；所以我虽然是您的，却又不是您的。我说得太啰嗦了，可是我的目的是要尽量拖延时间，不放您马上就去选择。

巴　让我选吧；我现在提心吊胆，才像给人拷问一样受罪呢。

鲍　给人拷问，巴散尼奥！那么你给我招认出来，在你的爱情之中，隐藏着什么奸谋？

巴　没有什么奸谋，我只是有点怀疑忧惧，但恐我的痴心化为徒劳；奸谋跟我的爱情正像冰炭一样，是无法相容的。

鲍　嗯，可是我怕你是因为受不住拷问的痛苦，才说这样的话。

巴　您要是答应赦我一死，我愿意招认真情。

鲍　好，赦你一死，你招认吧。

巴　"爱"便是我所能招认的一切。

---

47. **peize**:（源自法语词 peser）耽搁。

48. **eche**: 增加。

49. **enforced**: under compulsion，强迫。

Had been the very sum [50] of my confession.
O happy torment, when my torturer
Doth teach me answers for deliverance [51] !
But let me to my fortune and the caskets.

    Por.   Away then! I [52] am lock'd in one of them;
If you do love me, you will find me out.
Nerissa and the rest, stand all aloof.
Let music sound while he doth make his choice;
Then if he lose he makes a swan-like end [53],
Fading [54] in music. That the comparison
May stand more proper, my eye shall be the stream
And wat'ry death-bed for him. He may win,
And what is music then? Then music is
Even as the flourish when true subjects bow
To a new-crowned monarch; such it is
As are those dulcet sounds [55] in break of day
That creep into the dreaming bridegroom's ear,
And summon him to marriage. Now he goes,
With no less presence [56], but with much more love,
Than young Alcides [57], when he did redeem
The virgin tribute paid by howling Troy [58]
To the sea-monster. I stand for sacrifice [59];
The rest aloof are the Dardanian [60] wives,
With bleared [61] visages, come forth to view
The issue [62] of th'exploit. Go, Hercules,
Live thou [63], I live; with much, much more dismay
I view the fight than thon that mak'st the fray [64].

    A song, whilst Bassanio comments on the caskets to himself.

      Tell me where is fancy [65] bred [66],
      Or in the heart or in the head ?
      How begot, how nourished ?

---

50. **sum**: 全部，一切。
51. **deliverance**: 免罪。
52. **I**: 指她的雕像。
53. **swan-like end**: die singing, 天鹅的绝唱。
54. **Fading**: 死亡。
55. **dulcet sounds**: 欢快的乐曲。 **dulcet**: sweet.

56. **presence**: 尊严的外表。
57. **Alcides**: 即 Hercules，他从海怪那里救出了 Hesione，也就是下一行所说的 virgin tribute。
58. **howling Troy**: wailing or lamenting Trojans,悲伤的特洛埃人。

多谢我的刑官，您教给我怎样免罪的答话了！可是让我去瞧瞧那几个匣子，试试我的运气吧。

鲍 那么去吧！在那三个匣子中间，有一个里面锁着我的小像；您要是真的爱我，您会把我找出来的。聂莉沙，你跟其余的人都站开些。在他选择的时候，把音乐奏起来，要是他失败了，好让他像天鹅一样在音乐声中死去；把这譬喻说得更确当一些，我的眼睛就是他葬身的清流。也许他会胜利的；那么那音乐又像什么呢？那时候音乐就像忠心的臣子俯伏迎迓新加冕的君王的时候所吹奏的号角，又像是黎明时分送进正在做着好梦的新郎的耳中，催他起来举行婚礼的甜柔的琴韵。现在他去了，他的沉毅的姿态，就像少年赫邱里斯奋身前去，在特洛埃人的呼叫声中，把他们祭献给海怪的处女拯救出来一样，可是他心里却藏着更多的爱情；我站在这儿做牺牲，她们站在旁边，就像泪眼模糊的达达尼尔妇女们，出来看这场争斗的结果。去吧，赫邱里斯！我的生命悬在你手里，但愿你安然生还；我这观战的人心中，比你上场作战的人还要惊恐万倍。

巴散尼奥独白时，乐队奏乐唱歌。

> 告诉我爱情生长在何方？
> 还是在脑海？还是在心房？
> 它怎样发生？它怎样成长？

---

59. **I...sacrifice**: I stand here instead of Hesione, 替代 Hesione 作牺牲。
60. **Dardanian**: 指特洛埃。
61. **bleared**: weeping, 哭喊着的。
62. **issue**: 结果。
63. **Live thou**: if you live.
64. **fray**: 战斗。
65. **fancy**: 爱情。
66. **bred**: 产生, 同下行的 head 押韵, 暗示所选的盒子应为 lead, 这是 Portia 给 Bassanio 的暗示。

> *All*.   *Reply, reply.*
> *It is engend' red in the eyes,*
> *With gazing fed, and fancy dies*
> *In the cradle where it lies.*
> *Let us all ring fancy' s knell.*
> *I' ll begin it. Ding, dong, bell.*
> *All*.   *Ding, dong, bell.*

Bass.   So may the outward shows be least themselves [67] —
The world is still [68] deceiv' d with ornament.
In law, what plea so tainted and corrupt
But, being season' d with a gracious voice,
Obscures the show of evil? In religion,
What damned error but some sober brow
Will bless it, and approve [69] it with a text [70],
Hiding the grossness [71] with fair ornament?
There is no vice so simple [72] but assumes
Some mark of virtue on his outward parts.
How many cowards, whose hearts are all [73] as false
As stairs of sand, wear yet upon their chins
The beards of Hercules and frowning Mars [74]
Who inward search' d, have livers white as milk,
And these assume but valour' s excrement [75]
To render them redoubted [76]! Look on beauty,
And you shall see' tis purchas' d by the weight [77],
Which therein works a miracle in nature,
Making them lightest [78] that wear most of it.
So are those crisped [79] snaky golden locks,
Which make such wanton gambols with the wind
Upon supposed fairness [80], often known
To be the dowry [81] of a second head [82],

---

67. **So may...themselves**: outward appearances may bear no relation to their intrinsic worth, 外表和内容也许不一致。
68. **still**: ever, 总是。
69. **approve**: prove, 证实。
70. **text**: 指《圣经》中的段落。
71. **grossness**: 粗糙, 过失, 罪恶。
72. **simple**: 纯粹的。
73. **all**: just.

（众和。）回答我，回答我。

爱情的火在眼睛里点亮，

凝视是爱情生活的滋养，

它的摇篮便是他的坟场。

让我们把爱的丧钟鸣响，

　　叮当！叮当！

　　（众和。）叮当！叮当！

巴　外观往往和事物的本身完全不符，世人却容易为表面的装饰所欺骗。在法律上，哪一件卑鄙邪恶的陈诉，不可以用娓娓动听的言词掩饰它的罪状？在宗教上，哪一桩罪大恶极的过失，不可以引经据典，文过饰非，证明它的确上合天心？任何彰明昭著的罪恶，都可以在外表上装出一副道貌岸然的样子。多少没有胆量的懦夫，他们的颊上却长着天神一样的威武的须髯，剖开来一看，肝脏白得像奶。这种人摆出一副凶相，教人望而生畏！再看那些世间所谓美貌吧，那是完全靠着脂粉装点出来的，愈是轻浮的女人，所涂的脂粉也愈重；至于那些随风飘扬，像蛇一样的金丝卷发，看上去果然漂亮，不知道却是从坟墓中死人的骷髅上借下来的。

---

74. **The beards...Mars**：Hercules 的胡须和战神 Mars 的皱眉，都是男性和勇气的象征。

75. **excrement**：outgrowth（如胡须）。

76. **render them redoubted**：make themselves feared，本身看起来可怕。

77. **by the weight**：论斤两买的。（指上行说的化妆品）。

78. **lightest**：双关，(1)指不贞洁、轻浮；(2)指很轻。在此剧中莎士比亚多次用此词表双关意义。

79. **crisped**：curled，卷曲的。

80. **supposed fairness**：看起来漂亮。

81. **dowry**：占有。

82. **second head**：wig，假发。参见莎士比亚十四行诗第68 首：to live a second life on a second head.

The skull that bred them in the sepulchre.
Thus ornament is but the guiled [83] shore
To a most dangerous sea；the beauteous scarf
Veiling an Indian [84] beauty；in a word，
The seeming truth which cunning times put on
To entrap the wisest．Therefore then，thou gaudy gold，
Hard food for Midas [85]，I will none of thee；
Nor none of thee，thou pale and common drudge [86]
’Tween man and man；but thou，thou meagre [87] lead，
Which rather threaten’st than dost promise aught，
Thy paleness moves me more than eloquence，
And here choose I．Joy be the consequence！
　　Por．［*Aside*．］　How all the other passions fleet to air [88]，
As doubtful thoughts，and rash-embrac’d [89] despair，
And shudd’ring fear，and green-eyed [90] jealousy！
O love，be moderate，allay thy ecstasy，
In measure [91] rain thy joy，scant [92] this excess！
I feel too much thy blessing；make it less，
For Fear I surfeit [93]．
　　Bass．　　　　What find I here？　［*Opening the leaden casket*．］
Fair Portia’s counterfeit [94]！What demigod
Hath come so near creation？Move these eyes？
Or whether [95]，riding on the balls of mine，
Seem they in motion？Here are sever’d [96] lips．
Parted with sugar breath [97]；so sweet a bar
Should sunder [98] such sweet friends [99]．Here in her hairs
The painter plays the spider，and hath woven
A golden mesh t’entrap the hearts of men
Faster [100] than gnats in cobwebs．But her eyes—
How could he see to do them [101]？Having made one，
Methinks it should have power to steal both his [102]

- -

83. **guiled**：treacherous，危险的，有礁石的。
84. **Indian**：i.e.dark-complexioned，伊丽莎白时代的人不喜欢黑黝黝的皮肤。
85. **Midas**：Phrygian king，他能够把他所触摸的任何东西点化成金。结果食物也变成了金子，自己心爱的女儿也变成了金子。此乃神对贪婪的人的一种报复。见奥维德《变形记》第11卷。

86. **common drudge**：大众的贱奴，指银币铸成后成为流通货币，下一行中的’Tween man and man 也含同一意义。　’**Tween**=between.
87. **meagre**：不起眼的，朴素的。

所以装饰不过是一道把船只诱进凶涛险浪的怒海中去的陷人的海岸，又像是遮掩着一个黑丑蛮女的一道美丽的面幕，总而言之，它是狡诈的世人用来欺诱智士的似是而非的真理。所以，你炫目的黄金，米达斯王的坚硬的食物，我不要你；你惨白的银子，在人们手里来来去去的下贱的奴才，我也不要你；可是你，寒伧的铅，你的形状只能使人退走，一点没有吸引人的力量，然而你的质朴却比巧妙的言辞更能打动我的心，我就选了你吧，但愿结果美满！

鲍 （旁白。）一切纷杂的思绪，多心的疑虑，卤莽的绝望，战栗的恐惧，酸性的妒嫉，多么快地烟消云散了！爱情啊！把你的狂喜节制一下，不要让你的欢乐溢出界限，让你的情绪越过分寸，你使我感觉到太多的幸福，请你把它减轻几分吧，我怕我快要给快乐窒息而死了！

巴 这里面是什么？（开铅匣。）美丽的鲍细霞的副本！这是谁的神化之笔，描画出这样一位绝世的美人？这双眼睛是在转动吗？还是因为我的眼球在转动，所以仿佛它们也在随着转动？她的微启的双唇，是随着她嘴里吐出来的甘美芳香的气息而张合的，唯有这样甘美的气息才能分开这样甜蜜的朋友。画师在描画她的头发的时候，一定曾经化身为蜘蛛，织下了这么一个金丝的发网，来诱捉男子们的心；哪一个男子见了它，不会比飞蛾投入蛛网还牢牢地陷进网罗呢？可是她的眼睛！他怎么能够睁了眼睛把它们画出来呢？他在画了一只眼睛以后，我想它的逼人的光芒，一定会使他自己目眩神夺，

---

88. **fleet to air**：逃走。

89. **rash-embrac'd**：hasty，太快，匆忙。

90. **green-eyed**：绿色代表嫉妒。

91. **In measure**：适度地。

92. **scant**：diminish，减少。

93. **surfeit**：太多，承受不了。

94. **counterfeit**：指雕像，画像。

95. **Or whether**：or.

96. **sever'd**：parted，张开的。

97. **sugar breath**：香气，此行后面的 bar 也是指 breath。

98. **sunder**：分开。

99. **sweet friends**：指嘴唇。

100. **Faster**：more firmly，牢牢地。

101. **do them**：指画眼睛。　　**do**：paint.

102. **steal both his**：使他两眼昏花，变瞎。

And leave itself unfurnish'd [103]. Yet look how far
The substance of my praise doth wrong this shadow [104]
In underprizing it [105], so far this shadow
Doth limp behind the substance [106]. Here's the scroll,
The continent [107] and summary of my fortune.   [*Reads.*]

> *"You that choose not by the view,*
> *Chance as fair [108], and choose as true：*
> *Since this fortune falls to you,*
> *Be content, and seek no new.*
> *If you be well pleas'd with this,*
> *And hold [109] your fortune for your bliss,*
> *Turn you where your lady is,*
> *And claim her with a loving kiss."*

A gentle scroll. Fair lady, by your leave [110],   [*Kissing her.*]
I come by note [111], to give and to receive.
Like one of two contending in a prize [112],
That thinks he hath done well in people's eyes,
Hearing applause and universal shout,
Giddy in spirit, still gazing in a doubt
Whether those peals of praise be his [113] or no,
So, thrice-fair lady, stand I, even so,
As doubtful whether what I see be true,
Until confirm'd, sign'd, ratified by you.
    Por. You see me, Lord Bassanio, where I stand,
Such as I am. Though for myself alone
I would not be ambitious in my wish
To wish myself much better, yet for you,
I would be trebled twenty times [114] myself,
A thousand times more fair, ten thousand times more rich,
That only to stand high in your account [115],
I might in virtues, beauties, livings [116], friends,

---

103. **unfurnish'd**：使画家画不完另一只。
104. **shadow**：画像。
105. **underprizing it**：低估了它的美丽。
106. **the substance**：指 Portia 本人。
107. **The continent**=summary.
108. **Chance as fair**：幸运的冒险。
109. **hold**：regard.
110. **by your leave**：取得你的同意。

再也描画不成其余的一只。可是瞧，我用尽一切赞美的字句，还
不能充分形容出这一个画中幻影的美妙；然而这幻影跟它的实体
比较起来，又是多么望尘莫及！这儿是一纸手卷，宣判着我的命
运。（读。）

> "你选择不凭着外表，
> 果然给你直中鹄心！
> 胜利既已入你怀抱，
> 你莫再往别处追寻。
> 这结果倘使你满意，
> 就请接受你的幸运，
> 赶快回转你的身体，
> 给你的爱深深一吻。"

温柔的纶音！美人，请恕我大胆，（吻鲍。）
我奉命来把彼此的深情交换。
像一个夺标的健儿驰骋身手，
耳旁只听见沸腾的人声如吼，
虽然明知道胜利已在他手掌，
却不敢相信人们在向他赞赏。
绝世的美人，我现在神眩目晕，
仿佛闯进了一场离奇的梦境；
除非你亲口证明这一切是真，
我再也不相信我自己的眼睛。

鲍　巴散尼奥公子，您瞧我站在这儿，不过是这样的一个人。虽然为
了我自己的缘故，我不愿妄想自己比现在的我更好一点；可是为
了您的缘故，我希望我能够六十倍胜过我的本身，再加上一千倍
的美丽，一万倍的富有；我但愿我有无比的贤德，美貌，财产和
亲友，

---

111. **note**: 铅匣中的纸卷，即字条。
112. **prize**: competition，竞赛。
113. **his**: for him.

114. **trebled twenty times**: 六十倍。
115. **account**: estimation，估计。
116. **livings**: 财产。

Exceed account [117]. But the full sum of me
Is sum of nothing; which, to term in gross [118],
Is an unlesson'd girl, unschool'd, unpractis'd [119],
Happy [120] in this, she is not yet so old
But she may learn; happier than this,
She is not bred so dull but she can learn;
Happiest of all, is that her gentle spirit
Commits itself to yours to be directed;
As from [121] her lord, her governor, her king.
Myself, and what is mine, to you and yours
Is now converted. But now [122] I was the lord
Of this fair mansion, master of my servants,
Queen o'er myself; and even now, but now,
This house, these servants, and this same myself
Are yours—my lord's! —I give them with this ring,
Which when you part from, lose, or give away,
Let it presage the ruin [123] of your love,
And be my vantage to exclaim on you [124].

    Bass.　　Madam, you have bereft [125] me of all words,
Only [126] my blood speaks to you in my veins,
And there in such confusion in my powers [127],
As after some oration fairly spoke
By a beloved prince, there doth appear
Among the buzzing pleased multitude [128],
Where every something, being blent [129] together,
Turns to a wild of nothing [130], save [131] of joy
Express'd and not express'd. But when this ring
Parts from this finger, then parts life from hence [132];
O then be bold to say Bassanio's dead!

    Ner.　　My lord and lady, it is now our time,
That have stood by and seen our wishes prosper [133],
To cry good joy. Good joy, my lord and lady!

---

117. **account**: 计算。
118. **term in gross**: 总计。
119. **unpractis'd**: 没有经验。
120. **Happy**: fortunate, 幸运的。
121. **from**: by.
122. **But now**: just now.

123. **ruin**: decay, 指爱情的结束。
124. **And be...you**: be my opportunity to reproach you, 我便要借此机会指责你。　**vantage**: opportunity; **exclaim**: reproach.
125. **bereft**: 被夺去，失去。

好让我在您的心目中占据一个很高的位置。可是我这一身却是一无所有，我只是一个不学无术，没有教养的女子，幸亏她的年纪还不是顶大，来得及发奋学习；她的天资也不是顶笨，可以加以教导之功；尤其大幸的，她有一颗柔顺的心灵，愿意把它奉献给您，听从您的指导，把您当作她的主人，她的统治者和她的君王。我自己以及我所有的一切，现在都变成您的所有了；刚才我还拥有着这一座华丽的大厦，我的仆人都听从着我的指挥，我是支配我自己的女王，可是就在现在，这屋子，这些仆人和这一个我，都是属于您的了，我的夫君。凭着这一个指环，我把这一切完全呈献给您；要是您让这指环离开您的身边，或者把它丢了，或者把它送给别人，那就预示着您的爱情的毁灭，我可以因此责怪您的。

巴　小姐，您使我说不出一句话来，只有我的热血在我的血管里跳动着向您陈诉。我的精神是在一种恍惚的状态中，正像喜悦的群众在听到他们所爱戴的君王的一篇美妙的演辞以后那种心灵眩惑的神情，除了口头的赞叹和内心的欢乐以外，一切的一切都混合起来，化成白茫茫的一片模糊。可是这指环要是有一天离开这手指，那么我的生命也一定已经终结；那时候您可以放胆地说，巴散尼奥已经死了。

聂　姑爷，小姐，我们站在旁边，眼看我们的愿望成为事实，现在该让我们来道喜了。恭喜姑爷！恭喜小姐。

---

126. **Only**：应放在 you 之后，in 之前。但当时它的位置移动较灵活。

127. **powers**：faculties，才能，智能，官能。

128. **multitude**：人群。

129. **blent**：blended，混合，混杂。

130. **wild of nothing**：chaos，纷乱。

131. **save**：except.

132. **from hence**：从我这里。

133. **prosper**：realize，实现。

> *Gra.* My Lord Bassanio and my gentle lady,
> I wish you all the joy that you can wish;
> For I am sure you can wish none from me [134];
> And when your honours mean to solemnize
> The bargain of your faith [135], I do beseech you
> Even at that time I may be married too.
>   *Bass.* With all my heart, so [136] thou canst get a wife.
>   *Gra.* I thank your lordship, you have got me one.
> My eyes, my lord, can look as swift as yours:
> You saw the mistress, I beheld the maid;
> You lov'd, I lov'd; for intermission [137]
> No more pertains to [138] me, my lord, than you;
> Your fortune stood upon [139] the caskets there,
> And so did mine too as the matter falls [140];
> For wooing here until I sweat again [141],
> And swearing till my very roof [142] was dry
> With oaths of love, at last, if promise last.
> I got a promise of this fair one here
> To have her love, provided that your fortune
> Achiev'd [143] her mistress.
>   *Por.*   Is this true, Nerissa?
>   *Ner.* Madam, it is, so you stand pleas'd withal [144].
>   *Bass.* And do you, Gratiano, mean good faith?
>   *Gra.* Yes, faith, my lord.
>   *Bass.* Our feast shall be much honoured in your marriage.
>   *Gra.* We'll play [145] with them the first boy for a thousand ducats.
>   *Ner.* What, and stake down [146]?
>   *Gra.* No, we shall ne'er win at that sport, and stake down.
> But who comes here? Lorenzo and his infidel?
> What, and my old Venetian friend Salerio?

     Enter Lorenzo, Jessica, and Salerio.

---

134. **you...me**: i.e. you feel no need to be wished more joy by me (than you have already wished for yourselves). 不用我赞言"祝你们快乐"了。

135. **The bargain of your faith**: 缔结婚约, 成其好事, 指举行婚礼。

136. **so**: provided.

137. **intermission**: 迟疑。

138. **pertains to**: 属于。

139. **stood upon**: 取决于。

140. **falls**: happens, 发生。

141. **sweat again**: sweated repeatedly, 汗流浃背, 此处 sweat 是过去式, 因此 t 结尾而省掉 -ed。

葛 巴散尼奥大爷和我的温柔的夫人，愿你们尽情享受你们如愿以偿的一切快乐！我确信你们欢乐无涯，用不着我来多嘴祝愿了。我还有一个请求，要是你们决定在什么时候举行嘉礼，我也想跟你们一起结婚。

巴 很好，只要你能够找到一个妻子。

葛 谢谢大爷，您已经替我找到一个了。不瞒大爷说，我这一双眼睛瞧起人来，并不比您大爷慢；您瞧见了小姐，我也瞧见了使女；您产生了爱情，我也产生了爱情。我和您一样没有迟疑。您的命运靠那几个匣子决定，我也是一样；因为我在这儿千求万告，身上的汗出了一身又一身，指天誓日地说到唇干舌燥，才算得到了这位好姑娘的一句回音，答应我要是您能够得到她的小姐，我也可以得到她的爱情。

鲍 这是真的吗，聂莉莎？

聂 是真的，小姐，要是您赞成的话。

巴 葛莱西安诺，你也是出于真心吗？

葛 是的，大爷。

巴 我们的喜筵有你们的婚礼添兴，那真是喜上加喜了。

葛 我们要跟他们打赌一千块钱，看谁先养儿子。

聂 什么，要下赌注吗？

葛 不。若把下面堵住，那我们永远赢不了。可是谁来啦？罗伦佐和他的异教徒吗？什么！还有我那威尼斯老朋友萨莱里奥？

罗伦佐，吉雪加及萨莱里奥上。

---

142. **roof**: i.e. roof of the mouth，唇，腭。

143. **Achiev'd**: 赢得，得到。

144. **so...withal**: if you are pleased with it.　**so**: provided that;　**withal**: with it.

145. **play**: 打赌。

146. **and stake down**: 原文 stake 有两个意思，(1)赌注；(2)打桩。Nerissa 说此话时并无第二个意思，而下一行中 Gratiano 却开了一个淫猥的玩笑。

Bass．   Lorenzo and Salerio，welcome hither，
If that the youth of my new int' rest here [147]
Have power to bid you welcome．By your leave [148]，
I bid my very friends [149] and countrymen，
Sweet Portia，welcome．

　　Por．　　　　　　So do I，my lord，
They are entirely [150] welcome．

　　Lor．　　I thank your honour．For my part，my lord，
My purpose was not to have seen you here，
But meeting with Salerio by the way，
He did entreat me，past all saying nay，
To come with him along．

　　Sal．　　　　　　I did，my lord，
And I have reason for it．Signior Antonio
Commends him [151] to you．　[*Gives Bassanio a letter*．]

　　Bass．　　　　　　Ere I ope [152] his letter，
I pray you tell me how my good friend doth．

　　Sal．　　Not sick，my lord，unless it be in mind，
Nor well，unless in mind．His letter there
Will show you his estate．

　　Gra．　　Nerissa，cheer yond stranger [153]，bid her welcome．
Your hand，Salerio．What' s the news from Venice？
How doth that royal merchant [154]，good Antonio？
I know he will be glad of our success；
We are the Jasons [155]，we have won the fleece [156]．

　　Sal．　　I would you had won the fleece that he hath lost．

　　Por．　　There are some shrowd [157] contents in yond same paper
That steals the colour from Bassanio' s cheek —
Some dear friend dead，else nothing in the world
Could turn so much the constitution [158]
Of any constant [159] man．What，worse and worse！

---

147. **youth...here**：his newly acquired prerogative to give orders here. 刚做主人就有资格⋯ **youth** 刚刚；**int' rest**=interest, 权力。
148. **By your leave**：得到你的许可。
149. **very friends**：真正的朋友。　**very**：true.
150. **entirely**：heartily.
151. **Commends him**：sends his greetings，转达他的问候。
152. **Ere I ope**：before I open.

巴　罗伦佐，萨莱里奥，虽然我也是初履此地，让我借用着这里主人的名义，欢迎你们的到来，亲爱的鲍细霞，请您允许我接待我这几个同乡朋友。

鲍　我也是竭诚欢迎他们。

罗　谢谢。巴散尼奥大爷，我本来并没有想到要到这儿来看您，因为在路上碰见萨莱里奥，给他不由分说地硬拉着一块儿来啦。

萨　是我拉他来，大爷，我是有理由的。安东尼奥先生叫我替他向您致意。（给巴散尼奥一信。）

巴　在我没有拆开这信以前，请你告诉我我的好朋友近来好吗？

萨　他没有病，除非有点儿心病；也不怎么好，除非是在心里头。您看了他的信，就可以知道他的近况。

葛　聂莉莎，招待招待那位客人。对她表示欢迎。把你的手给我，萨莱里奥。威尼斯有些什么消息？那位善良的商人安东尼奥怎样？我知道他听见了我们的成功，一定会十分高兴；我们是两个伊阿宋，把金羊毛取了来啦。

萨　我希望你们能够把他失去的金羊毛取了回来，那就好了。

鲍　那信里一定有些什么坏消息，巴散尼奥的脸色都变白了；多半是一个什么好朋友死了，否则不会有别的事情会把一个堂堂男子激动到这个样子的。怎么，还有更坏的事情吗？

---

153. **cheer yond stranger**：**yond** 即 that；**stranger** 指 Jessica。

154. **royal merchant**：i. e. prince of merchants（？），指 Antonio。请参阅第四幕第一场中的"royal merchant"，那指的是"最富有的商人"。

155. **Jasons**：请参阅第一幕第一场，希腊英雄 Jason 渡海去 Colchis 寻找金羊毛。

156. **fleece**：兼指 Antonio 的船队（同船队 fleets 发音相似）。

157. **shrowd**：shrewd, grievous, 悲伤的。

158. **constitution**：state of mind, 心绪。

159. **constant**：steadfast, 修饰 man, 指男子汉。

With leave，Bassanio，I am half yourself，
And I must freely have the half of any thing
That this same paper brings you.
    Bass.   O sweet Portia，
Here are a few of the unpleasant'st words
That ever blotted paper！Gentle lady，
When I did first impart my love to you，
I freely told you all the wealth I had
Ran in my veins [160]：I was a gentleman；
And then I told you true. And yet，dear lady，
Rating myself at nothing，you shall see
How much I was a braggart [161]：when I told you
My state [162] was nothing，I should then have told you
That I was worse than nothing；for indeed
I have engag'd [163] myself to a dear friend，
Engag'd my friend to his mere [164] enemy，
To feed my means [165]. Here is a letter，lady，
The paper as the body of my friend，
And every word in it a gaping wound
Issuing life blood. But is it true，Salerio？
Hath all his ventures fail'd？What，not one hit [166]？
From Tripolis，from Mexico，and England，
From Lisbon [167]，Barbary [168]，and India，
And not one vessel scape the dreadful touch
Of merchant-marring [169] rocks？
    Sal.   Not one，my lord.
Besides，it should appear，that if he had
The present money [170] to discharge [171] the Jew.
He would not take it. Never did I know
A creature that did bear the shape of man
So keen [172] and greedy to confound [173] a man.

---

160. **in my veins**：在血脉里（指出身高贵）。
161. **braggart**：吹牛者。
162. **state**：estate，产业。
163. **engag'd**：pledged，指借债。
164. **mere**：absolute，绝对的，完全的。

165. **feed my means**：供我开销。   **feed**：supply.
166. **hit**：successful venture，成功的生意。
167. **Lisbon**：里斯本，葡萄牙首部。
168. **Barbary**：非洲西北一地名。

恕我冒渎，巴散尼奥，我是您自身的一半，这封信所带给您的任何不幸的消息，也必须让我分一半去。

巴　啊，亲爱的鲍细霞！这信里所写的，是自有纸墨以来最悲惨的字句。好小姐，当我初次向您倾吐我的爱慕之忱的时候，我坦白地告诉您，我的高贵的家世是我仅有的财产，那时我并没有向您说谎；可是，亲爱的小姐，单单把我说成一个两袖清风的寒士，还未免夸张过分，因为我不但一无所有，而且还负着一身的债务；不但欠了我的一个好朋友许多钱，还累他为了我的缘故，欠了他仇家的钱。这一封信，小姐，那信纸就像是我朋友的身体，上面的每一个字，都是一处血淋淋的创伤。可是，萨莱里奥，那是真的吗？难道他的船舶都一起遭难了？竟没有一艘平安到港吗？从的黎波里，从墨西哥，从英国，里斯本，巴巴里和印度来的船只，没有一艘能够逃过那些毁害商船的礁石的可怕的撞击吗？

萨　一艘也没有逃过。而且即使他现在有钱还那犹太人，那犹太人也不肯收他。我从来没有见过这样一个样子像人的家伙，一心一意只想残害他的同类；

---

169. **merchant-marring**: destructive to merchant ships, 摧毁商船的。

170. **The present money**: the ready, available money, 现钱。

171. **discharge**: 偿付债务。

172. **keen**: savage, 凶残的。

173. **confound**: ruin, 毁掉。

He plies [174] the Duke at morning and at night,
And doth impeach the freedom of the state [175].
If they deny him justice. Twenty merchants,
The Duke himself, and the magnificoes [176]
Of greatest port [177], have all persuaded with him,
But none can drive him from the envious [178] plea
Of forfeiture, of justice, and his bond.

     Jes.   When I was with him I have heard him swear
To Tubal and to Chus, his countrymen,
That he would rather have Antonio's flesh
Than twenty times the value of the sum
That he did owe him, and I know, my lord,
If law, authority and power deny not,
It will go hard with [179] poor Antonio.

     Por.   Is it your dear friend that is thus in trouble?

     Bass.   The dearest friend to me, the kindest man,
The best-condition'd and unwearied spirit [180]
In doing courtesies, and one in whom
The ancient Roman honour more appears
Than any that draws breath in Italy.

     Por.   What sum owes he the Jew?

     Bass.   For me, three thousand ducats.

     Por.   What, no more?
Pay him six thousand, and deface [181] the bond;
Double six thousand, and then treble that,
Before a friend of this description [182]
Shall lose a hair through Bassanio's fault.
First go with me to church and call me wife,
And then away to Venice to your friend;
For never shall you lie by Portia's side
With an unquiet soul [183]. You shall have gold
To pay the petty debt twenty times over.

---

174. **plies**: request, 请求, 缠着。

175. **And doth...state**: accuse the state of not guaranteeing the rights of its citizens, 指责国家不能保护公民的权益。　**freedom**: franchise, 权益。

176. **magnificoes** 〔意〕: grandees, 大公, 贵族。

177. **port**: dignity, 尊严。

178. **envious**: malicious, 恶意的。

179. **go hard with**: 遭遇不幸。

他不分昼夜地向公爵絮叨，说是他们倘不对他依法办事，那么威尼斯根本不成其为自由邦。二十个商人，公爵自己，还有那些最有名望的士绅，都曾劝过他，可是准也不能叫他回心转意，放弃他的狠毒的控诉；他一口咬定，要求按照约文的规定，处罚安东尼奥的违约。

吉　我在家里的时候，曾经听见他向杜拔尔和邱斯，他的两个同族的人谈起，说他宁可取安尔尼奥身上的肉，不愿收受比他的欠款多二十倍的钱。要是法律和威权不能拒绝他，那么可怜的安东尼奥恐怕难逃一死了。

鲍　遭到这样危难的人，是不是您的好朋友？

巴　我的最亲密的朋友，一个心肠最仁慈的人，热心为善，多情尚义，在他身上存留着比任何意大利人更多的古代罗马的仁侠精神。

鲍　他欠那犹太人多少钱？

巴　他为了我的缘故，向他借了三千块钱。

鲍　什么，只有这一点数目吗？还他六千块钱，把那借约毁了；两倍六千块钱，或者照这数目再倍三倍都可以，可是万万不能因为巴散尼奥的过失，害这样一个好朋友损伤一根毛发。先和我到教堂里去结为夫妇，然后你就到威尼斯去看你的朋友；鲍细霞决不让你抱着一颗不安宁的良心睡在她的身旁。你可以带偿还这笔小小借款的二十倍那么多的钱去；

---

180. **The...spirit**: 心肠最好的、最和善的一个人。
best condition′d: best-natured;
unwearied: most unwearied;
spirit: person.

181. **deface**: destroy, 销毁。

182. **this description**: of this kind, 这种。

183.**With an unquiet soul**: 带着不安的心绪。

When it is paid, bring your true friend along.
My maid Nerissa and myself mean time
Will live as maids and widows [184]. Come away!
For you shall hence upon your wedding-day.
Bid your friends welcome, show a merry cheer [185]
Since you are dear bought [186], I will love you dear.
But let me hear the letter of your friend.

 Bass. [*Reads*.] "Sweet Bassanio, my ships have all miscarried [187], my creditors grow cruel, my estate is very low, my bond to the Jew is forfeit; and since in paying it, it is impossible I should live, all debts are clear'd between you and I [188], if I might but see you at my death. Not withstanding, use your pleasure [189]; if your love [190] do not persuade you to come, let not my letter."

 Por. O love! dispatch [191] all business and be gone.

 Bass. Since I have your good leave to go away,
I will make haste: but till I come again,
No bed shall e'er be guilty of my stay [192].
Nor rest be interposer'twixt us twain [193]. [*Exeunt*.]

Scene III — Venice. A Street.

Enter Shylock, Solanio. Antonio, and the Jailer.

 Shy. Jailer, look to him, tell not me of mercy.
This is the fool that lent out money gratis.
Jailer, look to him.

 Ant.   Hear me yet, good Shylock.

 Shy. I'll have my bond, speak not against my bond,
I have sworn an oath that I will have my bond.
Thou call'dst me dog before thou hadst a cause,
But since I am a dog, beware my fangs [194].
The Duke shall grant me justice. I do wonder,

---

184. **Will...widows**: will be true to you and lament your absence, 指 Bassanio 不在时，Portia 会对他守贞洁。
185. **cheer**: countenance, 笑脸。
186. **dear bought**: obtained at a high price, dear, 昂贵。
187. **all miscarried**: all have been lost, 指船只失事。

188. **between you and I**: 你我之间。注意这里用的是主格"I"，而不是"me"。
189. **use your pleasure**: follow your own inclination, 自己保重，自己酌量。

债务清了以后，就带你的忠心的朋友到这儿来。我的侍女聂莉莎陪着我在家里，仍旧像未嫁的时候一样，守候着你们的归来。来，今天就是你结婚的日子，大家快快乐乐，好好招待你的朋友们。你既然是用这么大的代价买来的，我一定格外宠爱你。可是让我听听你朋友的信。

巴 （读信。）"巴散尼奥挚友如握：弟船只悉数遇难，债主煎迫，家业荡然。犹太人之约，业已愆期；履行罚则，殆无生望。足下前此欠弟债项，一切勾销，惟盼及弟未死之前，来相探视。若足下旧情淡漠，不来晤面，则亦不复相强，此信置之可也。"

鲍 啊，亲爱的，快把一切事情办好，立刻就去吧！

巴 既然蒙您允许，我就赶快收拾动身；可是——
　　此去经宵应少睡，长留魂魄系相思。（同下。）

第三场　威尼斯；街道

夏洛克，索拉尼奥，安东尼奥及狱吏上。

夏 狱官，留心看住他；不要对我讲什么慈悲。这就是那个放债不取利息的傻瓜。狱官，留心看住他。

安 再听我说句话，好夏洛克。

夏 我一定要照约实行；你倘然想推翻这一张契约，那还是请你免开尊口的好。我已经发过誓，非得照约实行不可。你曾经无缘无故骂我狗，既然我是狗，那么你可留心着我的狗牙齿吧。公爵一定会给我主持公道的。

---

190. **love**: 爱人。莎士比亚时代许多抽象名词可作具体名词用，如 vice 指恶人。隔一行中的"O love"，则是指"亲爱的"。

191. **dispatch**: 安排好，处理好。

192. **No bed…stay**: 直译：床铺决不会犯留我住宿之罪，即"我决不贪睡"之意。

193. **'twixt us twain**: between us two，我们两人之间，这里用 twain 是为了和 again 协韵。

194. **fangs**: 毒牙。

Thou naughty [195] jailer, that thou art so fond [196]
To come abroad [197] with him at his request.

  Ant. I pray thee hear me speak.

  Shy. I'll have my bond; I will not hear thee speak.
I'll have my bond, and therefore speak no more.
I'll not be made a soft and dull-ey'd [198] fool
To shake the head [199], relent, and sigh, and yield
To Christian intercessors. Follow not,
I'll have no speaking; I will have my bond. [*Exit.*]

  Sol. It is the most impenetrable cur [200]
That ever kept [201] with men.

  Ant.   Let him alone,
I'll follow him no more with bootless [202] prayers.
He seeks my life; his reason well I know:
I oft deliver'd from his forfeitures [203]
Many that have at times made moan to me [204];
Therefore he hates me.

  Sol.   I am sure the Duke
Will never grant this forfeiture to hold [205].

  Ant. The Duke cannot deny the course of law;
For the commodity [206] that strangers [207] have
With us in Venice, if it be denied,
Will much impeach the justice of the state,
Since that the trade and profit of the city
Consisteth of all nations. Therefore go.
These griefs and losses have so bated [208] me
That I shall hardly spare a pound of flesh
To-morrow to my bloody creditor.
Well, jailer, on. Pray God Bassanio come
To see me pay his debt, and then I care not [209]! [*Exeunt.*]

---

195. **naughty**: wicked, good-for-nothing, 糊涂的, 坏心肠的。

196. **fond**: foolish, 蠢。

197. **abroad**: out, 释放出来。

198. **dull-ey'd**: easily put upon, 易受骗的。

199. **shake the head**: 摇头。这里用定冠词不用所有格是受法语语法的影响。

200. **impenetrable cur**: 铁石心肠的狗。

201. **kept**: dwelt, 生活。

202. **bootless**: unavailing, useless, 无用的, 徒劳的。

你这糊涂的狱官，我真不懂你老是会答应他的请求，陪着他到外边来。

安 请你听我说。

夏 我一定要照约实行，不要听你讲什么鬼话，我一定要照约实行，所以请你闭嘴吧。我不像那些软心肠流眼泪的傻瓜们一样，听了基督徒的几句劝告，就会摇头叹气，懊悔屈服。别跟着我，我不要听你说话，我要照约实行。（下。）

索 这是人世间一头最顽固的恶狗。

安 别理他；我也不愿再费无益的唇舌向他哀求了。他要的是我的命，我也知道他的原因。常常有许多人因为不堪他的剥削，向我诉苦，是我帮助他们脱离他的压迫，所以他才恨我。

索 我相信公爵一定不会允许他执行这一种处罚。

安 公爵不能变更法律的规定，因为威尼斯的繁荣，完全倚赖着各国人民的来往通商，要是剥夺了异邦人应享的权利，一定会使人对威尼斯的法治精神发生重大的怀疑。去吧，这些不如意的事情，已经把我搅得心力交瘁，我怕到明天身上也许割不下一磅肉来，偿还我这位不怕血腥气的债主了。狱官，走吧。求上帝，让巴散尼奥来亲眼看见我替他还债，我就死而无怨了！（同下。）

---

203. **I.. .forfeitures**: 我常常帮人还债。　　**oft**〔古诗〕: often; **deliver'd**: rescued, 指解救那些欠 Shylock 债务的人，即下一行的 many（deliver'd 的宾语）。**forfeitures**: penalty, 惩罚。

204. **made moan to me**: begged me for assistance, 请求援助。

205. **hold**: 有效。

206. **commodity**: favourable trade privileges, 有利的商业贸易条款。

207. **strangers**: aliens, 外国人。

208. **bated**: reduced, 减少。

209. **I care not**: I'll not regret, 我无遗憾。

Scene Ⅳ — Belmont. A Room in Portia's House.

Enter Portia, Nerissa, Lorenzo, Jessica, and Balthazar.

  Lor. Madam, although I speak it in your presence,
You have a noble and a true conceit [210]
Of godlike amity [211], which appears most strongly
In bearing thus the absence of your lord.
But if you knew to whom you show this honour,
How true a gentleman you send relief,
How dear a lover of my lord your husband,
I know you would be prouder of the work
Than customary bounty can enforce you [212].

  Par. I never did repent for doing good,
Nor shall not now: for in companions
That do converse and waste [213] the time together,
Whose souls do bear an egall yoke of love [214],
There must be needs [215] a like proportion [216]
Of lineaments [217], of manners, and of spirit;
Which makes me think that this Antonio,
Being the bosom lover of my lord,
Must needs be like my lord. If it be so,
How little is the cost I have bestowed
In purchasing the semblance [218] of my soul,
From out [219] the state of hellish cruelty.
This comes too near the praising of myself,
Therefore no more of it. Hear other things:
Lorenzo, I commit into your hands
The husbandry and manage [220] of my house
Until my lord's return. For mine own part,
I have toward heaven breath'd a secret vow
To live in prayer and contemplation,

---

210. **conceit**: understanding, 理解。
211. **amity**: 友谊。
212. **Than...you**: it would give you greater satisfaction than any ordinary good deed could. **bounty**: benevolence, 慷慨; **enforce**: urge upon, 迫使; 给予。

213. **waste**: spend, 打发时间。
214. **egall yoke of love**: equal burden of love, 相同的爱的牵挂。
215. **needs**: 必要。
216. **proportion**: 对等, 相当。

 第四场　贝尔蒙脱；鲍细霞家中一室

鲍细霞，聂莉莎，罗伦佐，吉雪加及包尔萨泽上。

罗　夫人，不是我当面恭维您，您的确有一颗高贵真诚，不同凡俗的仁爱的心；尤其像这次敦促尊夫就道，宁愿割舍儿女的私情，这一种精神毅力，真令人万分钦佩。可是您倘使知道受到您这种好意的是个什么人，您所救援的是怎样一个正直的君子，他对于尊夫的交情又是怎样深挚，我相信您一定会格外因为做了这一件好事而自傲，超过普通的善举所能给您的喜悦。

鲍　我做了好事从来不后悔，现在也当然不会。因为凡是常在一块儿谈心游戏的朋友，彼此之间都有一种相互的友爱，他们在容貌上，风度上，习性上，也必定相去不远；所以在我想来，这位安东尼奥既然是我的丈夫的心腹好友，他的为人一定很像我的丈夫。要是我的猜想果然不错，那么我把一个跟我的灵魂相仿的人从残暴的迫害下救赎出来，花这一点儿代价，算得什么！可是这样的话，太近于自吹自擂了，所以别说了吧，还是谈些其他的事情。罗伦佐，在我的丈夫没有回来以前，我要劳驾您替我照管家里；我自己已经向天许下密誓，要在祈祷和默念中过着生活，

---

217. **lineaments**：外貌。
218. **semblance**：相似，指像 Bassanio.
219. **From out**：out of，从。

220. **husbandry and manage**：care and management，照看、管理，这两个词是近义词。
husbandry：housekeeping，管理家务。

Only attended by Nerissa here,
Until her husband and my lord's return.
There is a monast'ry two miles off,
And there we will abide. I do desire you
Not to deny this imposition [221],
The which my love and some necessity
Now lays upon you.
　　　Lor.　　　　　Madam, with all my heart,
I shall obey you in all fair commands.
　　　Por.　My people do already know my mind,
And will acknowledge you and Jessica
In place of Lord Bassanio and myself.
So fare you well till we shall meet again.
　　　Lor.　Fair thoughts and happy hours attend on you!
　　　Jes.　I wish your ladyship all heart's content.
　　　Por.　I thank you for your wish, and am well pleas'd
To wish it back on you. Fare you well, Jessica.
　　　　　　　　　[*Exeunt Jessica and Lorenzo.*　]
Now, Balthazar,
As I have ever found thee honest-true [222],
So let me find thee still. Take this same letter,
And use thou all th' endeavour of a man
In speed to Padua [223]. See thou render this
Into my cousin's hands, Doctor Bellario,
And look what notes and garments he doth give thee,
Bring them, I pray thee, with imagin'd speed [224]
Unto the traject [225], to the common [226] ferry
Which trades [227] to Venice. Waste no time in words,
But get thee gone. I shall be there before thee.
　　　Balth.　Madam, I go with all convenient [228] speed.　[*Exit*.　]
　　　Por.　Come on, Nerissa, I have work in hand
That you yet know not of. We'll see our husbands
Before they think of us.

---

221. **imposition**: charge, 任务, 责任, 嘱托。
222. **honest-true**: trustworthy, 值得信赖。
223. **Padua**: 当时有名的民法研究中心。
224. **imagin'd speed**: speed as quick as thought, （以）最快的速度。
225. **traject**: 渡船（源自意大利语 traghetto）。

　　只让聂莉莎一个人陪着我，直到我们两人的丈夫回来。在两哩路之外有一所修道院，我们就预备住在那儿。我向您提出这一个请求，不只是为了个人的私情，还有其他事实上的必要，请您不要拒绝我。

罗　夫人，您有什么吩咐，我无不乐于遵命。

鲍　我的仆人们都已知道我的决心，他们会把您和吉雪加当作巴散尼奥和我自己一样看待。后会有期，再见了。

罗　但愿美妙的思想和安乐的时光追随在您的身旁！

吉　愿夫人一切如意！

鲍　谢谢你们的好意，我也愿意用同样的愿望祝福你们。再见，吉雪加。（吉、罗下。）包尔萨泽，我一向知道你诚实可靠，希望你永远做一个诚实可靠的人。这一封信你给我火速送到帕多瓦，交给我的表兄斐拉里奥博士亲手收拆；要是他有什么回信和衣服交给你，你就赶快带着他们到码头上，乘公共渡船到威尼斯去。不要多说话，去吧；我会在威尼斯等你。

包　小姐，我尽快去就是了。（下。）

鲍　来，聂莉莎，我现在还要干一些你没有知道的事情，我们要在我们的丈夫还没有想到我们之前去跟他们相会。

---

226. **common**：public，公共的。

227. **trades**：plies back and forth，来回行驶。

228. **convenient**：due，适当的。

Ner.   Shall they see us?
Por.   They shall, Nerissa; but in such a habit [229]
That they shall think we are accomplished [230]
With that we lack. I'll hold thee any wager,
When we are both accoutered [231] like young men,
I'll prove the prettier fellow of the two,
And wear my dagger with the braver grace [232],
And speak between the change of man and boy
With a reed voice [233], and turn two mincing steps [234]
Into a manly stride; and speak of frays [235]
Like a fine bragging youth, and tell quaint [236] lies,
How honourable ladies sought my love,
Which I denying, they fell sick and died.
I could not do withal. Then I'll repent,
And wish, for all that, that I had not kill'd them;
And twenty of these puny [237] lies I'll tell,
That men shall swear I have discontinued school
Above a twelvemonth. I have within my mind
A thousand raw tricks of these bragging Jacks [238],
Which I will practice.
Ner.   Why, shall we turn to [239] men?
Por.   Fie, what a question's that,
If thou wert near a lewd interpreter [240]!
But come, I'll tell thee all my whole device [241]
When I am in my coach, which stays for us
At the park-gate; and therefore haste away,
For we must measure [242] twenty miles to-day.   [*Exeunt*.]

Scene **V** — The Same. A Garden.

Enter Launcelot and Jessica.

Laun.   Yes, truly, for look you, the sins of the father are to be
laid upon the children; therefore, I promise [243] you, I fear [224] you. I was
always plain with you, and so now I speak my agitation [245] of the matter;

---

229. **habit**: costume，服装。
230. **accomplished**: equipped，装备。
231. **accoutered**: 打扮起来。
232. **braver grace**: 威武。
233. **reed voice**: 男孩的尖声。
234. **mincing steps**: 细步。
235. **frays**: 打架。
236. **quaint**: 精心编造的。

聂　我们要让他们看见我们吗？

鲍　他们将会看见我们，聂莉莎，可是我们要打扮得叫他们认不出我们的本来面目。我可以拿无论什么东西跟你打赌，要是我们都扮成了少年男子，我一定比你漂亮点儿，带起刀子来也比你格外神气点儿；我会沙着喉咙讲话，就像一个正在发育的男孩子一样；我会把两个姗姗细步并成一个男人家的阔步；我会学着那些爱吹牛的哥儿们的样子，谈论一些击剑比武的玩意儿，再随口编造些巧妙的谎话，什么谁家的千金小姐爱上了我啦，我不接受她的好意，她害起病来死啦，我怎么心中不忍，后悔不该害了人家的性命啦，以及二十个诸如此类的无关重要的谎话，人家听见了，一定以为我走出学校的门还不过一年多，这些爱吹牛的娃娃们的鬼花样儿我有一千种在脑袋里，都可以搬出来应用。

聂　怎么，我们要扮成男人吗？

鲍　嗳，这是什么话，要是你身边有坏人听了把话传出去。来，车子在门口等着我们，我们上了车，我可以把我的整个计划一路告诉你。快去吧，今天我们要赶二十里路呢。（同下。）

第五场　同前；花园

朗西洛脱及吉雪加上。

朗　真的，不骗您，父亲的罪恶是要子女承当的，所以我倒真的在替您捏着一把汗呢。我一向喜欢对您说老实话，所以现在我也老老实实地把我心里所担忧的事情告诉您；

---

237. **puny**：petty，childish，小的，幼稚的。
238. **bragging Jacks**：吹牛的家伙。
239. **turn to**：change into，变成。
240. **lewd interpreter**：下流的传话的人。
241. **device**：plan，计划，打算。
242. **measure**：travel，旅行。
243. **promise**：说实话。
244. **fear**：fear for，为……担忧。
245. **agitation**：cogitation，（想法）之误用。

therefore be' a good cheer [246], for truly I think you are damn'd. There is but one hope in it that can do you any good, and that is but a kind of bastard hope [247] neither [248].

Jes. And what hope is that, I pray thee?

Laun. Marry, you may partly hope that your father got [249] you not, that you are not the Jew's daughter.

Jes. That were a kind of bastard hope indeed; so the sins of my mother should be visited [250] upon me.

Laun. Truly then I fear you are damn'd both by father and mother; thus when I shun Scylla, your father, I fall into Charybdis, your mother [251]. Well, you are gone both ways.

Jes. I shall be sav'd by my husband [252], he hath made me a Christian!

Laun. Truly, the more to blame he; we were Christians enow [253] before, e'en as many as could well live one by another [254]. This making of Christians will raise the price of hogs. If we grow all to be [255] porkeaters, we shall not shortly have a rasher [256] on the coals for money [257].

Enter Lorenzo.

Jes. I'll tell my husband, Launcelot, what you say. Here he comes.

Lor. I shall grow jealious [258] of you shortly, Launcelot, if you thus get my wife into corners [259]!

Jes. Nay, you need not fear us, Lorenzo, Launcelot and I are out [260]. He tells me flatly there's no mercy for me in heaven because I am a Jew's daughter; and he says you are no good member of the common-wealth, for in converting Jews to Christians, you raise the price of pork.

Lor. I shall answer that better to the commonwealth than you can the getting up [261] of the Negro's belly; the Moor is with child by you, Launcelot.

---

246. **'a good cheer**: to be cheerful, 宽心，开心。　**'a**=of.
247. **bastard hope**: 不正当的希望。
248. **neither**: 强调前面的否定含义 (=that isn't much of a hope either)。
249. **got**: begot, 出生。
250. **visited**: 惩罚。
251. **I...mother**: **Scylla** 为意大利半岛南端的岩石，**Charybdis** 则为意大利与西西里海峡中的漩涡。两者都是船只容易出事的地点。

　　您放心吧，我想您总免不了下地狱。只有一个希望也许可以帮帮您的忙，可是那也是个不大高妙的希望。

吉　请问你，是什么希望呢？

朗　嗯，您可以存着一半儿的希望，希望您不是您的父亲所生，不是这个犹太人的女儿。

吉　这个希望可真的太不高妙啦；这样说来，我的母亲的罪恶又要降到我的身上来了。

朗　那倒也是真的，您不是为您的父亲下地狱，就是为您的母亲下地狱；逃过了凶恶的礁石，逃不过危险的漩涡。好，您下地狱是下定了。

吉　我可以靠着我的丈夫得救；他已经使我变成一个基督徒了。

朗　这就是他大大的不该。咱们本来已经有很多的基督徒，简直快要挤都挤不下啦；要是再这样把基督徒一批一批制造出来，猪肉的价钱一定会飞涨，大家吃起猪肉来，恐怕我们有钱也买不到一片薄薄的咸肉了。

　　罗伦佐上。

吉　朗西洛脱，你这样胡说八道，我一定要告诉我的丈夫。他来啦。

罗　朗西洛脱，你要是再拉着我的妻子在壁角里说话，我真的要吃起醋来了。

吉　不，罗伦佐，你放心好了，我已经跟朗西洛脱翻脸啦。他老实不客气地告诉我，上天不会对我发慈悲，因为我是一个犹太人的女儿；他又说你不是国家的好公民，因为你把犹太人变成了基督徒，提高了猪肉的价钱。

罗　要是政府向我质问起来，我自有话说。可是，朗西洛脱，你把那黑人的女儿弄大了肚子，教她怀了孕，这该是什么罪名呢？

---

252. **I...husband**：参见《新约·圣经·哥林多前书》第7章第14节："the unbelieving wife is sanctified by the husband"（不信的妻子就因着丈夫成了圣洁）。

253. **enow**：enough，足够。莎士比亚运用这种形式仅作为名词复数的修饰语。

154. **one by another**：together.

255. **grow all to be**：all become，都变成。

256. **rasher**：slice of bacon，咸肉片。

257. **on the coals**：烧，烤。　**for money**：at any price，无论用多少钱。

258. **jealous**：jealous，嫉妒。

259. **into corners**：密谈。

260. **out**：at odds，不和，吵架。

26l. **getting up**：弄大了（肚子）。

Laun.   It is much that the Moor should be more than reason [262]; but if she be less than an honest woman, she is indeed more than I took her for.

Lor.   How every fool can play upon the word [263]! I think the best grace of wit [264] will shortly turn into silence, and discourse grow commendable in none only but [265] parrots. Go in, sirrah, bid them prepare for dinner.

Laun.   That is done, sir, they have all stomachs [266]!

Lor.   Goodly Lord, what a wit-snapper [267] are you! then bid them prepare dinner.

Laun.   That is done too, sir, only "cover [268]" is the word.

Lor.   Will you cover then, sir?

Laun.   Not so, sir, neither, I know my duty.

Lor.   Yet more quarrelling with occasion [269]! wilt thou show the whole wealth of thy wit in an instant? I pray thee understand a plain man in his plain meaning: go to thy fellows, bid them cover the table, serve in the meat [270], and we will come in to dinner.

Laun.   For the table, sir, it shall be serv'd in; for the meat, sir, it shall be cover'd; for your coming in to dinner, sir, why, let it be as humours and conceits [271] shall govern.   [*Exit.*]

Lor.   O dear discretion [272], how his words are suited [273]!
The fool hath planted [274] in his memory
An army of good words, and I do know
A many fools, that stand in better place,
Garnish'd [275] like him, that for a tricksy [276] word
Defy the matter [277]. How cheer'st thou [278], Jessica?
And now, good sweet [279], say thy opinion,
How dost thou like the Lord Bassanio's wife?

Jes.   Past all expressing [280]. It is very meet [281]
The Lord Bassanio live an upright life,
For having such a blessing in his lady,

---

262. **more than reason**: larger than is reasonable, 肚子大得不得了。

263. **play upon the word**: 做文字游戏,指 Launcelot 用 Moor 和 more。

264. **best grace of wit**: 才子的精湛口才。 **grace**: excellence, 精湛。

265. **only but**. 除开。

266. **stomachs**: 胃口,食欲。

267. **wit-snapper**: 说俏皮话的人。

268. **cover**: 有二义:(1)准备开饭;(2)戴帽。Launcelot 故意玩弄这两个字义。下一行中的 cover 是第二种含义。

269. **quarreling with occasion**: 抓住每次机会说俏皮话。**quarreling**: quibbling or making perverse remarks,

270. **meat**: 莎士比亚时代 meat 泛指任何食物。

朗　要求这黑姑娘更有理智，那大可不必；可是如果她不是一个诚实的女人，那可出乎我的意料。

罗　每一个傻瓜都会说俏皮话！我想不多久口才最好的才子也只好哑口无言，只有鹦鹉对答如流。给我进去，小鬼，叫他们预备好吃饭了。

朗　先生，他们早已预备好了；他们都是有肚子的呢。

罗　老天爷，你的嘴真尖利！我要你叫他们把饭菜预备起来。

朗　都已经预备好了，先生，只消说一声"开饭"就行了。

罗　那么你就去"开"好吗？

朗　那可不敢，我知道我自己的地位。

罗　说话很会兜圈子！你是不是要把你的机智的全部家当都兜出来？我求你啦，理解一个简单人说的简单话：去对你那些同伴们说，桌子可以铺起来，饭菜可以端上来，我们要进来吃饭啦。

朗　是，先生，我就去叫他们把饭菜铺起来，桌子端上来；至于您进不进来吃饭，那可悉随尊便。（下。）

罗　啊，分辨得真清楚，用字多么恰当！这傻瓜在脑子里塞满了一大堆好字眼。我知道有许多傻瓜，地位比他高，跟他一样喜欢咬文嚼字，为了说一句双关话，不惜搅乱常识。你好吗，吉雪加？亲爱的好人儿，现在告诉我，你对于巴散尼奥的夫人有什么意见？

吉　好到没有话说。巴散尼奥大爷娶到这样一位好夫人，享尽了人世天堂的幸福，

---

271. **humours and conceits**: as your whims and notions shall determine, 悉听尊便。

272. **discretion**: discrimination, 分辨。

273. **suited**: adapted to suit the occasion, 灵活地使用。

274. **planted**: put, 装满。

275. **Garnish'd**: furnished(with words), 塞满词汇。

276. **tricksy**: ingenious, clever but with no regard to the subject under discussion, 指好说俏皮话，玩弄字眼，但与话题无关，不切题。

277. **defy the matter**: disdain the meaning, 不着边际，言不及"义"。

278. **How cheer'st thou**: what cheer, 过得快活吗？

279. **sweet**: sweetheart, 心上人。

280. **Past all expressing**: 非言语所能形容，意为"非常喜欢"。

281. **meet**: proper, 适当。

He finds the joys of heaven here on earth,
And if on earth he do not merit it,
In reason he should never come to heaven!
Why, if two gods should play some heavenly match,
And on the wager lay two earthly women,
And Portia one, there must be something else
Pawn'd [282] with the other, for the poor rude world
Hath not her fellow [283].

  Lor.   Even such a husband
Hast thou of me as she is for a wife.

  Jes. Nay, but ask my opinion too of that.

  Lor. I will anon, first let us go to dinner.

  Jes. Nay, let me praise you while I have a stomach [284].

  Lor. No, pray thee, let it serve for table-talk;
Then howsome'er [285] thou speak'st, 'mong [286] other things
I shall disgest it.

  Jes.   Well, I'll set you forth [287]. [*Exeunt*.]

---

282. **Pawn'd**: staked，下赌注，当，押。
283. **her fellow**: her equal，和她旗鼓相当的人。
284. **stomach**: 双关，(1)appetite(胃口)；(2)inclination
(情绪)。
285. **howsome'er**: howsoever，无论。

自然应该不会走上邪路了。如果他不规矩，那么他永远也进不了天堂。要是有两个天神打赌，各自拿一个人间的女子作赌注，如其一个是鲍细霞，那么还有一个必须另外加上些什么，才可以彼此相抵，因为这一个寒伧的世界还不能产生一个跟她同样好的人来。

罗　他娶到了她这么一个好妻子，你也嫁着了我这么一个好丈夫。

吉　那可要先问问我的意见。

罗　可以可以，可是先让我们吃了饭再说。

吉　不，让我趁着胃口没有倒之前，先把你恭维两句。

罗　不，你有话还是留到吃饭的时候说吧；那么不论你说得好说得坏，我都可以连着饭菜一起吞下去。

吉　好，你且等着听我怎样说你吧。（同下。）

---

286. ' mong〔诗〕：among 的缩略形式。

287. **set you forth**：（1）serve you up，给你开饭；（2）praise you extravagantly，着实地恭维你几句。

ACT IV

Scene I — Venice. A Court of Justice.

Ener the Duke, the Magnificoes, Antonio, Bassanio,

Gratiano, Salerio, Solanio, and others.

Duke.　　What, is Antonio here?

Ant.　　Ready [1], so please your Grace.

Duke.　　I am sorry for thee. Thou art come to answer

A stony adversary, an inhuman wretch,

Uncapable of pity, void and empty

From any dram of mercy [2].

　　Ant.　　I have heard

Your Grace hath ta'en great pains to qualify [3]

His rigorous course [4], but since he stands obdurate,

And that no lawful means can carry me

Out of his envy's [5] reach, I do oppose

My patience to his fury [6], and am arm'd [7]

To suffer, with a quietness of spirit,

The very tyranny and rage of his.

　　Duke.　　Go one [8], and call the Jew into the court.

　　Sal.　　He is ready at the door; he comes, my lord.

Enter Shylock.

Duke.　　Make room, and let him stand before our face.

Shylock, the world thinks, and I think so too,

That thou but leadest this fashion of thy malice [9]

To the last hour of act [10], and then 'tis thought

Thou'lt show thy mercy and remorse more strange [11]

Than is thy strange apparent cruelty;

And where [12] thou now exact'st [13] the penalty,

Which is a pound of this poor merchant's flesh,

---

1. **Ready...Grace**: 有，听候殿下吩咐。
2. **From...mercy**: 毫无怜悯之心。　**From**: of; **dram**: smallest amount.
3. **qualify**: moderate, 减轻。
4. **course**: 法律诉讼。
5. **envy's**: 凶恶的。
6. **fury**: 愤怒; 凶暴。
7. **arm'd**: prepared, 准备好。
8. **Go one**: （对衙役）来人。
9. **leadest...malice**: pretend to carry through this spiteful action, 装出狠毒的样子。　**fashion**: form, pretence.

第四幕

第一场　威尼斯；法庭

公爵，众绅士，安东尼奥，巴散尼奥，葛莱西安诺，萨莱里奥，索拉尼奥及余人等同上。

公爵　安东尼奥有没有来？

安　有，殿下。

公爵　我很替你不快乐；你是来跟一个心如铁石的对手当庭对质，一个不懂得怜悯，没有一丝慈悲心的不近人情的恶汉。

安　听说殿下曾经用尽力量劝他不要过为已甚，可是他一味坚执，不肯略作让步。既然没有合法的手段可以使我脱离他的怨毒的掌握，我只有用默认迎受他的愤怒，安心等待着他的残暴的处置。

公爵　来人，传那犹太人到庭。

萨　他在门口等着；他来了，殿下。

夏洛克上。

公爵　大家让开些，让他站在我的面前。夏洛克，人家都以为你不过故意装出这一副凶恶的姿态，到了最后关头，就会显出你的仁慈恻隐来，比你现在这种表面上的残酷更加出人意料，现在你虽然坚持着照约处罚，一定要从这个不幸的商人身上割下一磅肉来，

---

10. **act**：performance，行为，表演。
11. **remorse more strange**：更加同情。　**strange**：extra-ordinary，尤其，更加。
12. **where**：whereas，然而。
13. **exact'st**：要求（偿付）；坚持。

Thou wilt not only loose [14] the forfeiture,
But touch'd with humane gentleness and love.
Forgive a moi'ty [15] of the principal,
Glancing an eye of pity on his losses,
That have of late so huddled [16] on his back,
Enow to press a royal merchant down,
And pluck commiseration of his state
From brassy bosoms and rough hearts of flints,
From stubborn Turks and Tartars [17] never train'd
To offices [18] of tender courtesy.
We all expect a gentle answer, Jew!

    Shy.   I have possess'd [19] your Grace of what I purpose,
And by our holy Sabaoth [20] have I sworn
To have the due and forfeit [21] of my bond.
If you deny it, let the danger [22] light
Upon your charter and your city's freedom!
You'll ask me why I rather choose to have
A weight of carrion flesh [23] than to receive
Three thousand ducats. I'll not answer that;
But say it is my humour [24], is it answer'd?
What if my house be troubled with a rat,
And I be pleas'd to give ten thousand ducats
To have it ban'd [25]? What, are you answer'd yet?
Some men there are love not a gaping pig [26];
Some that are mad if they behold [27] a cat;
And others, when the bagpipe [28] sings i' th' nose,
Cannot contain their urine: for affection [29],
Mistress of passion, sways it to the mood
Of what it likes or loathes. Now for your answer:
As there is no firm reason to be rend'red [30]
Why be cannot abide a gaping pig;
Why he, a harmless necessary cat [31];

---

14. **loose**: give up, forget, 放弃。在莎士比亚时代 loose 和 lose 是一对同源词，莎翁可能用的是 lose（忘记）的词义。
15. **moi'ty**=moiety, 一部分。
16. **huddled**: crowded, 堆压在。
17. **stubborn Turks and Tartars**: 凶恶的土耳其人和鞑靼人。当时欧洲人认为土耳其人和鞑靼人是野蛮民族。
18. **offices**: acts, 行为。
19. **possess'd**: informed.
20. **Sabaoth**: 指 Sabbath, 这里指礼拜六。Sabaoth 是个希伯莱字，意思是 "armies" 或 "hosts"，通常容易与 Sabbath 混淆。
21. **due and forfeit**: 债务和惩罚。

到了那时候，你不但愿意放弃这一种处罚，而且因为受到良心上的感动，说不定还会豁免他一部分的欠款。人家都是这样说，我也是这样猜想着。你看他最近接连遭逢的巨大损失，足以使无论怎样富有的商人倾家荡产，即使铁石一样的心肠，从来不知道人类同情的野蛮人，也不能不对他的境遇发生怜悯。犹太人，我们都在等候你一句温和的回答。

夏　我的意思已经向殿下告禀过了；我也已经指着我们的圣安息日起誓，一定要照约执行处罚；要是殿下不准许我的请求，那您的宪章就会失去效力，您的城邦也将不成其为自由邦。您要是问我为什么不愿接受三千块钱，宁愿拿一块腐烂的臭肉，那我可没有什么理由可以回答您，我只能说我欢喜这样，这是不是一个回答？要是我的屋子里有了耗子，我高兴出一万块钱叫人把它们赶走，谁管得了我？这不是回答了您吗？有的人不爱看张开嘴的烤猪，有的人瞧见一头猫就要发脾气，还有人听见人家吹风笛的声音，就忍不住要小便；因为一个人的感性支配着心灵内部喜恶的情愫，谁也做不了自己的主。现在我就这样回答您：为什么有人受不住一头张开嘴的烤猪，有人受不住一头有益无害的猫，

---

22. **danger**: harm，危害。意指威尼斯如不秉公断案，将丧失其作为自由城市的地位和司法特权。

23. **carrion flesh**: 烂肉，死肉。

24. **humour**: whim，心血来潮，一时冲动。

25. **ban'd**: poisoned，下毒药。

26. **gaping pig**: roasted pig with its mouth open，张开嘴的烤猪。

27. **behold**: 看到。

28. **bagpipe**: 苏格兰风笛。

29. **affection**: instinctual feelings，本能的情感。

30. **rend'red**: 提出。

31. **necessary cat**: 捉老鼠的猫。

Why he a woollen bagpipe, but of force [32]
Must yield to such inevitable shame
As to offend, himself being offended;
So can I give no reason, nor I will not,
More than a lodg'd [33] hate and a certain [34] loathing
I bear Antonio, that I follow thus
A losing suit [35] against him. Are you answered?

     ***Bass*.** This is no answer, thou unfeeling man,
To excuse the current [36] of thy cruelty.

     ***Shy*.** I am not bound to please thee with my answers.

     ***Bass*.** Do all men kill the things they do not love?

     ***Shy*.** Hates any man the thing he would not kill?

     ***Bass*.** Every offense is not a hate at first.

     ***Shy*.** What, wouldst thou have a serpent sting thee twice?

     ***Ant*.** I pray you think [37] you question [38] with the Jew:
You may as well go stand upon the beach
And bid the main flood [39] bate his usual height;
You may as well use question with the wolf
Why he hath made the ewe bleak [40] for the lamb;
You may as well forbid the mountain pines
To wag their high tops, and to make no noise
When they are fretten [41] with the gusts of heaven;
You may as well do any thing most hard
As seek to soften that — than which what's harder? —
His Jewish heart! Therefore I do beseech you
Make no more offers, use no farther means,
But with all brief and plain conveniency [42]
Let me have judgment and the Jew his will.

     ***Bass*.** For thy three thousand ducats here is six.

     ***Shy*.** If every ducat in six thousand ducats
Were in six parts, and every part a ducat,
I would not draw [43] them, I would have my bond.

---

32. **of force**: 必要地。
33. **lodg'd**: 积怨很深的。
34. **certain**: 确定的。
35. **A losing suit**: unprofitable case, 吃亏的官司。

36. **current**: tenor, drift, 意向。
37. **think**: bear in mind, 记住。
38. **question**: argue, 争论。

还有人受不住咿咿唔唔的风笛的声音，这些都是毫无充分的理由的，只是因为天生的癖性，使他们一受到感触，就会情不自禁地现出丑相来；所以我不能举什么理由，也不愿举什么理由，除了因为我对于安东尼奥抱着久积的仇恨和深刻的反感，所以才会向他进行这一场对于我自己并没有好处的诉讼。现在您不是已经得到我的回答了吗？

巴　你这冷酷无情的家伙，这样的回答可不能作为你的残忍的辩解。

夏　我的回答本来不是为要讨你的欢喜。

巴　难道人们对于他们所不喜欢的东西，都一定要置之死地吗？

夏　哪一个人会恨他所不愿意杀死的东西？

巴　初次的冒犯，不应该就引为仇恨。

夏　什么！你愿意给毒蛇咬两次吗？

安　请你想一想，你现在跟这个犹太人讲理，就像站在海滩上，叫那大海的怒涛减低它的奔腾的威力，责问豺狼为什么害母羊为了失去它的羔羊而哀啼，或是叫那山上的松柏，在受到天风吹拂的时候，不要摇头摆脑，发出谡谡的声音。要是你能够叫这个犹太人的心变软——世上还有什么东西比它更硬呢？——那么还有什么难事不可以做到？所以我请你不用再跟他商量什么条件，也不用替我想什么办法，让我爽爽快快受到判决，满足这犹太人的心愿吧。

巴　借了你三千块钱，现在拿六千块钱还你好不好？

夏　即使这六千块钱中间的每一块都可以分作六份，每一份都可以变成一块钱，我也不要它们；我只要照约处罚。

---

39. **main flood**: high tide，海潮。

40. **bleak**: bleat，羊叫。

41. **fretten**: fretted，使发愁，使摇曳。

42. **conveniency**: fitness，合适。

43. **draw**: take，接受。

Duke.　　How shalt thou hope for mercy, rend'ring none [44]?

　Shy.　　What judgment shall I dread, doing no wrong?

You have among you many a purchas'd slave,

Which like your asses, and your dogs and mules,

You use in abject and in slavish parts [45],

Because you bought them. Shall I say to you,

"Let them be free! Marry them to your heirs!

Why sweat they under burthens [46]? Let their beds

Be made as soft as yours, and let their palates

Be season'd with such viands [47]"? You will answer,

"The slaves are ours." so do I answer you:

The pound of flesh which I demand of him

Is dearly bought as mine, and I will have it.

If you deny me, fie upon [48] your law!

There is no force in the decrees of Venice.

I stand for judgment. Answer — shall I have it?

　Duke.　　Upon [49] my power I may dismiss this court,

Unless Bellario, a learned doctor,

Whom I have sent for to determine this,

Come here to-day.

　　Sal.　　　　　My lord, here stays without [50]

A messenger with letters [51] from the doctor,

New [52] come from Padua.

　Duke.　　Bring us the letters; call the messenger.

　Bass.　　Good cheer, Antonio! what, man, courage yet!

The Jew shall have my flesh, blood, bones, and all,

Ere thou shalt lose for me one drop of blood.

　Ant.　　I am a tainted wether [53] of the flock,

Meetest [54] for death; the weakest kind of fruit

Drops earliest to the ground, and so let me.

You cannot better be employ'd, Bassanio,

Than to live still [55] and write mine epitaph.

---

44. **rend'ring none**: without providing mercy, 不给别人怜悯。

45. **parts**: tasks, 苦工。

46. **burthens**: burdens.

47. **season'd...viands**: 品尝同样的肉食。　**season'd**: 加调料。

48. **fie upon**: 见鬼，混账。

49. **upon**: by, in accordance with.

50. **stays without**: waits outside, 等在外面。

51. **letters**: a letter, 一封信。

52. **New**: newly, 刚刚。

公爵　你这样一点没有慈悲之心，将来怎么能够希望人家对你慈悲呢？

夏　我又不干错事，怕什么刑罚？你们买了许多奴隶，把他们当作驴狗骡马一样看待，叫他们做种种卑贱的工作，因为他们是你们出钱买来的。我可不可以对你们说，让他们自由，叫他们跟你们的子女结婚吧；为什么他们要在重担之下流着血汗呢？让他们的床铺得跟你们的床同样柔软，让他们的舌头也尝尝你们所吃的东西吧，你们会回答说："这些奴隶是我们所有的。"所以我也可以回答你们：我向他要求的这一磅肉，是我出了很大的代价买来的；它是我的所有，我一定要把它拿到手里。您要是拒绝了我，那么让你们的法律见鬼去吧！威尼斯的法令只是一纸空文！我现在等候着判决，请快些回答我，我可不可以拿到这一磅肉？

公爵　我已经差人去请裴拉里奥，一位有学问的博士，来替我们审判这件案子；要是他今天不来，我可以有权宣布延期判决。

萨　殿下，外面有一个使者刚从帕多瓦来，带着这位博士的书信，等候着殿下的召唤。

公爵　把信拿来给我；叫那使者进来。

巴　高兴起来吧，安东尼奥！喂，老兄，不要灰心！这犹太人可以把我的肉，我的血，我的骨头，我的一切都拿去，可是我决不让你为了我的缘故流一滴血。

安　我是羊群里一头不中用的病羊，死是我的应分；最软弱的果子最先落到地上，让我也就这样结束了我的一生吧。你应当继续活下去，巴散尼奥；我的墓志铭除了你以外，是没有人写得好的。

---

53. **tainted wether**：染病的阉羊。　**tainted**：infected with disease，得病的；　**wether**：a castrated ram，阉割了的公羊。

54. **Meetest**：most fit，最该；最适合。

55. **live still**：go on living，活下去。

Enter Nerissa dressed like a lawyer's clerk.

Duke.　　Came you from Padua, from Bellario?
Ner.　　From both, my lord. Bellario greets your Grace.
　　　　　　　　　　　　　　　　　　[*Presenting a letter.*]
Bass.　　Why dost thou whet thy knife so earnestly?
Shy.　　To cut the forfeiture from that bankrout there.
Gra.　　Not on thy sole [56], but on thy soul, harsh Jew,
Thou mak'st thy knife keen; but no metal can,
No, not the hangman's axe [57], bear half the keenness
Of thy sharp envy [58]. Can no prayers pierce thee [59]?
Shy.　　No, none that thou hast wit enough to make.
Gra.　　O, be thou damn'd, inexecrable [60] dog!
And for thy life [61] let justice be accus'd.
Thou almost mak'st me waver in my faith
To hold opinion with Pythagoras [62],
That souls of animals infuse themselves
Into the trunks [63] of men. Thy currish spirit
Govern'd a wolf, who hang'd for human slaughter,
Even from the gallows did his fell [64] soul fleet,
And whilst thou layest in thy unhallowed dam [65],
Infus'd itself in thee; for thy desires
Are wolvish, bloody, starv'd, and ravenous.
Shy.　　Till thou canst rail the seal from off my bond,
Thou but offend'st [66] thy lungs to speak so loud.
Repair thy wit, good youth, or it will fall
To cureless [67] ruin. I stand here for law.
Duke.　　This letter from Bellario doth commend [68]
A young and learned doctor to our court.
Where is he?
Ner.　　He attendeth here hard by [69]
To know your answer, whether you'll admit him [70].

- -

56. **sole**："鞋底"，同 soul"心"谐音。
57. **hangman's axe**：刽子手的斧头。
58. **envy**：恶意。
59. **pierce thee**：穿透你，指打动你的心。
60. **inexecrable**：可憎恶的，坏透的。这里的前缀 in 并没有否定意义。inexecrable 等于 that cannot be execrated enough。

61. **for thy life**: because you are permitted to live.
62. **Pythagoras**：毕达哥拉斯，灵魂轮回说的创立者，认为人死后来世可以为兽，兽死来世亦可为人。

聚莉莎扮律师书记上。

公爵 你是从帕多瓦裴拉里奥那里来的吗？

聂 是，殿下。裴拉里奥叫我向殿下致意。（呈上一信。）

巴 你这样使劲儿磨着刀干么？

夏 从那破产的家伙身上割下那磅肉来。

葛 狠心的犹太人，你的刀不应该放在你的靴底磨，应该放在你的灵魂里磨，才可以磨得锐利；就是刽子手的钢刀，也赶不上你的刻毒的心肠厉害。难道什么恳求都不能打动你吗？

夏 不能，无论你说得多么婉转动听，都没有用。

葛 万恶不赦的狗，看你死后不下地狱！让你这种东西活在世上，真是公道不生眼睛。你简直使我的信仰发生动摇，相信起毕达哥拉斯所说畜生的灵魂可以转生人体的议论来了，你的前生一定是一头豺狼，因为吃了人给人捉住吊死，它那凶恶的灵魂就从绞架上逃了出来，钻进了你那老娘的肮脏的胎里，因为你的性情正像豺狼一样残暴贪婪。

夏 除非你能够把我这一张契约上的印章骂掉，否则像你这样拉开了喉咙直嚷，不过白白伤了你的肺，何苦来呢？好兄弟，我劝你还是修养修养你的聪明吧，免得它将来一起毁坏得不可收拾。我在这儿要求法律的裁判。

公爵 裴拉里奥在这封信上介绍一位年轻有学问的博士出席我们的法庭。他在什么地方？

聂 他就在这儿附近等着您的答复，不知道殿下准不准许他进来？

---

63. **trunks**：躯体。
64. **fell**：cruel，残酷的。
65. **unhallowed dam**：邪恶的母狗。
    unhallowed：impious；**dam**：母兽。
66. **offend'st**：injurest，伤害。
67. **cureless**：incurable，不可救药。
68. **commend**：recommend，推荐。
69. **hard by**：nearby，附近。
70. **admit him**：让他进来。

Duke.   With all my heart.   Some three or four of you
Go give him courteous conduct [71] to this place.
Mean time the court shall hear Bellario's letter.

Clerk.   [*Reads*.]   "Your Grace shall understand that at the receipt
of your letter I am very sick, but in the instant that your messenger
came, in loving visitation [72] was with me a young doctor of Rome.   His
name is Balthazar.   I acquainted him with the cause in controversy
between the Jew and Antonio the merchant. We turn'd o'er many books
together. He is furnish'd with my opinion, which better'd with his
own learning, the greatness whereof I cannot enough commend [73], comes
with him, at my importunity [74], to fill up [75] your Grace's request in my
stead [76].   I beseech you let his lack of years be no impediment to let him
lack [77] a reverend estimation, for I never knew so young a body with so
old a head. I leave him to your gracious acceptance, whose trial [78] shall
better publish [79] his commendation."

Duke.   You hear the learn'd Bellario, what he writes,
And here I take it is the doctor come.

Enter Portia, dressed like a doctor of Laws.

Give me your hand.   Come you from old Bellario?
   Por.   I did, my lord.
   Duke.   You are welcome, take your place.
Are you acquainted with the difference [80]
That holds this present question in the court?
   Por.   I am informed throughly [81] of the cause [82].
Which is the merchant here?   and which the Jew?
   Duke.   Antonio and old Shylock, both stand forth.
   Por.   Is your name Shylock?
   Shy.   Shylock is my name.
   Por.   Of a strange nature is the suit you follow,
Yet in such rule [83] that the Venetian law

---

71. **conduct**: escort，陪伴。
72. **in loving visitation**: on a friendly visit，（进行）友好访问。
72. **the greatness...commend**: 此君学识渊博，实难罄述。
    cannot enough commend: 说不尽，夸不完。
74. **importunity**: 请求。
75. **fill up**: comply with，遵从。
76. **in my instead**: 代替我。
77. **let him lack**: which will deprive him of，使他失去，使他得不到。
78. **whose trial**: 对他的考验。

公爵　非常欢迎。来，你们去三四个人，恭恭敬敬领他到这儿来。现在让我们把裴拉里奥的来信当庭宣读。

书记　（读信。）"尊翰到时，鄙人抱疾方剧；适有一青年博士包尔萨泽君自罗马来此，致其慰问，因与详讨犹太人与安东尼奥一案，偏稽群籍，折衷是非，遂恳其为鄙人庖代，以应殿下之召。凡鄙人对此案所具意见，此君已深悉无遗；其学问才识，虽穷极赞辞，亦不足道其万一，务希勿以其年少而忽之，盖如此少年老成之士，实鄙人生平所仅见也。倘蒙延纳，必能不辱使命。敬祈钧裁。"

公爵　你们已经听到了博学的裴拉里奥的来信。这儿来的大概就是那位博士了。

　　　　鲍细霞扮律师上。

公爵　把您的手给我。足下是从裴拉里奥老前辈那儿来的吗？

鲍　正是，殿下。

公爵　欢迎欢迎，请上坐。您有没有明了今天我们在这儿审理的这件案子的两方面的争点？

鲍　我对于这件案子的详细情形已经完全知道了。这儿哪一个是那商人，哪一个是犹太人？

公爵　安东尼奥，夏洛克，你们两人都上来。

鲍　你的名字就叫夏洛克吗？

夏　夏洛克是我的名字。

鲍　你这场官司打得倒也奇怪，可是按照威尼斯的法律，

---

79. **publish**：make known，使大家知道。
80. **difference**：dispute，案件的分歧所在。
81. **throughly**：thoroughly，彻底地。

82. **cause**：case.
83. **rule**：order，手续。

Cannot impugn [84] you as you do proceed. — [*To Antonio.*]
You stand within his danger [85], do you not?

   Ant. Ay, so he says.

   Por. Do you confess the bond?

   Ant. I do.

   Por. Then must the Jew be merciful.

   Shy. On what compulsion [86] must I ? tell me that.

   Por. The quality of mercy is not strain'd [87],
It droppeth as the gentle rain from heaven
Upon the place beneath. It is twice blest [88]:
It blesseth him that gives and him that takes.
'Tis mightiest in the mightiest, it becomes
The throned monarch better than his crown.
His sceptre shows the force of temporal power [89],
The attribute to [90] awe and majesty,
Wherein doth sit [91] the dread and fear of kings;
But mercy is above this sceptred sway [92],
It is enthroned in the hearts of kings,
It is an attribute to [93] God himself;
And earthly power doth then show likest God's
When mercy seasons [94] justice. Therefore, Jew,
Though justice be thy plea, consider this,
That in the course of justice, none of us
Should see salvation [95]. We do pray for mercy,
And that same prayer [96] doth teach us all to render
The deeds of mercy. I have spoke [97] thus much
To mitigate [98] the justice of thy plea.
Which if thou follow, this strict court of Venice
Must needs give sentence'gainst the merchant there.

   Shy. My deeds upon my head [99]! I crave the law,
The penalty and forfeit of my bond.

   Por. Is he not able to discharge [100] the money?

---

84. **impugn**: 驳回。

85. **You...danger**: you are at his mercy, 你的命运操在他的手里。danger是法律术语，源自拉丁语dominium，即jurisdiction，根据法律提出的要求。

86. **compulsion**: 充分理由。

87. **The quality...strain'd**: 慈悲的美德并不是勉强的。
  quality: 美德；　**strained**: 勉强；等于constrained。

这是Portia针对Shylock的compulsion一语所发的议论。此段话历来被认为是莎士比亚杰作之一，但对Shylock讲基督教义可谓是对牛弹琴。

88. **twice blest**: 双重的福佑。

89. **temporal power**: 人间的权威。　**temporal**: to this life or this world.

你的控诉是可以成立的。（向安。）你的生死现在操在他的手里，是不是？

安　他是这样说的。

鲍　你承认这借约吗？

安　我承认。

鲍　那么犹太人应该慈悲一点。

夏　为什么我应该慈悲一点？把您的理由告诉我。

鲍　慈悲不是出于勉强，它是像甘霖一样从天上降下尘世；它给人双重的祝福，不但给幸福于受施的人，也同样给幸福于施与的人；它有超乎一切的无上威力，比皇冠更足以显出一个帝王的高贵：御杖不过象征着俗世的威权，使人民对于君王的尊严凛然生畏；慈悲的力量却高出于权力之上，它深藏在帝王的内心，是一种属于上帝的德性，执法的人倘能把慈悲调剂着王法，人间的权力就和上帝的神力没有差别。所以，犹太人，虽然你所要求的是王法，可是请你想一想，要是真的按照王法执行起赏罚来，谁也没有死后得救的希望；我们既然祈祷着上帝的慈悲，就应该自己做一些慈悲的事。我说了这一番话，为的是希望你能够从你的法律的立场上作几分让步；可是如果你坚持着原来的要求，那么威尼斯的法庭是执法无私的，只好把那商人宣判定罪了。

夏　我只要求法律允许我照约执行处罚。

鲍　他是不是不能清还你的债款？

---

90. **The attribute to**: visible symbol of, 明显的标志，指 scepter。

91. **sit**: 存在着。

92. **sceptred sway**: 国王的权力。

93. **an attribute to**: 特点，和上文 the attribute 意义不同。

94. **seasons**: tempers, 调剂。

95. **salvation**: 灵魂得到拯救。接基督教的原罪说，灵魂被拯救的人才得以升天堂。

96. **that same prayer**: 指《圣经》中的主祷文。

97. **spoke**: spoken。

98. **mitigate**: 不要坚持，让步。

99. **My deeds upon my head！**：我做的事报应在我自己身上（我要对我自己的行为负责！我敢作敢为，不要慈悲）！注意此处 deeds 与前面 Portia 所说的 the deeds of mercy 相对应。

100. **discharge**: 偿付。

Bass.　　Yes,　here I tender [101] it for him in the court,
Yea.　twice the sum.　If that will not suffice,
I will be bound to pay it ten times o'er,
On forfeit of my hands,　my head,　my heart.
If this will not suffice,　it must appear
That malice bears down truth [102].　　*[To the Duke.]*　　And I beseech you
Wrest once the law to your authority [103]:
To do a great right,　do a little wrong,
And curb this cruel devil of his will.
　　Por.　　It must not be,　there is no power in Venice
Can alter a decree established.
'Twill be recorded for a precedent,
And many an error by the same example
Will rush into the state.　It cannot be.
　　Shy.　　A Daniel [104] come to judgment!　yea,　a Daniel!
O wise young judge,　how I do honour thee!
　　Por.　　I pray you let me look upon the bond.
　　Shy.　　Here'tis,　most reverend doctor,　here it is.
　　Por.　　Shylock,　there's thrice thy money off'red thee.
　　Shy.　　An oath,　an oath,　I have an oath in heaven!
Shall I lay perjury upon my soul?
No,　not for Venice.
　　Por.　　　　　　Why,　this bond is forfeit,
And lawfully by this the Jew may claim
A pound of flesh,　to be by him cut off
Nearest the merchant's heart.　Be merciful,
Take thrice thy money,　bid me tear the bond.
　　Shy.　　When it is paid according to the tenure.
It doth appear you are a worthy judge;
You know the law,　your exposition [105]
Hath been most sound.　I charge you by the law,
Whereof you are a well-deserving pillar,

---

101. **tender**: 付给；还清。
102. **bears down truth**: overthrows righteousness，推翻公
　　理。
103. **Wrest...authority**: For once twist the law a little and
　　subject it to your authority，行使你的权力将法律变
　　通一次。　　**wrest**: strain，改变。

巴　不，我愿意替他当庭还清；照原数加倍也可以；要是这样他还不满足，那么我愿意签署契约，还他十倍的数目，倘然不能如约，他可以割我的手，砍我的头，挖我的心；要是这样还不能使他满足，那就是存心害人，不顾天理了。（向公爵。）请大人运用权力，把法律稍为变通一下，犯一次小小的错误，积一次大大的功德，别让这个残忍的恶魔逞他杀人的兽欲。

鲍　那可不行，在威尼斯谁也没有权力变更既成的法律；要是开了这一个恶例，以后谁都可以藉口有例可援，什么坏事都可以干了。这是不行的。

夏　一个但尼尔来做法官了！真的是但尼尔再世！聪明的青年法官啊，我真佩服你！

鲍　请你让我瞧一瞧那借约。

夏　在这儿，可尊敬的博士；请看吧。

鲍　夏洛克，他们愿意出三倍的钱还你呢。

夏　不行，不行，我已经对天发过誓啦，难道我可以让我的灵魂背上毁誓的罪名吗？不，把整个儿的威尼斯给我，我都不能答应。

鲍　好，那么就应该照约处罚；根据法律，这犹太人有权要求从这商人的胸口割下一磅肉来。还是慈悲一点，把三倍原数的钱拿去，让我撕了这张约吧。

夏　等他按照约中所载条款受罚以后，再撕也不迟。您瞧上去像是一个很好的法官；您懂得法律，您讲的话也很有道理，不愧是法律界的中流砥柱，所以现在我就用法律的名义，

---

104. **Daniel**: 但尼尔（旧译"但以理"），据《旧约·圣经·但以理书》，Daniel 是希伯莱预言家，又是著名法官，善断冤狱。

105. **exposition**: 理解。

Proceed to judgment. By my soul I swear
There is no power in the tongue of man
To alter me: [106] I stay here on my bond.

  Ant. Most heartily I do beseech the court
To give the judgment.

  Por.   Why then thus it is:
You must prepare your bosom for his knife—

  Shy. O noble judge, O excellent young man!

  Por. For the intent and purpose of the law
Hath full relation to the penalty [107],
Which here appeareth due upon the bond.

  Shy. 'Tis very true. O wise and upright judge!
How much more elder [108] art thou than thy looks!

  Por. Therefore lay bare your bosom.

  Shy.   Ay, his breast,
So says the bond, doth it not, noble judge?
"Nearest his heart," those are the very words.

  Por. It is so. Are there balance [109] here to weigh
The flesh?

  Shy. I have them ready.

  Por. Have by some surgeon, Shylock, on your charge [110],
To stop his wounds, lest he do bleed to death.

  Shy. Is it so nominated in the bond?

  Por. It is not so express'd, but what of that?
'Twere [111] good you do so much for charity.

  Shy. I cannot find it, 'tis not in the bond.

  Por. You, merchant, have you anything to say?

  Ant. But little; I am arm'd and well prepar'd.
Give me your hand, Bassanio, fare you well.
Grieve not that I am fall'n to this [112] for you;
For herein Fortune [113] shows herself more kind
Than is her custom. It is still her use [114]
To let the wretched man outlive his wealth,

---

106. **To alter me**: 改变我的决定。
107. **the intent...penalty**: 制定法律的（意图和）目的跟
 （契约上所订的）惩罚是完全一致的。 **Hath...to**:
 完全承认（其）有效性。
108. **more elder**: 形容词比较级和最高级同时使用分析
 式和综合式，是伊丽莎白时代英语的一个特征，如
 more nearer, more better, most unkindest。

请您立刻进行宣判，凭着我的灵魂起誓，谁也不能用他的口舌改变我的决心。我现在只等着执行原约。

安　我也诚心请求大人从速宣判。

鲍　好，那么就是这样：你必须准备让他的刀子刺进你的胸膛。

夏　啊，尊严的法官！好一位优秀的青年！

鲍　因为这约上所订定的惩罚，对于法律条文的涵义并无抵触。

夏　很对很对！啊，聪明正直的法官！想不到你瞧上去这样年轻，见识却这么老练！

鲍　所以你应该把你的胸膛袒露出来。

夏　对了，"他的胸部"，约上是这么说的；——不是吗，尊严的法官？——"附近心口的所在"，约上写得明明白白的。

鲍　不错，称肉的天平有没有预备好？

夏　我已经带来了。

鲍　夏洛克，你应该自己拿出钱来，请一位外科医生替他堵住伤口，免得他流血而死。

夏　约上有这样的规定吗？

鲍　约上并没有这样的规定；可是那又有什么相干呢？为了人道起见，你应该这样做的。

夏　我找不到，约上没有这一条。

鲍　商人，你还有什么话说吗？

安　我没有多少话要说；我已经准备好了。把你的手给我，巴散尼奥，再会吧！不要因为我为了你的缘故遭到这种结局而悲伤，因为命运对我已经特别照顾了：她往往让一个不幸的人在家产荡尽以后继续活下去，

---

109. **balance**：等于 balances，形式上与单数并无区别，动词却要用复数形式 are。

110. **on your charge**：at your expense，该你出钱。

111. **'Twere**：it would be，将会。

112. **fall'n to this**：处于这种地步。

113. **Fortune**：命运之神。

114. **use**：habit，custom，习惯。莎士比亚常把 use 作"习惯"用。

To view with hollow eye and wrinkled brow
An age of poverty; from which ling'ring penance
Of such misery doth she cut me off.
Commend me to your honourable wife,
Tell her the process [115] of Antonio's end,
Say how I lov'd you, speak me fair in death;
And when the tale is told, bid her be judge [116]
Whether Bassanio had not once a love [117].
Repent but [118] you that you shall lose your friend,
And he repents not that he pays your debt;
For if the Jew do cut but deep enough,
I'll pay it instantly with all my heart.

  Bass. Antonio, I am married to a wife
Which [119] is as dear to me as life itself,
But life itself, my wife, and all the world,
Are not with me esteem'd above thy life.
I would lose all, ay, sacrifice them all
Here to this devil, to deliver you.

  Por. Your wife would give you little thanks for that
If she were by to hear you make the offer.

  Gra. I have a wife who I protest [120] I love;
I would she were in heaven, so she could
Entreat some power to change this currish Jew.

  Ner. 'Tis well you offer it behind her back,
The wish would make else an unquiet house [121].

  Shy. [*Aside.*] These be the Christian husbands.
  I have a daughter —
Would any of the stock of Barrabas [122]
Had been her husband rather than a Christian!
—We trifle time. I pray thee pursue sentence [123].

  Por. A pound of that same merchant's flesh is thine,
The court awards it, and the law doth give it.

  Shy. Most rightful judge!

---

115. **process**: story, 故事。

116. **bid her be judge**: 请她判断。be 前省略不定式符
  号 to。

117. **love**: 这里作"好朋友"，不作"情人"解，lover 也可
  以指朋友，如 Being the bossom lover of my lord。

118. **Repent but**: grieve only, 只为……而懊悔。

119. **Which**: 指 wife，莎士比亚时代的英语中 which 可
  以指人，who 可以指物，并不像现在这样严格区分。

120. **I protest**: 我承认。 protest: declare.

  用他凹陷的眼睛和满是皱纹的额角去挨受贫困的暮年；这一种拖延时日的刑罚，她已经把我豁免了。替我向尊夫人致意，告诉她安东尼奥的结局；对她说我怎样爱你，说我从容地面对死亡，等到你把这一段故事讲完以后，再请她作出判断，巴散尼奥是不是曾经有一个真心爱他的朋友。只要你为了失去一个朋友而悲伤，替你还债的人就死而无怨；只要那犹太人的刀刺得深一点，我就可以在一刹那的时间一心一意把那笔债完全还清。

巴 安东尼奥，我爱我的妻子，就像爱我自己的生命一样；可是我的生命，我的妻子，以及整个世界，在我的眼中都不比你的生命更为贵重；我愿意丧失一切，把它们献给这恶魔做牺牲，来救出你的生命。

鲍 尊夫人要是就在这儿听见您说这样的话，恐怕不见得会感谢您吧。

葛 我有一个妻子，我可以发誓我是爱她的；可是我希望她马上归天，好去求告上帝改变这恶狗一样的犹太人的心。

聂 幸亏尊驾在她的背后说这样的话，否则府上一定要吵得鸡犬不宁了。

夏 （旁白。）这些便是相信基督教的丈夫！我有一个女儿，我宁愿她嫁给强盗的子孙，不愿她嫁给一个基督徒，别再浪费光阴了；请快些宣判吧。

鲍 那商人身上的一磅肉是你的；法庭判给你，法律许可你。

夏 公平正直的法官！

---

121. **else...house**: 不然的话，你妻子总是要和你吵架。
  else: otherwise.
122. **stock of Barrabas**: Barrabas 的后裔。Barrabas 是和耶稣同时被囚的一个犯人。罗马驻犹太的行政长官（Pilate）问众人要释放谁，众人要求释放 Barrabas，于是耶稣被钉死在十字架上。参见《新约·圣经·马可福音》第 15 章第 6—15 节。
123. **pursue sentence**: 作出判决。pursue 重音在第一个音节上。

Por.　And you must cut this flesh from off his breast,
The law allows it, and the court awards it.

　　Shy.　Most learned judge, a sentence! Come prepare!

　　Por.　Tarry a little [124], there is something else.
This bond doth give thee here no jot of blood;
The words expressly are "a pound of flesh."
Take then thy bond, take thou thy pound of flesh,
But in the cutting it, if thou dost shed
One drop of Christian blood, thy lands and goods
Are by the laws of Venice confiscate [125]
Unto the state of Venice.

　　Gra.　O upright judge! Mark, Jew. O learned judge!

　　Shy.　Is that the law?

　　Por.　　　　　　　Thyself shalt see the act;
For as thou urgest justice, be assur'd
Thou shalt have justice more than thou desir'st.

　　Gra.　O learned judge! Mark [126], Jew, a learned judge!

　　Shy.　I take this offer then; pay the bond thrice
And let the Christian go.

　　Bass.　　　　　　Here is the money.

　　Por.　Soft [127],
The Jew shall have all [128] justice. Soft, no haste.
He shall have nothing but the penalty.

　　Gra.　O Jew! an upright judge, a learned judge!

　　Por.　Therefore prepare thee to cut off the flesh.
Shed thou no blood, nor cut thou less nor more
But just a pound of flesh [129]. If thou tak'st more
Or less than a just pound, be it but so much
As makes it light or heavy in the substance [130]
Or the division of the twentith part
Of one poor scruple [131], nay, if the scale do turn
But in the estimation of a hair [132],
Thou diest, and all thy goods are confiscate.

---

124. **Tarry a little**: wait a while,等一会儿。

125. **confiscate**：系过去分词，由拉丁语过去式词尾-atus演变而来，现在由于类推作用，在这类词后面再加上词尾-(e)d.

126. **Mark**: 注意。

127. **Soft**: 且慢,相当于 tarry。

128. **all**: only.

129. **But...flesh** 整整的一磅肉。　**just**: exact.

130. **substance**: gross weight, 总重量。

鲍　你必须从他的胸前割下这磅肉来，法律许可你，法庭判给你。

夏　博学多才的法官！判得好！来，预备！

鲍　且慢，还有别的话哩。这约上并没有允许你取他的一滴血，只是写明着"一磅肉"；所以你可以照约拿一磅肉去，可是在割肉的时候，要是流下一滴基督徒的血，你的土地财产，按照威尼斯的法律，就要全部充公。

葛　啊，公平正直的法官！听着，犹太人；啊，博学多才的法官！

夏　法律上是这样说的吗？

鲍　你自己可以去查查明白。既然你要求王法，我就给你王法，而且比你要求的还多。

葛　啊，博学多才的法官！听着，犹太人；好一个博学多才的法官！

夏　那么我愿意接受还款；照约上的数目三倍还我，放了那基督徒吧。

巴　钱在这儿。

鲍　别忙！这犹太人必须得到绝对的王法。别忙！他除了照约处罚以外，不能接受其他的赔偿。

葛　啊，犹太人！一个公平正直的法官，一个博学多才的法官！

鲍　所以你准备着动手割肉吧。不准流一滴血，也不准割得超过或是不足一磅的重量；要是你割下来的肉，比一磅略微轻一点或是重一点，即使相差只有一丝一毫，或者仅仅一根汗毛之微，也要把你抵命，你的财产全部充公。

---

131. **scruple**: 斯克鲁普尔，等于二十个格令（格令是古罗马最小的衡量单位。1 grain=1/20 scruple.），极少量地。

132. **But...hair**: by a hair's breadth，只差一丝一厘。

Gra.   A second Daniel! a Daniel, Jew!
Now, infidel, I have you on the hip [133].
　　　Por.   Why doth the Jew pause?   Take thy forfeiture.
　　　Shy.   Give me my principal [134], and let me go.
　　　Bass.   I have it ready for thee, here it is.
　　　Por.   He hath refus'd it in the open court;
He shall have merely justice and his bond.
　　　Gra.   A Daniel, still say I, a second Daniel!
I thank thee, Jew, for teaching me that word.
　　　Shy.   Shall I not have barely [135] my principal?
　　　Por.   Thou shalt have nothing but the forfeiture,
To be so taken at thy peril, Jew.
　　　Shy.   Why then the devil give him good of it!
I'll stay no longer question [136].
　　　Por.   Tarry, Jew,
The law hath yet another hold [137] on you.
It is enacted in the laws of Venice,
If it be proved against an alien,
That by direct or indirect attempts
He seek the life of any citizen,
The party 'gainst the which he doth contrive [138]
Shall seize [139] one half his goods; the other half
Comes to the privy coffer of the state [140],
And the offender's life lies in the mercy
Of the Duke only, 'gainst all other voice [141]:
In which predicament I say thou stand'st;
For it appears, by manifest [142] proceeding,
That indirectly, and directly too,
Thou hast contrived against the very life
Of the defendant; and thou hast incurr'd
The danger formerly by me rehears'd [143].
Down [144] therefore, and beg mercy of the Duke.

---

133. **I...hip**: I have you at my mercy, 我让你向我求饶。
134. **principal**: 本金。
135. **barely**: merely, 仅仅。
136. **I'll...question**: I'll remain here no longer to be questioned, 不再在这里等待案情的判决。

137. **hold**: 约束力。
138. **contrive**: plot, 图谋。
139. **seize**: take possession of, 获得, 法律用语。

葛 一个再世的但尼尔，一个但尼尔，犹太人！现在你可掉在我的手里了，你这异教徒！

鲍 那犹太人为什么还不动手？快执行处罚吧。

夏 把我的本钱还给我，放我去吧。

巴 钱我已经预备好在这儿，你拿去吧。

鲍 他已经当庭拒绝过了；我们现在只能给他王法，让他履行原约。

葛 好一个但尼尔，一个再世的但尼尔！谢谢你，犹太人，你教会我说这句话。

夏 难道我不能单单拿回我的本钱吗？

鲍 犹太人，除了冒着你自己的生命的危险，割下那一磅肉以外，你不能拿一个钱。

夏 好，那么魔鬼保佑他去享用吧！我不打这场官司了。

鲍 等一等，犹太人，法律还要向你追究。威尼斯的法律规定凡是一个异邦人企图用直接或间接手段，谋害任何公民，查明确有实据者，他的财产的半数应当归被企图谋害的一方所有，其余的半数没收入公库，犯罪者的生命悉听公爵处置，他人不得过问。你现在刚巧陷入这一法网，因为根据事实的发展，已经足以证明你确有运用直接或间接手段，危害被告生命的企图，所以你已经遭逢着我刚才所说起的那种危险了。快快跪下来，请公爵开恩吧。

---

140. **privy...state**：国库的财产。

141. **voice**：jurisdiction，法律范围。

142. **manifest**：明显的。

143. **formerly...rehears'd**：我刚才叙述过的。 **re-hearsed**：enumerated.

144. **Down**：下跪。

  Gra. Beg that thou mayst have leave to hang thyself,
And yet thy wealth being forfeit to the state.
Thou hast not left the value of a cord [145];
Therefore thou must be hang'd at the state's charge.
  Duke. That thou shalt see the difference of our spirit,
I pardon thee thy life before thou ask it.
For half thy wealth, it is Antonio's;
The other half comes to the general state,
Which humbleness may drive unto a fine [146].
  Por. Ay, for the state, not for Antonio [147].
  Shy. Nay, take my life and all, pardon not that：
You take my house when you do take the prop [148]
That doth sustain my house; you take my life
When you do take the means whereby I live.
  Por. What mercy can you render him, Antonio?
  Gra. A halter gratis [149] — nothing else, for God's sake.
  Ant. So please my lord the Duke and all the court
To quit [150] the fine for one half of his goods,
I am content; so [151] he will let me have
The other half in use [152], to render it
Upon his death unto the gentleman [153]
That lately stole his daughter.
Two things provided more, that for this favour
He presently [154] become a Christian;
The other, that he do record [155] a gift,
Here in the court, of all he dies possess'd
Unto his son Lorenzo and his daughter.
  Duke. He shall do this, or else I do recant [156]
The pardon that I late [157] pronounced here.
  Por. Art thou contented, Jew? what dost thou say?
  Shy. I am content.
  Por.   Clerk, draw a deed of gift [158].

---

145. **cord**：上吊用的绳子。
146. **Which...fine**：if you repent and bear yourself humbly, this may be reduced to a mere fine, 如果你悔过，可以把你那一半财产免于充公，而只取罚款。
  drive：作 reduce 解。
147. **for the state, not for Antonio**：这里指充公的那一部分，属 Antonio 的一半应悉数归他，不可减免。
148. **prop**：支柱，这单指财产。
149. **halter gratis**：a free rope, 免费奉赠上吊用绳子一根。**gratis**：免费。
150. **quit**：免除。

葛　求公爵开恩，让你自己去寻死；可是你的财产现在充了公，一根绳子也买不起啦，所以还是要让公家破费把你吊死。

公爵　让你瞧瞧我们基督徒的精神，你虽然没有向我开口，我自动饶恕了你的死罪。你的财产一半划归安东尼奥，还有一半没收入公库；要是你能够诚心悔过，这一半也许还可以免予没收而减为罚款。

鲍　这是说没收入公库的一部分，不是说划归安东尼奥的一部分。

夏　不，把我的生命连着财产一起拿了去吧，我不要你们的宽恕。你们搬走了支撑屋子的栋梁，就是拆毁了我的屋子；你们夺去了我的养家活命的根本，就是活活的要了我的命。

鲍　安东尼奥，你能不能给他一点慈悲？

葛　白送给他一根上吊的绳子吧；看在上帝的面上，不要给他别的东西！

安　要是殿下和法庭愿意从宽发落，免予没收他的财产的一半而只处以罚款，我就十分满足了；只要他能够让我接管他的另外一半的财产，等他死了以后，把它交给最近和他的女儿私奔的那位绅士；可是还要有两个附带的条件：第一，他接受了这样的恩典，必须立刻改信基督教；第二，他必须当庭写下一张文契，声明他死了以后，他的全部财产传给他的女婿罗伦佐和他的女儿。

公爵　他必须履行这两个条件，否则我就撤销刚才所宣布的赦令。

鲍　犹太人，你满意吗？你有什么话说？

夏　我满意。

鲍　书记，写下一张授赠产业的文契。

---

151. **so**: provided，如果。
152. **in use**: 代管。
153. **the gentleman**: 指 Lorenzo。
154. **presently**: 马上，立刻。
155. **record**: 书写记录。
156. **recant**: 收回。
157. **late**: 适才，刚刚。
158. **a deed of gift**: 捐赠的契约。

Shy.　　I pray you give me leave to go from hence,
I am not well.　Send the deed after me,
And I will sign it.
　　Duke.　　　　Get thee gone.　but do it.
　　Gra.　　In christ'ning shalt thou have two godfathers:
Had I been judge,　thou shouldst have had ten more [159],
To bring thee to the gallows,　not to the font.　[*Exit Shylock.*]
　　Duke.　　Sir, I entreat you home with me to dinner.
　　Por.　　I humbly do desire your Grace of pardon,
I must away this night toward Padua,
And it is meet I presently set forth.
　　Duke.　　I am sorry that your leisure serves you not [160].
Antonio,　gratify [161] this gentleman,
For in my mind you are much bound to [162] him.

　　　　　　　　[*Exeunt Duke，　Magnificoes，　and Train.*]
　　Bass.　　Most worthy gentleman,　I and my friend
Have by your wisdom been this day acquitted [163]
Of grievous penalties,　in lieu whereof [164]
Three thousand ducats,　due unto the Jew,
We freely cope your courteous pains [165] withal.
　　Ant.　　And stand indebted,　over and above [166],
In love and service to you evermore.
　　Por.　　He is well paid that is well satisfied,
And I,　delivering you,　am satisfied,
And therein do account [167] myself well paid.
My mind was never yet more mercenary.
I pray you know me when we meet again;
I wish you well,　and so I take my leave.
　　Bass.　　Dear sir,　of force I must attempt [168] you further.
Take some remembrance [169] of us as a tribute [170],
Not as fee [171].　Grant me two things,　I pray you,
Not to deny me,　and to pardon me.

---

159. **ten more**: Gratiano 在奚落 Shylock。受洗礼时，由两位教父陪同，但受审时要由十二人组成陪审团定罪。所以还需增加十人。这是英国法律规定，威尼斯无此做法。
160. **your...not**: 您没空闲。
161. **gratify**: reward, 酬谢。
162. **bound to**: obliged to, 感谢。
163. **acquitted**: 免于。
164. **in lieu whereof**: 作为回报，归还。
165. **We...pains**: we freely offer repayment for your courteous service, 对您的辛劳，我等应尽量报答。

夏　请你们允许我退庭，我身子不太舒服，文契写好了送到我家里，我在上面签名就是了。

公爵　去吧，可是临时变卦是不成的。

葛　你在受洗礼的时候，可以有两个教父；要是我做了法官，我一定给你请十二个教父，不是领你去受洗，是送你上绞架。

（夏下。）

公爵　先生，我想请您到舍间去用餐。

鲍　请殿下多多原谅，我今天晚上要回帕多瓦去，必须现在就动身，恕不奉陪了。

公爵　你这样贵忙，不能容我略尽寸心，真是抱歉得很。安东尼奥，谢谢这位先生，你这回全亏了他。（公爵、众士绅及侍从等下。）

巴　最可尊敬的先生，我跟我这位敝友今天多赖您的智慧，免去了一场无妄之灾；为了表示我们的敬意，这三千块钱本来是预备还那犹太人的，现在就奉送给先生，聊以报答您的辛苦。

安　您的大恩大德，我们是永远不会忘记的。

鲍　一个人做了心安理得的事，就是得到了最大的酬报；我这次帮了两位的忙，总算没有失败，已经引为十分满足，用不着再谈什么酬谢了。但愿咱们下次见面的时候，两位仍旧认识我。我现在就此告辞了。

巴　好先生，我不能不再向您提出一个请求，请您随便从我们身上拿些什么东西去，不算是酬谢，只算是留个纪念。请您答应接受我两件礼物，赏我这一个面子，原谅我的礼轻意重。

---

166. **over and above**: 十分，非常。

167. **account**: 认为。

168. **attempt**: 请求。

169. **remembrance**: 纪念品。

170. **tribute**: 敬意。

171. **fee**: 报酬。

Por.　You press me far, and therefore I will yield.
[*To Antonio*.]　Give me your gloves, I'll wear them for your sake,
[*To Bassanio*.]　And for your love I'll take this ring from you.
Do not draw back your hand, I'll take no more,
And you in love shall not deny me this!
　　Bass.　This ring, good sir, alas, it is a trifle!
I will not shame [172] myself to give you this.
　　Por.　I will have nothing else but only this,
And now methinks I have a mind to it.
　　Bass.　There's more depends on this than on the value.
The dearest ring in Venice will I give you,
And find it out by proclamation [173];
Only for this, I pray you pardon me.
　　Por.　I see, sir, you are liberal in offers.
You taught me first to beg, and now methinks
You teach me how a beggar should be answer'd [174].
　　Bass.　Good sir, this ring was given me by my wife,
And when she put it on, she made me vow
That I should neither sell, nor give, nor lose it.
　　Por.　That 'scuse [175] serves many men to save their gifts,
And if your wife be not a mad woman,
And know how well I have deserv'd this ring,
She would not hold out enemy for ever
For giving it to me. Well, peace be with you [176]!

　　　　　　　　　　　　　　　[*Exeunt Portia and Nerissa*.]

　　Ant.　My Lord Bassanio, let him have the ring.
Let his deservings and my love withal [177]
Be valued 'gainst your wive's commandement [178].
　　Bass.　Go, Gratiano, run and overtake him;
Give him the ring, and bring him, if thou canst,
Unto Antonio's house. Away, make haste.　[*Exit Gratiano*.]

- -

172. **shame myself**: 使我自己蒙羞，使我自己感到羞耻。　174. **be answer'd**: 被拒绝。
173. **proclamation**: 通过广告征求。

鲍 你们这样殷勤，我只好却之不恭了。（向安。）把您的手套送给我，让我戴在手上留个纪念吧；（向巴。）为了纪念您的盛情，让我拿了这戒指去。不要缩回您的手，我不再向您要别的什么了；您既然是一片诚意，想来总也不会拒绝我吧。

巴 这指环吗，好先生？唉！它是个不值钱的玩意儿；我不好意思把这东西送给您。

鲍 我什么都不要，就是要这指环；现在我想我非得把它要来不可。

巴 这指环的本身并没有什么价值，可是因为有其他的关系，我不能把它送人。我愿意出通告征求威尼斯最贵重的一枚指环送给您，可是这一枚却只好请您原谅了。

鲍 先生，您原来是个口头上慷慨的人；您先教我怎样伸手求讨，然后再教我怎样回答一个叫化子。

巴 好先生，这指环是我的妻子给我的，她把它套上我的手指的时候，曾经叫我发誓永远不把它出卖，送人，或是遗失。

鲍 人们在吝惜他们的礼物的时候，都可以用这样的话做推托的。要是尊夫人不是一个疯婆子，她知道我对于这指环是多么受之无愧，一定不会因为您把它送掉了而跟您长久反目的。好，愿你们平安！（鲍、聂同下。）

安 我的巴散尼奥少爷，让他把那指环拿去吧；他的功劳和我的交情就算是重于尊夫人的命令吧。

巴 葛莱西安诺，你快追上他们，把这指环送给他；要是可能的话，领他到安东尼奥的家里去。去，赶快！（葛下。）

---

175. **'scuse**: excuse, 借口, 托辞。
176. **peace be with you**: 祝你们平安。
177. **withal**: at the same time, 同时。

178. **commandement**: command, 命令。在莎士比亚时代这个词常读成四个音节。

Come, you and I will thither [179] presently,
And in the morning early will we both
Fly toward Belmont. Come, Antonio. [*Exeunt.*]

Scene **II** — The Same. A Street.

Enter Portia and Nerissa.

Por. Inquire the Jew's house out, give him this deed.
And let him sign it. We'll away tonight,
And be a day before our husbands home.
This deed will be well welcome to Lorenzo.

Enter Gratiano.

Gra. Fair sir, you are well o'erta'en [180].
My Lord Bassanio upon more advice [181]
Hath sent you here this ring, and doth entreat [182]
Your company at dinner.
Por.   That cannot be.
His ring I do accept most thankfully,
And so I pray you tell him; furthermore,
I pray you show my youth old Shylock's house.
Gra. That will I do.
Ner.   Sir, I would speak with you.
[Aside to Portia.] I'll see if I can get my husband's ring,
Which I did make him swear to keep for ever.
Por. [*Aside to Nerissa.*] Thou mayst, I warrant. We shall have old
swearing [183]
That they did give the rings away to men;
But we'll outface [184] them, and outswear [185] them too. —
Away, make haste. Thou know'st where I will tarry.
Ner. Come, good sir, will you show me to this house? [*Exeunt.*]

- -

179. **thither**: 那里，到那里。
180. **you...o'erta'en**: I am lucky to have overtaken you, 追
　　上你真算幸运。
181. **more advice**: further reflection or consideration, 再
　　次考虑。
182. **entreat**: 恳求。

来，我就陪着你到你府上；明天一早咱们两人就赶到贝尔蒙脱去。
来，安东尼奥。（同下。）

第二场　同前；街道

鲍细霞及聂莉莎上。

鲍　打听打听这犹太人住在什么地方，把这文契交给他，叫他签了字。
我们要比我们的丈夫先一天到家，所以一定得在今天晚上动身。
罗伦佐拿到了这一张文契，一定高兴得不得了。

葛莱西安诺上。

葛　好先生，我好容易追上了您。我家大爷巴散尼奥再三考虑之下，
决定叫我把这指环拿来送给您，还要请您赏光陪他吃一顿饭。

鲍　那可没法应命，他的指环我收下了，请你替我谢谢他。我还要请
你给我这小兄弟带路到夏洛克老头儿家里。

葛　可以可以。

聂　大哥，我要向您说句话儿。（向鲍旁白。）我要试一试我能不能把
我丈夫的指环拿下来。我曾经叫他发誓永远不离手。

鲍　（向聂旁白。）你一定能够。我们回家以后，一定可以听听他们指
天誓日，说他们把指环送给了别人；可是我们要压倒他们，比他
们发更厉害的誓。你快去吧，你知道我会在什么地方等你。

聂　来，大哥，请您给我带路。（各下。）

---

183. **old swearing**: 许下庄重诺言。
　　　old: plentiful or great，当时口语中这样使用。
184. **outface**: 羞辱。

185. **outswear**: 骂人骂个够。注意莎士比亚时代有许
多动词前面可以加"out"，表示"exceed"的意思。

ACT Ⅴ

Scene — Belmont. The Avenue to Portia's House.

Enter Lorenzo and Jessica.

Lor.   The moon shines bright.   In such a night as this,
When the sweet wind did gently kiss the trees,
And they did make no noise, in such a night
Troilus [1] methinks mounted the Troyan walls,
And sigh'd his soul toward the Grecian tents,
Where Cressid [2] lay that night.

Jes.   In such a night
Did Thisby [3] fearfully o'ertrip the dew,
And saw the lion's shadow ere himself,
And ran dismayed away.

Lor.   In such a night
Stood Dido [4] with a willow in her hand
Upon the wild Sea-banks, and waft her love
To come again to Carthage.

Jes.   In such a night
Medea [5] gathered the enchanted herbs
That did renew old Aeson [6].

Lor.   In such a night
Did Jessica steal from the wealthy Jew,
And with an unthrift [7] love did run from Venice,
As far as Belmont.

Jes.   In such a night
Did young Lorenzo swear he lov'd her well,
Stealing her soul with many vows of faith,
And ne'er a true one.

------

1. **Troilus**：特洛埃勒斯是特洛埃王子，与克蕾雪达相爱。在特洛埃十年战争期间，克蕾雪达作为交换战俘的人质离开特洛埃。临行前两人山盟海誓，但克蕾雪达到了希腊军营，立即接受了希腊将领狄俄墨得斯的求爱。特洛埃勒斯痛不欲生，到希腊军营前要求与情敌决一死战，在杀死不少希腊人后，自己也阵亡了。参见乔叟（1340—1400）的长诗和莎翁的有关剧本。

2. **Cressid**：克蕾雪德即克蕾雪达（Cressida）。见上注。

3. **Thisby**：雪丝佩，巴比伦之美女，与其情人匹拉麦斯相约在城外幽会。雪丝佩先到，被狮子吓跑，掉落纱巾于地上。匹拉麦斯后至幽会地点，看到狮子口衔染血的纱巾，误以为雪丝佩已死，便拔剑自刎。雪丝佩后来赶到，见匹拉麦斯死了，也自杀身亡。参

第 五 幕

 贝尔蒙脱;通至鲍细霞住宅的林荫路

罗伦佐及吉雪加上。

罗 好皎洁的月色！正像这样一个夜晚，微风轻轻地吻着树枝，不发出一点声响；我想正是在这样一个夜里，特洛埃勒斯登上特洛埃的城墙，遥望着克蕾雪达所寄身的希腊人的营幕，发出他的深心中的悲叹。

吉 正是在这样一个夜里，雪丝佩心惊胆战地踩着霜露，去赴她情人的约会，因为看见了一头狮子的影子，吓得远远逃走。

罗 正是在这样一个夜里，黛陀手里执着柳枝，站在辽阔的海滨，招她的爱人回到迦泰基来。

吉 正是在这样一个夜里，迷迭霞采集了灵芝仙草，使衰迈的伊孙返老还童。

罗 正是在这样一个夜里，吉雪加从犹太富翁的家里逃了出来，跟着一个不中用的情郎从威尼斯一直走到贝尔蒙脱。

吉 正是在这样一个夜里，年轻的罗伦佐发誓说他爱她，用许多忠诚的盟言偷去了她的灵魂，可是没有一句话是真的。

见莎剧《仲夏夜之梦》。

4. **Dido**: 黛陀，迦泰基女王，爱上了在特洛埃城陷落后漂泊到迦泰基的英雄伊尼阿斯，旋被他遗弃。见维吉尔诗歌中的有关部分。柳枝为失恋之象征。

5. **Medea**: 迷迭霞，出自希腊神话: 迷迭霞是科尔喀斯国王的女儿，她帮助伊阿宋取得了金羊毛。伊阿宋在科尔喀斯时，曾向她起誓,答应娶她为妻，后伊阿宋变心，又娶了克瑞翁国王的女儿为妻。迷迭霞为了报复他，亲手杀死了自己的两个孩子。

6. **Aeson**: 伊孙即伊阿宋的父亲，迷迭霞会魔术，使公公返老还童。

7. **unthrift**: prodigal, 浪荡的，这里是戏谑的说法。

Lor.　　　　　In such a night
Did pretty Jessica（like a little shrow [8]）
Slander her love，and he forgave it her.

　　Jes.　I would out-night [9] you，did nobody come：
But hark，I hear the footing [10] of a man.

Enter Stephano.

　　Lor.　Who comes so fast in silence of the night?

　　Steph.　A friend.

　　Lor.　A friend! what friend? your name，I pray you，friend?

　　Steph.　Stephano is my name，and I bring word
My mistress will before the break of day
Be here at Belmont. She doth stray about
By holy crosses [11]，where she kneels and prays
For happy wedlock hours.

　　Lor.　　　　　　Who comes with her?

　　Steph.　None but a holy hermit and her maid.
I pray you，is my master yet return'd?

　　Lor.　He is not，nor we have not heard from him.
But go we in，I pray thee，Jessica，
And ceremoniously let us prepare [12]
Some welcome for the mistress ofthe house.

Enter Launcelot.

　　Laun.　Sola [13]，sola! Wo ha，ho! Sola，sola!

　　Lor.　Who calls?

　　Laun.　Sola! did you see Master Lorenzo? Master Lorenzo，sola，
sola!

　　Lor.　Leave hollowing [14]，man — here.

　　Laun.　Sola! Where，where?

　　Lor.　Here!

---

8. **shrow**：shrew，泼妇。

9. **out-night**：指不断地用 in such a night 对答，抒发情怀，妙语惊人，超过罗伦佐。莎士比亚是运用 out 构造新词的能手. 如第四幕第二场的 outswear；又如："it out-herods Herod"《哈姆雷特》第三幕第二场）。意思是：其残暴超过了希律王；比残暴的希律王还要残暴。

10. **footing**：footsteps，脚步声。

11. **doth...crosses**：makes pilgrimage from one sacred shrine to another：一遇到神殿、神龛或圣祠，就要停下来祈祷。在英国和意大利许多道路交叉口或山顶都有这类圣祠。

罗 正是在这样一个夜里，可爱的吉雪加像一个小泼妇似的，信口毁谤她的情人，可是他饶恕了她。

吉 倘不是有人来了，我可以搬弄出比你所知道的更多的夜的典故来。可是听！这不是一个人的脚步声吗？

史梯番诺上。

罗 谁在这静悄悄的深夜里跑得这么快？

史 一个朋友。

罗 一个朋友！什么朋友？请问朋友尊姓大名？

史 我的名字是史梯番诺，我来向你们报个信，我家女主人在天明以前，就要到贝尔蒙脱来了；她一路上看见圣十字架，便停下步来，长跪祷告，祈求着婚姻的美满。

罗 谁陪她一起来？

史 没有什么人，只是一个修道的隐士和她的侍女。请问我家主人有没有回来？

罗 他没有回来，我们也没有听到他的消息。可是，吉雪加，我们进去吧；让我们按照着礼节，准备一些欢迎这屋子的女主人的仪式。

朗西洛脱上。

朗 索拉，索拉！哦哈呵！索拉！索拉！

罗 谁在那儿嚷？

朗 索拉！你看见罗伦佐大爷吗？罗伦佐大爷！索拉！索拉！

罗 别嚷啦，朋友；他就在这儿。

朗 索拉！哪儿？哪儿？

罗 这儿。

---

12. **ceremoniously...prepare:** let us prepare some ceremonious welcome，准备欢迎仪式。

13. **Sola:** 拟声词，可能是模仿信使的喇叭声。

14. **Leave hollowing:** stop shouting.

  Laun. Tell him there's a post [15] come from my master, with his horn full of good news. My master will be here ere morning. *[Exit.]*

  Lor. Sweet soul, let's in, and there expect [16] their coming.
And yet no matter; why should we go in?
My friend Stephano, signify [17], I pray you,
Within the house, your mistress is at hand,
And bring your music forth into the air. *[Exit Stephano.]*
How sweet the moonlight sleeps upon this bank!
Here will we sit, and let the sounds of music
Creep in our ears. Soft stillness and the night
Become the touches of sweet harmony [18].
Sit, Jessica. Look how the floor of heaven
Is thick inlaid with patens [19] of bright gold.
There's not the smallest orb which thou behold'st
But in his motion like an angel sings,
Still quiring [20] to the young-ey'd [21] cherubins;
Such harmony is in immortal souls,
But whilst this muddy vesture of decay [22]
Doth grossly [23] close it in, we cannot hear it.

     Enter Musicians.

Come ho, and wake Diana [24] with a hymn,
With sweetest touches pierce your mistress' ear,
And draw her home with music. *[Music.]*

  Jes. I am never merry when I hear sweet music.

  Lor. The reason is, your spirits are attentive [25];
For do but note a wild and wanton [26] herd
Or race [27] of youthful and unhandled colts,
Fetching [28] mad bounds, bellowing and neighing loud,
Which is the hot condition [29] of their blood,
If they but hear perchance a trumpet sound,

---

15. **post**: 信使。
16. **expect**: 等待。
17. **signify**: 宣布；通知。
18. **Become...harmony**: befit the notes on musical instrument, 适宜演奏和谐的音乐。 **Become**: befit; **touches**: notes, the fingering of an instrument, 指用手演奏。

19. **patens**: metal plates or disks, 金属圆盘，指闪闪发亮的星星。
20. **quiring**: choiring, singing in harmony, 歌唱，和唱。
21. **young-ey'd**: eternally keen-sighted, 目光敏锐的。

朗　对他说我家主人差一个人带了许多好消息来了；他在天明以前就要回家来啦。（下。）

罗　亲爱的，我们进去，等着他们回来吧。不，还是不用进去。我的朋友史梯番诺，请你进去通知家里的人，你们的女主人就要回来啦，叫他们准备好乐器到门外来迎接。（史下。）月光多么恬静地睡在山坡上！我们就在这儿坐下来，让音乐的声音悄悄送进我们的耳中；柔和的静寂和夜色，是最足以衬托出音乐的甜美的。坐下来，吉雪加。瞧，天宇中嵌满了多少灿烂的金钱；你所看见的每一颗微小的天体，在转动的时候都会发出天使般的歌声，永远应和着嫩眼的天婴的妙唱。在永生的灵魂里也有这一种音乐，可是当它套上这一具泥土制成的俗恶易朽的皮囊以后，我们便再也听不见了。

　　众乐工上。

罗　来啊！奏起一支圣歌来唤醒黛安娜女神；用最温柔的节奏倾注到你们女主人的耳中，让她被乐声吸引着回来。（音乐。）

吉　我听见了柔和的音乐，总觉得有些惆怅。

罗　这是因为你有一个敏感的灵魂。你只要看一群狂放不羁的野兽或是未驯服的小驹，逞着它们奔放的血气，乱跳狂奔，高声嘶叫；倘然偶尔听到一声喇叭，

---

22. **muddy...decay**：the clothing of mortal flesh，泥土做成的躯壳，即凡人肉体。按基督教教义宣传，人是上帝用泥土做成的。

23. **grossly**：世俗的，肉体的。

24. **Diana**：黛安娜。罗马神话中的月亮女神和狩猎女神。在诗歌中象征月亮。

25. **spirits are attentive**：faculties are concentrated，全神贯注。

26. **wanton**：untrained，未加驯服的，下一行中的 unhandled 意思相近。

27. **race**：兽群。

28. **Fetching**：taking，指跳跃的动作。

29. **hot condition**：血性的特点。

Or any air of music touch their ears,
You shall perceive them make a mutual stand [30],
Their savage eyes turn'd to a modest gaze,
By the sweet power of music; therefore the poet [31]
Did feign [32] that Orpheus [33] drew [34] trees, stones, and floods;
Since nought so stockish [35], hard, and full of rage [36],
But music for the time doth change his nature.
The man that hath no music in himself,
Nor is not moved with concord of sweet sounds,
Is fit for treasons, stratagems [37], and spoils [38];
The motions of his spirit are dull as night,
And his affections dark as Erebus [39]:
Let no such man be trusted. Mark the music.

Enter Portia and Nerissa, at a distance.

Por.   That light we see is burning in my hall.
How far that little candle throws his beams!
So shines a good deed in a naughty [40] world.

Net.   When the moon shone, we did not see the candle.

Por.   So doth the greater glory dim the less:
A substitute [41] shines brightly as a king
Until a king be by, and then his state [42]
Empties itself, as doth an inland brook
Into the main of waters [43]. Music, hark!

Ner.   It is your music, madam, of the house.

Por.   Nothing is good, I see, without respect [44];
Methinks it sounds much sweeter than by day.

Ner.   Silence bestows that virtue on it, madam.

Por.   The crow doth sing as sweetly as the lark
When neither is attended [45]; and I think
The nightingale, if she should sing by day

---

30. **mutual stand**: all stand still, 全都站着一动不动。
31. **the poet**: 指希腊诗人奥维德（43 B.C.—17A.D.）。他
　　在《变形记》中提到色累斯的音乐家 Orpheus。
32. **feign**: 编造。
33. **Orpheus**: 奥菲厄斯, 希腊神话中的音乐和诗歌之神,
缪斯女神们教他学习弹琴和唱歌。他美妙的歌声
能使猛兽俯首, 顽石点头, 树木随之起舞。
34. **drew**: 吸引。
35. **nought so stockish**: nothing so solid（冥顽不化）。

或是任何乐调，就会一齐立定，它们狂野的眼光，因为中了音乐的魅力，变成温和的注视。所以诗人会造出奥菲厄斯用音乐感动木石，平息风浪的故事，因为无论怎样坚硬顽固狂暴的事物，音乐都可以立刻改变它们的性质；灵魂里没有音乐，或是听了甜蜜和谐的乐声而不会感动的人，都是擅于为非作恶，使奸弄诈的；他们的灵魂像黑夜一样昏沉，他们的感情像鬼域一样幽暗；这种人是不可信任的。听这音乐！

鲍细霞及聂莉莎自远处上。

鲍　那灯光是从我家里发出来的。一支小小的蜡烛，它的光照耀得多么远！一件善事也正像这支蜡烛一样，在这罪恶的世界上发出广大的光辉。

聂　月光明亮的时候，我们就瞧不见烛光。

鲍　小小的荣耀也正是这样给更大的光荣所遮掩。摄政的威权未尝不就像一个君主，可是一到国王回来，他的威权就归于乌有，正像溪涧中的细流注入大海一样。音乐！听！

聂　小姐，这是我们家里的音乐。

鲍　没有比较，就显不出长处，我觉得它比在白天好听得多啦。

聂　小姐，那是因为晚上比白天静寂的缘故。

鲍　没有欣赏的人时，乌鸦的歌声也就和云雀一样，要是夜莺在白天混杂在群鹅的聒噪里歌唱，

---

36. **rage**: 野性未驯。
37. **stratagems**: deceptive tricks, 花招, 阴谋。
38. **spoils**: 掠夺。
39. **Erebus**: 希腊神话中灵魂到阴曹地府去时所经过的黑暗地方。
40. **naughty**: wicked, 罪恶的。
41. **substitute**: 替身，代替。
42. **state**: 威严。
43. **main of waters**: ocean, 大海。
44. **without respect**: 没有参照、陪衬。
45. **When...attended**: when each sings alone.

When every goose is cackling, would be thought
No better a musician than the wren.
How many things by season season'd are [46]
To their right praise and true perfection!
Peace ho! the Moon sleeps with Endymion [47],
And would not be awak'd. [*Music ceases.*]

   Lor.   That is the voice,
Or I am much deceiv'd, of Portia.

   Por. He knows me as the blind man knows the cuckoo,
By the bad voice!

   Lor.   Dear lady, welcome home!

   Por. We have been praying for our husbands' welfare,
Which speed [48] we hope the better for our words.
Are they return'd?

   Lor.   Madam, they are not yet;
But there is come a messenger before,
To signify their coming.

   Por.   Go in, Nerissa.
Give order to my servants that they take
No note [49] at all of our being absent hence—
Nor you, Lorenzo — Jessica, nor you. [*A tucket* [50] *sounds.*]

   Lor. Your husband is at hand, I hear his trumpet.
We are no tell-tales, madam, fear you not [51].

   Por. This night methinks is but the daylight sick,
It looks a little paler. 'Tis a day,
Such as the day is when the sun is hid.

   Enter Bassanio, Antonio, Gratiano, and their Followers.

   Bass. We should hold day with the Antipodes,
If you would walk in absence of the sun [52].

   Por. Let me give light, but let me not be light [53],

---

46. **by...are**: are matured by favourable occasion, 机会、环境的陪衬。
47. **Endymion**: 希腊神话中的美少年, 月亮女神 Diana 与他一见倾心, 每当他睡在 Latmos 山上, 月神必吻之并与之同眠。
48. **Which speed**: who thrive, (希望)他们走运。
49. **take no note**: 不要提及。
50. **tucket**: 一连串清晰的喇叭声。
51. **fear you not**: 你不用担心。

人家决不以为它比鹪鹩唱得更美。多少事情因为逢到有利的环境，才能够达到尽善的境界，博得一声恰当的赞赏！喂，静下来！月亮正在拥着她的情郎酣睡，不肯就醒来呢。

（音乐停止。）

罗　要是我没有听错，这分明是鲍细霞的声音。

鲍　我的声音太难听，所以一下子就给他听出来了，正像瞎子能够辨认杜鹃一样。

罗　好夫人，欢迎您回来！

鲍　我们在外边为我们的丈夫祈祷平安，希望他们能够因我们的祈祷而多福。他们已经回来了吗？

罗　夫人，他们还没有来；可是刚才有人来送过信，说他们就要回来了。

鲍　进去，聂莉莎，吩咐我们的仆人们，叫他们就当我们两人没有出去过一样；罗伦佐，您也给我保守秘密；吉雪加，您也不要多说。

（喇叭声。）

罗　您的丈夫来啦，我听见他的喇叭的声音。我们不是搬嘴弄舌的人，夫人，您放心好了。

鲍　这样的夜色就像一个昏沉的白昼，不过略微惨淡点儿；没有太阳的白天，瞧上去也不过如此。

巴散尼奥，安东尼奥，葛莱西安诺及侍从等上。

巴　要是您在没有太阳的地方走路，我们就可以和地球那一面的人共同享有着白昼。

鲍　让我发出光辉，可是不要让我像光一样轻浮；

---

52. **we...sun**：即使在晚上，我们仍可以和地球那一面的人同过白天，因为您的美貌像太阳一样照耀着。

53. **light**：双关语，①光；②轻浮。

54. **heavy**：双关语，①重；②悲哀。

For a light wife doth make a heavy [54] husband,
And never be Bassanio so for me —
But God sort all [55]! You are welcome home, my lord.
　　Bass. I thank you, madam. Give welcome to my friend;
This is the man, this is Antonio,
To whom I am so infinitely bound.
　　Por. You should in all sense [56] be much bound to him,
For as I hear he was much bound for you [57].
　　Ant. No more than I am well acquitted of [58].
　　Por. Sir, you are very welcome to our house.
It must appear in other ways than words,
Therefore I scant this breathing courtesy [59].
　　Gra. [*To Nerissa*.] By yonder moon I swear you do me wrong;
In faith, I gave it to the judge's clerk.
Would he were gelt [60] that had it, for my part,
Since you do take it, love, so much at heart.
　　Por. A quarrel ho already! what's the matter?
　　Gra. About a hoop of gold, a paltry ring
That she did give me, whose posy [61] was
For all the world [62] like cutler's poetry
Upon a knife, "Love me, and leave me not."
　　Ner. What talk you of the posy or the value?
You swore to me, when I did give it you,
That you would wear it till your hour of death,
And that it should lie with you in your grave.
Though not for me, yet for your vehement oaths,
You should have been respective [63] and have kept it.
Gave it a judge's clerk! no, God's my judge,
The clerk will ne'er wear hair on's face [64] that had it.
　　Gra. He will, and if he live to be a man.
　　Ner. Ay, if a woman live to be a man.

---

55. **But God sort all！**：上帝支配一切。　**sort**：dispose，支配。
56. **In all sense**：in every reason，确实应该。
57. **bound for you**：双关语，①感谢；②受牵连。
58. **acquitted of**：解脱。
59. **scant...courtesy**：cut short this wordy politeness，不再说客套话。　**scant**：make brief，长话短说。　**breathing courtesy**：utterance of welcome，客套话。

　　因为一个轻浮的妻子，是会使丈夫的心头沉重的，我决不愿意巴散尼奥为了我而心头沉重。可是一切都是上帝做主！欢迎您回家来，夫君！

巴　谢谢您，夫人。请您给我这位朋友欢迎；这就是安东尼奥，我曾经受过他无穷的恩惠。

鲍　他的确使您受惠无穷，因为我听说您曾经使他受累无穷呢。

安　没有什么，现在一切都已经圆满解决了。

鲍　先生，我们非常欢迎您的光临；可是口头的空言不能表示诚意，所以一切客套的话，我都不说了。

葛　（向聂。）我凭着那边的月亮起誓，你冤枉了我；我真的把它送给了那法官的书记。好人，你既然把这件事情看得这么重，那么我但愿拿了去的人是个割掉了鸡巴的。

鲍　啊！已经在吵架了吗？为了什么事？

葛　为了一个金圈圈儿，她给我的一个不值钱的指环，上面刻着的诗句，就跟那些刀匠们刻在刀子上的差不多，什么"爱我毋相弃"。

聂　你管它什么诗句，什么值钱不值钱？我当初给你的时候，你曾经向我发誓，说你要戴着它直到死去，死了就跟你一起葬在坟墓里；即使不为我，为了你所发的重誓，你也应该把它看重，好好地保存着，送给一个法官的书记！呸！上帝可以替我判断，拿了这个指环的那个书记，一定是个脸上永远不会出毛的。

葛　他年纪大起来，自然会出胡子的。

聂　一个女人也会长成男子吗？

---

60. **gelt**: gelded，阉割。

61. **posy**: 戒指内侧雕刻的一句格言或诗句。
posy=poesy.

62. **For all the world**: 完全。

63. **respective**: mindful，小心注意。

64. **wear hair on's face**: wear beard on his face，脸上长胡子。

Gra.　　Now，by this hand，I gave it to a youth，
A kind of boy，a little scrubbed-boy [65]，
No higher than thyself，the judge's clerk，
A prating [66] boy，that begg'd it as a fee.
I could not for my heart deny it him.
　　Por.　　You were to blame，I must be plain with you，
To part so slightly with your wive's first gift，
A thing stuck on with oaths upon your finger，
And so riveted with faith unto your flesh.
I gave my love a ring，and made him swear
Never to part with it，and here he stands.
I dare be sworn for him he would not leave it，
Nor pluck it from his finger，for the wealth
That the world masters [67]. Now，in faith，Gratiano，
You give your wife too unkind a cause of grief；
And 'twere to me [68] I should be mad at it.
　　Bass.　[*Aside.*]　　Why，I were best [69] to cut my left hand off，
And swear I lost the ring defending it.
　　Gra.　　My Lord Bassanio gave his ring away
Unto the judge that begg'd it，and indeed
Deserv'd it too；and then the boy，his clerk，
That took some pains in writing，he begg'd mine，
And neither man nor master would take aught [70]
But the two rings.
　　Por.　　　　　What ring gave you my lord?
Not that，I hope，which you receiv'd of me.
　　Bass.　　If I could add a lie unto a fault [71]，
I would deny it；but you see my finger
Hath not the ring upon it，it is gone.
　　Por.　　Even so void is your false heart of truth.
By heaven，I will ne'er come in your bed
Until I see the ring!

- -

65. **scrubbed boy**: stunted boy，个子不高的男孩。　　67. **masters**: possesses，拥有。
66. **prating**: babbling；boastful，唠叨，多嘴的。　　68. **'twere to me**: if it were I，若是我的话。

葛　我举手起誓，我的确把它送给一个少年人，一个年纪小小，发育不全的孩子；他的个儿并不比你高，这个法官的书记。他是个多话的孩子，一定要我把这指环给他做酬劳，我实在不好意思不给他。

鲍　恕我说句不客气的话，这是你的不对；你怎么可以把你妻子的第一件礼物随随便便给了人？你已经发过誓把它套在你的手指上，它就是你身体上不可分的一部分。我也曾经送给我的爱人一个指环，使他发誓永不把它抛弃；他现在就在这儿，我敢代他发誓，即使把世间所有的财富向他交换，他也不肯丢掉它或是把它从他的手指上取下来。真的，葛莱西安诺，你太对不起你的妻子了；倘然是我的话，我早就气疯了。

巴　（旁白。）哎哟，我应该把我的左手砍掉了，那就可以发誓说，因为强盗要我的指环，我不肯给他，所以连手都给砍下来了。

葛　巴散尼奥大爷也把他的指环给了那法官了，因为那法官一定要向他讨那指环；其实他就是拿了那指环去，也一点不算过分。那个孩子，那法官的书记，因为写了几个字，也就讨了我的指环去做酬劳。他们主仆两人什么都不要，就是要这两个指环。

鲍　我的爷，您把什么指环送了人哪？我想不会是我给您的那一个吧？

巴　要是我可以用说谎来加重我的过失，那么我会否认的；可是您瞧我的手指上没有指环；它已经没有了。

鲍　正像你的虚伪的心里没有一丝真情。我对天发誓，除非我见到了这指环，我再也不跟你同床共枕。

---

69. **I were best**: it would have been better for me，我最好是。
70. **aught**: nothing.
71. **add...fault**: 做错事再撒谎。

    Ner.   Nor I in yours
Till I again see mine!
    Bass.   Sweet Portia,
If you did know to whom I gave the ring,
If you did know for whom I gave the ring,
And would conceive [72] for what I gave the ring,
And how unwillingly I left the ring,
When nought would be accepted but the ring,
You would abate the strength of your displeasure.
    Por.   If you had known the virtue [73] of the ring,
Or half her worthiness that gave the ring,
Or your own honour to contain [74] the ring,
You would not then have parted with the ring.
What man is there so much unreasonable,
If you had pleas'd to have defended it
With any terms of zeal, wanted the modesty [75]
To urge [76] the thing held as a ceremony [77]?
Nerissa teaches me what to believe —
I'll die for't [78] but some woman had the ring!
    Bass. No, by my honour, madam, by my soul [79],
No woman had it, but a civil doctor [80],
Which [81] did refuse three thousand ducats of me,
And begg'd the ring, the which I did deny him,
And suffer'd him to go displeas'd away—
Even he that had held up the very life
Of my dear friend. What should I say, sweet lady?
I was enforc'd to send it after him,
I was beset with shame and courtesy,
My honour would not let ingratitude
So much besmear it. Pardon me, good lady,
For by these blessed candles of the night [82],

---

72. **conceive**: 完全理解。
73. **virtue**: efficacy, 力量, 功效。
74. **contain**: retain, 得到。
75. **wanted the modesty**: lack the prudence, 鲁莽。

76. **urge**: 坚持要求。
77. **ceremony**: 神圣的信物。
78. **I'll die for't**: I'll wager my life on it, 拿生命打赌。

聂　要是我看不见我的指环，我也再不跟你同床共枕。

巴　亲爱的鲍细霞，要是您知道我把这指环送给什么人，要是您知道我为了谁的缘故把这指环送人，要是您能够想到为了什么理由我把这指环送人，我又是多么舍不下这个指环，可是人家偏偏什么也不要，一定要这个指环，那时候您就不会生这么大的气了。

鲍　要是你知道这指环的价值，或是把这指环给你的那人的一半好处，或是你自己保存着这指环的光荣，你就不会把这指环抛弃。只要你用诚恳的话向他剀切解释，世上哪有这样不讲理的人，会好意思硬要人家留作纪念品的东西？聂莉莎讲的话一点不错，我可以用我的生命赌咒，一定是什么女人把这指环拿了去了。

巴　不，夫人，我用我的名誉，我的灵魂起誓，并不是什么女人拿去，的确是送给那位法学博士的；他不接受我送给他的三千块钱，一定要讨这指环，我不答应，他就老大不高兴地去了。就是他救了我的好朋友的性命；我应该怎么说呢，好太太？我没有法子，只好叫人追上去送给他；人情和礼貌逼着我这样做，我不能让我的名誉沾上忘恩负义的污点。原谅我，好夫人；凭着天上的明灯起誓，

---

79. **by my soul**: 以灵魂为誓。
80. **civil doctor**: 民法博士。
81. **Which**: who.
82. **blessed...night**: 满天星斗。

Had you been there, I think you would have begg'd
The ring of me to give the worthy doctor.

    Por.   Let not that doctor e'er come near my house.
Since he hath got the jewel that I loved,
And that which you did swear to keep for me,
I will become as liberal[83] as you,
I'll not deny him any thing I have,
No, not my body nor my husband's bed.
Know him I shall, I am well sure of it.
Lie not a night from[84] home. Watch me like Argus[85];
If you do not, if I be left alone,
Now by mine honour, which is yet mine own,
I'll have that doctor for my bedfellow.

    Ner.   And I his clerk; therefore be well advis'd[86]
How you do leave me to mine own protection.

    Gra.   Well, do you so; let not me take him then,
For if I do, I'll mar the young clerk's pen[87].

    Ant.   I am th'unhappy subject of these quarrels.

    Por.   Sir, grieve not you, you are welcome notwithstanding.

    Bass.   Portia, forgive me this enforced wrong,
And in the hearing of these many friends
I swear to thee, even by thine own fair eyes,
Wherein I see myself —

    Por.   Mark you but that[88]!
In both my eyes he doubly sees himself,
In each eye, one. Swear by your double[89] self,
And there's an oath of credit[90].

    Bass.   Nay, but hear me.
Pardon this fault, and by my soul I swear
I never more will break an oath with thee.

---

83. **liberal**: 双关语，①慷慨大方；②性放纵。
84. **from**: away from.
85. **Argus**: 阿耳戈斯，希腊神话中的百眼巨人。阿耳戈斯有百眼，睡觉时每次只闭两只眼，其余都睁着，在额前脑后如同星星一样闪闪发光。
86. **be well advised**: 好好听着。
87. **pen**: 双关语，①笔；②阳具。
88. **Mark you but that**: 你们注意他说的话。

　要是那时候您也在那儿，我想您一定会恳求我把这指环送给这位贤能的博士的。

鲍　让那博士再也不要走近我的屋子。他既然拿去了我所珍爱的宝物，又是你所发誓的永远为我保存的东西，那么我也会像你一样慷慨；我会把我所有的一切都给他，即使他要我的身体，或是我的丈夫的眠床，我都不会拒绝他。我总有一天会认识他的；你还是一夜也不要离开家里，像个百眼怪人那样看守着我吧；否则我可以凭着我的尚未失去的贞操起誓，要是你让我一个人在家里，我一定要跟这个博士睡在一床的。

聂　我也要跟他的书记睡在一床；所以你还是留心不要走开我的身边。

葛　好，随你的便，只要不让我碰到他；要是他给我捉住了，我就折断那个少年书记的那支笔。

安　都是我的不是，引出你们这一场吵闹。

鲍　先生，这跟您没有关系，您来我们是很欢迎的。

巴　鲍细霞，饶恕我这一次出于不得已的错误，当着这许多朋友们的面前，我向你发誓，凭着你这一双美丽的眼睛，在它们里面我可以看见我自己——

鲍　你们听他的话！他在我的一双眼睛里看见了两个自己，一只眼睛里有一个。你用你的两重人格发誓，我还能够相信你吗？

巴　不，听我说，原谅我这一次错误，凭着我的灵魂起誓，我以后再不违背对你所作的誓言。

---

89. **double**：双关语，①两个；②欺骗，如 doubledealer，两　　90. **of credit**：可信的。
面派。

***Ant*.   I once did lend my body for his wealth [91],
Which but for him that had your husband's ring
Had quite miscarried [92], I dare be bound again,
My soul upon the forfeit, that your lord
Will never more break faith advisedly [93].
    ***Por*.   Then you shall be his surety. Give him this.
And bid him keep it better than the other.
    ***Ant*.   Here, Lord Bassanio, swear to keep this ring.
    ***Bass*.   By heaven, it is the same I gave the doctor!
    ***Por*.   I had it of him. Pardon me, Bassanio,
For by this ring, the doctor lay [94] with me.
    ***Ner*.   And pardon me, my gentle Gratiano,
For that same scrubbed boy, the doctor's clerk,
In lieu of [95] this last night did lie with me.
    ***Gra*.   Why, this is like the mending of highways
In summer, where the ways are fair enough.
What, are we cuckolds ere we have deserv'd it [96]?
    ***Por*.   Speak not so grossly, you are all amaz'd [97].
Here is a letter, read it at your leisure.
It comes from Padua, from Bellario.
There you shall find that Portia was the doctor,
Nerissa there her clerk. Lorenzo here
Shall witness I set forth as soon as you,
And even but now return'd; I have not yet
Enter'd my house. Antonio, you are welcome,
And I have better news in store for you
Than you expect. Unseal this letter soon;
There you shall find three of your argosies
Are richly come to harbour suddenly.
You shall not know by what strange accident
I chanced on this letter.

---

91. **wealth**: welfare, 利益。
92. **miscarried**: died, 死亡。
93. **advisedly**: deliberately, 有意地。
94. **lay**: 睡觉。

安　我曾经为了他的幸福，把我自己的身体向人抵押，倘不是幸亏那个把您丈夫的指环拿去的人，几乎送了性命；现在我敢再立一张契约，把我的灵魂作为担保，保证您的丈夫决不会再有故意背信的行为。

鲍　那么就请您做他的保证人，把这个给他，叫他比上回那一个保存得牢一些。

安　拿着，巴散尼奥；请您发誓永远保存着这一个指环。

巴　天哪！这就是我给那博士的那一个！

鲍　我就是从他手里拿来的。原谅我，巴散尼奥，因为凭着这个指环，那博士已经跟我睡过觉了。

聂　原谅我，我的好葛莱西安诺；就是那个发育不全的孩子，那个博士的书记，因为我向他讨这个指环，昨天晚上已经跟我睡在一起了。

葛　哎哟，这就像是在夏天把铺得好好的道路重新翻造。嘿！我们就这样冤枉地做起王八来了吗？

鲍　不要说得那么难听。你们人家都有点莫名其妙；这儿有一封信，拿去慢慢地念吧，它是裴拉里奥从帕多瓦寄来的，你们从这封信里，就可以知道那位博士就是鲍细霞，她的书记便是这位聂莉莎。罗伦佐可以向你们证明，当你们出发以后，我就立刻动身；我回家来还没有多少时候，连大门也没有进去过呢。安东尼奥，我们非常欢迎您到这儿来；我还带着一个您所意料不到的好消息给您，请您拆开这封信，您就可以知道您有三艘商船，已经满载而归，快要到港了。您再也想不出这封信怎么会那么巧地到了我的手里。

---

95. **In lieu of**: 作为回报。

96. **deserv'd it**: 享受做丈夫的权利。

97. **amaz'd**: 糊涂了。

    Ant.   I am dumb.

    Bass.   Were you the doctor, and I knew you not?

    Gra.   Were you the clerk that is to make me cuckold?

    Ner.   Ay, but the clerk that never means to do it,

Unless he live until he be a man.

    Bass.   Sweet doctor, you shall be my bedfellow —

When I am absent, then lie with my wife.

    Ant.   Sweet lady, you have given me life and living [98],

For here I read for certain that my ships

Are safely come to road [99].

    Por.   How now, Lorenzo?

My clerk hath some good comforts [100] too for you.

    Ner.   Ay, and I'll give them him without a fee.

There do I give to you and Jessica,

From the rich Jew, a special deed of gift,

After his death, of all he dies possess'd of.

    Lor.   Fair ladies, you drop manna [101] in the way

Of starved people.

    Por.   It is almost morning,

Ant yet I am sure you are not satisfied

Of these events at full [102]. Let us go in,

And charge us there upon inter'gatories [103],

And we will answer all things faithfully.

    Gra.   Let it be so. The first inter'gatory

That my Nerissa shall be sworn on is,

Whether till the next night she had rather stay,

Or go to bed now, being two hours to day [104].

But were the day come, I should wish it dark

Till were couching [105] with the doctor's clerk.

Well, while I live I'll fear [106] no other thing

So sore [107], as keeping safe Nerissa's ring [108].   [*Exeunt*.]

---

98. **living**: 财产。

99. **road**: harbour.

100. **good comforts**: 好东西。

101. **manna**: 玛哪,《旧约·圣经》中所说古以色列人经过旷野时获得的神赐食物。见《出埃及记》第 16 章第 14 节。

102. **at full**: 充分、完全。

103. **charge...inter'gatories**: 向我们提出问题。inter'gatories=interogatories(疑问,质问)。

安　我话都说不出来了。

巴　你就是那个博士，而我没有认出你来吗？

葛　你就是要叫我当王八的那个书记吗？

聂　是的，可是除非那书记会长成一个男子，他再也不能叫你当王八。

巴　好博士，你今晚就陪我睡觉吧；当我不在的时候，你可以睡在我
　　妻子的床上。

安　好夫人，您救了我的命，又给了我一条活路；我从这封信里得到
　　了确实可靠的消息，我的船只已经平安到港了。

鲍　喂，罗伦佐！我的书记也有一件好东西要给您哩。

聂　是的，我可以免费送给他。这儿是那犹太富翁亲笔签署的一张授
　　赠产业的文契，声明他死了以后，全部遗产都传给您和吉雪加，
　　请你们收下吧。

罗　两位好夫人，你们像是散播玛哪的天使，救济着饥饿的人们。

鲍　天已经差不多亮了，可是我知道你们还想把这些事情知道得详细
　　一点。我们大家进去吧；你们还有什么疑惑的地方，尽管再向我
　　们发问，我们一定老老实实地回答一切的问题。

葛　很好，我要我的聂莉莎宣誓答复的第一个问题，是现在离白昼只
　　有两小时了，我们还是就去睡觉呢，还是等明天晚上再睡？正是
　　——

　　不惧黄昏近，但愁白日长；
　　翩翩书记俊，今夕喜同床。
　　金环束指间，灿烂自生光，
　　为恐娇妻骂，莫将弃道旁。（众下。）

---

104. **day**: 天亮。

105. **couching**: 睡觉。

106. **fear**: be concerned about, 担忧。

107. **So sore**: so intensely, 非常，极度。

108. **ring**: 双关语，①戒指；②女性生殖器官。

附录:《威尼斯商人》主要中文资料索引

1.《女律师》，包天笑译，《女学生》年刊第二期，1911 年。

2.《威尼斯商人》，曾广勋译，新文化出版社，1924 年。

3.《威尼斯商人》，顾仲彝译，上海新月书店，1930 年 5 月；上海商务印书馆，1931 年。

4.《威尼斯商人》，梁实秋译，上海商务印书馆，1936 年；上海商务印书馆，1947 年 3 月；《莎士比亚全集》（上），内蒙古文化出版社，1995 年。

5.《威尼斯商人》，曹未风译，贵阳文通书局，1942 年；《莎士比亚全集》丛书，文化合作公司，1946 年 6 月。

6.《威尼斯商人》，朱生豪译，《莎士比亚戏剧全集》（一）（三卷版），世界书局，1949 年 4 月；《莎士比亚戏剧全集》（一）（十二卷版），作家出版社，1954 年 5 月；《莎士比亚全集》（三）（十一卷版），人民文学出版社，1978 年 4 月。

7.《威尼斯商人》序言，顾仲彝附《威尼斯商人》，上海新月书店，1930 年 5 月。

8.'威尼斯商人'的意义，梁实秋，《人公报》，1934 年 7 月 4 日。

9. 关于《威尼斯商人》，梁实秋，《介绍莎士比亚特刊》，国立戏剧学校，1937 年 6 月。

10. 歇洛克，袁昌英，《介绍莎士比亚特刊》，国立戏剧学校，1937 年 6 月。

11.《威尼斯商人》——冲突和解决，吴兴华，《文学评论》，1963 年第 6 期。

12. 读 [《威尼斯商人》——冲突和解决] 后的几点意见，赵守垠，龙文佩，《文学评论》，1964 年第 4 期。

13. 论《威尼斯商人》，朱维之，《外国文学研究》，1978 年第 1 期。

14.《威尼斯商人》选场分析，陈惇，《北京师范大学学报》，1978 年第 2 期。

15.《威尼斯商人》简论，阮珅，《外国文学研究》，1978 年第 2 期。

16. 浅谈《威尼斯商人》，刘念兹，《山东师院学报》，1978 年第 3 期。

17. 《威尼斯商人》浅论，贺祥麟，《广西师院学报》，1979 年第 2 期。

18. 浅谈《威尼斯商人》，赵澧，《世界文学名著选评》第二辑，江西人民出版社，1979 年 12 月。

19. 论夏洛克，方平，《外国文学研究集刊》第一辑，中国社会科学出版社，1979 年；《和莎士比亚交个朋友吧》，四川人民出版社，1983 年。

20. 莎士比亚的《威尼斯商人》，陈瘦竹，《现代剧作家散论》，江苏人民出版社，1979 年。

21. 《威尼斯商人》分析，贺祥麟，《外国文学作品选讲》，广西人民出版社，1980 年。

22. 金羊毛的追逐者——《威尼斯商人》人物小议，方平，《外国文学研究》，1980 年第 1 期；《和莎士比亚交个朋友吧》，四川人民出版社，1983 年。

23. 《威尼斯商人》中的安东尼奥和夏洛克是一丘之貉吗？——与方平同志商榷，于乐庆，《戏剧学习》，1980 年第 4 期。

24. 喜剧《威尼斯商人》，石璞著，《欧洲文学史》（上），四川人民出版社，1980 年 7 月。

25. 揭示反面人物的灵魂——江水扮演的夏洛克，铁池写文，世椿速写，《北京晚报》，1980 年 10 月 21 日。

26. 剧协就话剧《威尼斯商人》召开座谈会——对夏洛克的艺术处理提出异议，铁池，《北京晚报》，1980 年 10 月 24 日。

27. 既要大胆出新　也要忠实原作——评中国青年艺术剧院演出的《威尼斯商人》，周培桐，《人民戏剧》，1981 年第 1 期；中国人民大学复印报刊资料《戏剧研究》，1981 年第 2 期。

28. 论夏洛克，张隆溪，《外国戏剧》，1981 年第 1 期。

29. 夏洛克的性格及其它，阮珅，《武汉大学学报》，1981 年第 3 期；中国人民大学复印报刊资料《戏剧研究》，1981 年第 6 期。

30. 关于"莎士比亚式喜剧"和《威尼斯商人》（一）"莎士比亚式喜剧"（二）《威尼斯商人》的特点与成就，孙家琇，《戏剧学习》，1981 年第 4 期。

31. 论《威尼斯商人》，（英）威尔逊·奈特著，张隆溪译，《莎士比亚评论汇编》（下），中国社会科学出版社，1981 年 11 月。

32. 浅谈《威尼斯商人》的主题、人物及情节，陈周方，《莎士比亚研究文集》，陕西人民出版社，1982 年 6 月。

33. 喜剧《威尼斯商人》和波希霞的喜剧性格，方平，《和莎士比亚交个朋友吧》，四川人民出版社，1983 年。

34. 《威尼斯商人》评析，赵澧，"浅谈《威尼斯商人》"，《世界文学名著选评》第二辑，江西人民出版社，1979 年 12 月；《外国文学参考资料》上册，地质出版社，1984 年 2 月。

35. 《威尼斯商人》与《论犹太人问题》，阮珅，《莎士比亚研究》第二辑，浙江文艺出版社，1984 年 10 月。

36. 从《威尼斯商人》与《合同文学》的比较略论中西文化的差异，张乘健，《温州师范学院学报》（哲社版），1988 年第 4 期。

37. 夏洛克复仇辨，方达，《安庆师院学报》，1990 年第 2 期。

38. 《威尼斯商人》性质再界定，周运增，《黄淮学刊》（社科版），1992 年第 4 期。

39. 夏洛克形象之我见，王录，《佳木斯师专学报》，1993 年第 2 期。

40. 《威尼斯商人》中的风险意识，姚志勇、吾文泉，《扬州师院学报》（社科版），1994 年第 2 期。

41. 《威尼斯商人》主要形象和情节艺术，张明非，《锦州师院学报》（哲社版），1994 年第 3 期。

42. 《威尼斯商人》研究述评，李鸿泉，《内蒙古师范大学学报》（哲社版），1994 年第 4 期。

43. 莎士比亚与基督教：从《威尼斯商人》说开去，陈惇，《北京师范大学学报》（社科版），1995 年第 5 期。

（朱禾　辑）